DEC 0 3 2019

Stolen

Heart

A Novel

By

K. L. McKee

Cameo Mountain Press

Palisade, CO 81526

Copyright ©2019 by Karen Lea McKee

All Rights Reserved.

Cover Photo—Mount Lamborn

Photographer K. L. McKee

First Edition

Book #2 in the North Fork Series

Scripture quotations are from THE HOLY BIBLE, THOMPSON CHAIN-REFERENCE® NEW INTERNATIONAL VERSION®, NIV® Copyright © 1982, by THE B. B. KIRKBRIDE BIBLE COMPANY, INC. and THE ZONDERVAN CORPORATION. Used by permission. All rights reserved worldwide.

Dedication

To my parents, Ray and Nina and my Aunt Ethel—all three taught me the meaning of faith, honesty, and integrity which they lived each day.

Proverbs 11:3a "The integrity of the upright guides them..."

Notes and Acknowledgments

None of the characters in *Stolen Heart* exist except in my imagination and bear no resemblance to people living or dead or any relation to persons of the same name.

Some geographic locations in the book are real. Although the North Fork Valley is an actual location in Western Colorado, the town of North Fork does not exist. It is here that I took liberties with geography, creating the fictional town of North Fork, set against the West Elk Mountain Range and the Castle Range. Mount Lamborn, mentioned in *Stolen Heart,* is real with an elevation of 11,402 feet.

When I was growing up, my uncle had a dog named Spur who was extremely intelligent. I couldn't put all of his abilities in this book, but I hope I have given a small taste of what an incredible dog he was.

As with all books, numerous individuals contributed to the writing of this book. Many thanks to Andy Wick, president and owner (along with wife Polly Jo and son Jeff) of Upper Valley Holsteins, Inc., and his crew for showing me the dairy operation and explaining the intricacies of that business. Thanks also to Pat and Carol Oglesby for their expertise in the art of fly fishing. Pat has gone on to fly fishing the rivers of heaven and is missed. I hope I've given a small glimpse of the joy of fly fishing. Dick Conkle was extremely helpful in detailing the difficult task of mine rescue. I took some slight liberties for the purpose of my story, but hope I kept the initial details of mine rescue true to fact. Without these individuals, my story would not be authentic. The author takes full responsibility for any errors or misunderstandings concerning the dairy industry, fly fishing, and mine rescue.

Every writer needs a support group. Patti Hill, Lucinda Stein, Pamela Larson, Joyce Anderson, and Brenda Evers became my friends, my best critics, and my cheering section. They kindly but firmly caught my mistakes and put me on the right track to make the words of this story come alive. A special thanks to Donna Bettencourt for proofreading.

And last, my husband, Steve, blessed me with his support and understanding during my many hours "chained" to my computer in order to put my story into words.

Most of all, I thank the farmers and miners who help keep this country supplied with food and fuel necessary for the rest of us to enjoy easier living. My respect goes out to all of you and your families.

Stolen Heart

A NOVEL

Prologue

$\mathcal{A}$ jet contrail sliced the azure sky and an automobile horn blared in the distance, but twenty-year-old Abby Stewart didn't notice. She stared at the carnation- and- rose draped casket. The words of the minister droned on, failing to register. She raised her coat collar to ward off the March chill. Anger and loss rose within her.

Abby's mother, who encouraged her dreams, who reassured her when everything went wrong, who loved her and laughed with her, was stolen in the prime of her life by the cancer that left her weak, thin, and in constant pain. Abby had no mother, no family, no one to turn to for love and support.

Tears streamed down Abby's face as the minister, her mother's few acquaintances, and the hospice nurses stopped to pay their respects and utter kind words about their friend, Nancy Stewart. Abby barely heard them. She wanted her mother back, healthy and vibrant.

Sitting by her mother's bedside day after day for the last month had left Abby exhausted and hurting beyond anything she could have imagined. She watched helplessly as her mother battled the pain, struggling for courage and dignity as she faced death. Abby would have done anything to help her mother, except the one thing her mother asked of her.

The day she died, Nancy Stewart directed Abby to a thick manila envelope. When Abby produced the envelope, her mother mustered the last of her strength and lucidity.

"Contained in that envelope, Abby, is an accounting of the debts your father left behind." Nancy wheezed and labored to take air into her lungs. "You must...promise me...you'll finish paying them off."

Abby gripped the envelope and fought back her temper. "Mother, I can't. These are *not* my debts, and they aren't yours either. Daddy accumulated these debts because of his dishonesty. *He* was responsible for them. Not you and especially not me. Don't ask me, Mother. *Please*."

"Abby, honey, you're so wrong." Tears formed in Nancy's eyes, but Abby couldn't tell whether her tears were from physical pain or the heartache Abby's father had inflicted. "Your father was a good man. He...he did the best he knew how. Things just never worked out for him."

"I don't want any part of this. He should have paid the debts a long time ago."

"His debts are our debts, Abby. We're his family. I

4

promised all those people their money. By paying his debts we keep his reputation...our reputation...clean."

"He never cared about me. Why should I care about his reputation?"

"Oh, honey, he did care about you, in his own way."

"He never showed it." Tears stung Abby's eyes. Wind rattled the windows as another storm front threatened. Foot-deep snow already blanketed the ground. Abby shivered. "I love you, Mother, but please don't ask me to save Daddy's reputation. He doesn't deserve it. Besides, he's dead so what does it matter?"

Abby watched her mother's tears trickle onto her pillow and regretted the comment. "I'm sorry. I just don't see what his dishonesty has to do with me."

Nancy's whispered words stung. "You're his daughter, like it or not." Her eyes closed. The soft but fierce comment took most of the energy Nancy had left.

Abby didn't know what to say. She held her breath until she saw the blanket covering her mother rise ever so slightly. Abby closed her own eyes and tried to picture her mother before the cancer consumed her beauty. Nancy Stewart's once shiny auburn hair was dull; her skin transparent; her lips colorless.

In the silence that filled the room to overflowing, Abby slipped the papers from the envelope, gritted her teeth, and stared at them, appalled at the amount still owed. Her mother had made arrangements with every creditor to pay off each debt—no doubt to keep Abby's father out of jail—and she kept a careful accounting of payments and balances. Abby stared at her mother and stifled a sob.

Nancy slowly opened her eyes, every physical effort adding to her pain. "Abby, if you won't do it for him, do it for me," her mother whispered. "*I* promised all those people they'd get their money back. Please...keep my promises for me." Her breathing grew more labored and shallow.

"Oh, Mother," Abby sobbed.

"Please, Abby. It's important to me."

Abby took a deep breath and wiped the tears from her cheeks. "All right, Mother, I promise. Somehow, some way, I'll pay it all back."

A smile graced Nancy's face as she closed her eyes. An hour later she had slipped into a coma, and then death.

Chapter 1

Denver, Colorado—June 2000

*A*bby Stewart stared at the email from her boss, Kevin Karlson, and fumed. How dare he ask her to cheat on his taxes. She sighed. Maybe cheat was too harsh a word. No, cheat sounded about right. She might not be perfect, but she wasn't dishonest like her father. Abby hit reply.

"Kevin—Suggestion of mileage deduction and entertainment for weekend of April 22nd as a business expense will not wash with IRS. Be advised that if you are audited, they will not only disallow, but add hefty penalties. I will not compromise my integrity so you can gain a few dollars in savings on your taxes. Abby"

There, that ought to get his hackles up. Mental note—

update résumé and check newspaper for job openings.

Abby leaned back in her chair and closed her eyes. A dull ache moved from the back of her neck to her forehead. She massaged her neck with her fingers and settled down to work. An hour passed before the inevitable summons came. The intercom line buzzed and Abby's heart skipped a beat. She sucked in a deep breath and picked up the receiver. "Abby."

"I need to see you immediately. Drop whatever you're doing."

"Good morning to you, too, Kevin."

"*Now.*"

"Right." Abby slowly replaced the receiver.

She needed this job. It paid better than any job she'd ever held, plus benefits far better than most employers provided. Few women her age were business managers of a nationally known advertising and PR firm. Finding the same type of position elsewhere would be difficult at best and set her back at least six months, maybe more.

A few months earlier, she'd paid the last of her student loans and reduced her father's debts to $50,000. If she could manage to keep her job, which she doubted at the moment, and stick with her tight budget, living off Ramen noodles and pot pies, the debts would disappear in five years. When she finished what her mother started, she'd feel more flexible where her career was concerned. She'd always dreamed of having her own accounting firm.

Abby steeled herself for the inevitable and walked the short distance to Kevin's office. Evelyn, Kevin's personal assistant, waved Abby through the open door.

Kevin glanced up from the scattered papers on his desk. "Close the door and sit down, Abby." A smile appeared on Kevin's face but failed to reach his eyes. Abby settled into the chair facing his desk and waited.

"Would you care for something to drink?" Kevin rose from his chair. At the wet bar, he poured himself some coffee.

"No thank you." Abby shifted in her chair, trying to find a comfortable position. She clenched and unclenched her hands.

Kevin returned to his chair. "How long have you worked for this firm, Abby?"

"Five years."

"Long enough to know I don't ask a lot of favors of my employees."

"Look, Kevin, I meant what I said in my email. You're treading on thin ice."

He frowned. "Email?"

Abby took a deep breath. "The one I sent about an hour ago. About the mileage and entertainment deduction. It won't wash with the IRS."

It was typical of Kevin to make this difficult for her. Since he'd taken over the firm three years ago, she hadn't cared for the way he conducted business, which always seemed to her a tad above shady. But that was his problem. As long as she kept her responsibility to the business honest and above board, she didn't care what he did, or what he told his clients. Accounting would remain squeaky clean while she was in charge, which was about to change, she reminded herself.

"I just got in a few minutes ago. I haven't checked my email yet. Apparently I should." He raised an eyebrow.

Abby took note of his dull and bloodshot eyes. "Then this isn't about—"

He rubbed his forehead. "We'll worry about that later. What I want to talk to you about is more...personal."

Abby bit the inside of her lip and relaxed her hands.

"I'm sure you're aware that I recently became engaged."

Abby nodded. Four months ago, office gossip had focused on Kevin's engagement for over two weeks.

"Unfortunately, Gail has suddenly decided I won't quite do for a husband. She broke off the engagement this weekend." His eyes narrowed.

"I'm sorry, Kevin, but what has that got to do with me?"

He set his coffee aside and leaned forward, resting his arms on his desk. "You and Gail are about the same size and coloring, and lucky for me, your given name is Abigail." He cleared his throat. "I'd like you to pose as my fiancée for about three weeks."

Abby stared. "I'm sorry, did you say you wanted me to pose as your *fiancée*?"

"That's exactly what I said."

"Surely you're not serious."

"I'm very serious."

"What possible reason could you have for wanting—?"

"Maybe I should start at the beginning."

"Maybe you should."

Instinct told Abby to get up and walk out, but curiosity refused to let her move. She waited as Kevin rose and paced behind his desk.

"I was raised in a small town. Population 2500, not counting the outlying farms and ranches. All four years of high school I played varsity football, basketball, and baseball. Star athlete, valedictorian of my class, and recipient of a football scholarship to CU. You get the picture."

Abby got it and didn't care. She hoped he would get to the point before lunch.

"Anyway, every Fourth of July, alumni from North Fork High School hold their class reunions, and the outstanding alumnus for the year is picked from one of the classes. This year is my tenth reunion, and I've been picked as the outstanding alumnus for this year." He paused and glanced at Abby.

"Congratulations, Kevin. That's quite an honor, but what has that got to do with Gail breaking off your engagement?"

"When I accepted the honor, I told the committee I would be bringing my fiancée with me."

"Then call them and tell them she won't be coming. That seems simple enough."

Kevin gripped the back of his chair. "I can't. You see, when I was in school, I could have dated any number of girls, played the field, but instead I chose to date the same girl my junior and senior year. Everyone thought we'd eventually get married. I broke off with her during my freshman year of college. She was heartbroken. She'll be at the reunion, and according to my mom, has been asking about me. She's never married, and I don't want to give her the idea I'm available."

"Maybe you can make amends with Gail before then. Turn on your charm. She's bound to come around." Abby smiled. Any one of the single women in the office would love to have the handsome, blond, blue-eyed Kevin show them the least bit of interest. Anyone but Abby. Kevin was too much like her father—handsome, personable, dishonest.

"It's over between us. And I need a fiancée for a few short weeks."

"I don't think so, Kevin. I guess you'll just have to tell the truth." *A new concept for you.* Abby rose to go.

"Wait. Hear me out, then give me your answer."

Abby settled back in her chair. This was too good to pass up. Observing the always-confident Kevin squirm was new territory, yet begging lurked on the tip of his tongue. It was worth a few extra minutes out of her day for the chance to see him grovel.

"My family can't wait to meet Gail, and I haven't the heart to tell them she isn't coming. With a fiancée, I won't have to answer my Mom's incessant questions about my love life, and I won't have to fend off my old girlfriend. I think she'd still like something to happen between us, and I don't want to hurt her feelings. Besides, the banquet numbers have been set for over a month. It would only be for three weeks. A few weeks after we return to Denver, I'll tell my family I've broken off the engagement, and no one will be the wiser." Kevin perched on the edge of his desk and waited for Abby to respond.

She rose. "Nice try, Kevin, but no." She moved toward the door, a smile on her face.

"Wait."

Abby stopped and turned toward Kevin.

"How much?" He narrowed his eyes

"Excuse me?"

"How much will it cost me for you to do this?"

"I told you, I'm not interested." She opened the door to leave.

"You'll get three weeks of paid vacation plus a bonus."

"I already have plans for my vacation. And I already get a bonus."

"This would be in addition to what you usually get."

Her hand on the doorknob, her curiosity piqued. "How much more?" she asked.

"How much do you want?"

Abby stared at him, positive he was joking. "You can't afford me," she said.

"Try me."

Abby's mouth went dry. She had never seen him so serious...or desperate. "You're afraid of what people will think, aren't you? You can't admit that you can't control everything and everyone you deal with. You'd do anything to insure that you look successful— that you can't fail." She shook her head. "How sad for you."

"Come on, Abby, what harm can it do? I save face and you get an extra three weeks of paid vacation plus a hefty bonus."

"Believe me, Kevin, if I agreed, I wouldn't be doing it to save your face."

"Look, in a weak moment, I promised my family I'd spend some time with them. I can't spend three weeks with my family without some kind of distraction." He smiled his trademark you-can't-deny-me-anything smile. "It will be fun."

"No."

"How much?"

Abby opened the door. "$50,000. *After* taxes," she said and closed the door behind her.

Chapter 2

*K*evin glanced at Abby as she slept, and then turned his gaze back to the road. Much to his delight, she had agreed to pose as his fiancée. He accepted Abby's terms because, although he hated to admit it, he was desperate. Gail had jilted him at the last minute, and for that, he would never forgive her.

The moon and stars must be in the right alignment, he mused. Why else would a slim, beautiful redhead named Abigail be so conveniently available? The five-carat plus diamond ring Gail had thrown at him fit Abby perfectly. Yes, he definitely lived a charmed life.

Kevin turned the radio up a notch as Springsteen belted out "A Good Man is Hard to Find." Life was good. Abby exacted a high price for her part in his charade, but no matter.

Money got you the important things in life, like respect, a luxury condominium, and a new Corvette. He wanted to show off the sporty car, but he couldn't fit all their luggage into it. Oh well, he had plenty to show off, including the BMW he'd rented for the trip. His business was more than successful. Money wasn't a problem. He grinned. Not bad for the son of a dairy farmer.

Once he had recovered from the initial shock of Abby's demand for $50,000 after taxes, he had marched into her office and demanded to know why so much.

"That's none of your business," Abby said, "as long as I do my part."

Kevin planted his hands on her desk and leaned toward her. "If I'm going to fork out nearly $70,000 dollars, I have a right to know why."

Abby glared at him, but didn't flinch. "Fair enough. Sit down." Kevin sat, and Abby continued. "I'm going to use it to pay off the remainder of the debts my father left behind when he died."

"I didn't know your father had died."

"He died over ten years ago. And I don't miss him."

Kevin stared at her for a moment. He didn't care to be around his parents much, but he didn't hate them. Though they were too "down home" for him, he would be sorry to lose either of his parents. Unless he read her comments wrong, Abby harbored nothing but hatred for her father.

"What about your mother, can't she pay off the debts?"

"She died a couple of years after my father died, and I promised her I'd pay back everything he owed. Otherwise, I wouldn't bother."

"Oh," Kevin said. They sat in silence for a few moments before Kevin spoke. "I figured you wanted the money to buy something expensive."

"Why is it a man always thinks a woman needs *expensive* things to make her happy?"

"Because it's true," Kevin replied, "at least the women I've known."

"I'm not one of those women. *Things* won't make me happy."

Kevin studied her a moment. "What would make you happy, Abby?"

"A good man," she said, a wry grin gracing her mouth. "But you know what they say—'a good man's hard to find.'"

"Present company excluded, of course."

"Present company *included*." Abby's smile disappeared.

"Humph," Kevin snorted and rose to go. "Well, since I'm willing to pay your price, be at my place by seven tonight. We have plans to make." He closed the door behind him before Abby had a chance to react or change her mind.

He had wasted little time fulfilling his part of the bargain, and now Abby sat beside him on the way to his hometown, ready to fulfill her part.

Out of the corner of his eye, Kevin saw Abby stir. *She is beautiful. I'll be the envy of every man in North Fork, including Jake.* He pictured the look of envy on his brother's face, and smiled.

~

Abby opened her eyes and glanced around her. Kevin guided the BMW along a winding canyon road. A river to her left cascaded over rocks and around boulders toward its destination, the water clear and clean. Pine and cedar along with current, chokecherry, and serviceberry bushes covered the hillside outside her window. Snowcapped mountains loomed ahead, boxing them in. Thankful to have left the city far behind, Abby thrilled at the spectacular peaks and forests so near.

"Where are we?" she asked as she straightened in her seat.

"Crystal River Valley," Kevin answered. "We'll be heading up McClure Pass in a few minutes. Did you get some sleep?"

"I rested." Besides the memories of her mother, Abby couldn't shake the guilt she had about agreeing to Kevin's proposal. But paying off her con-artist father's debts from money paid by another con artist had tempted her beyond reason. She couldn't help herself.

She clenched and unclenched her hands. In a little while I'll meet Kevin's family, she thought. *What am I worried about? I'm sure they're no different from Kevin. Good, honest people don't turn out sons like Kevin. Just twenty days, and then I can get back to my normal life.*

She thought about the envelopes she'd dropped in the mail. As soon as she deposited the money, she wrote three checks to three different individuals, varying in amounts, but "paid in full" written on each one. She no longer had her father's dishonesty ruling her life, or her promise to her mother hanging over her head. So why didn't she feel relieved?

Uneasiness slithered down her spine. She shoved it aside. Her short-lived charade would harm no one, she reasoned, and she'd be that much closer to giving Kevin her notice and opening her own accounting firm. She could hardly wait.

"Penny for your thoughts," Kevin said.

"Just wondering how much longer to North Fork."

"About an hour, give or take a few minutes."

Kevin steered the BMW around a curve and the car sped up a long incline, the valley receding below them.

"This is beautiful," Abby remarked. Kevin didn't comment. "Tell me again about your family. It won't hurt to refresh my memory."

"Sure, why not." Kevin shrugged. "Mom and Dad have lived on the farm since they were married, a little over thirty-two years ago. My brother, Jake, took over the dairy when he graduated from college. That was about nine years ago. Dad's crippled and can't do much. The dairy supports the three of them. Jake has kept it producing as best he can. He works day and night. Of course, he has no family, so I guess it doesn't matter. Mom works as a cook for the school district."

The tone of Kevin's voice made "crippled" and "cook" sound like dirty words. She assumed Kevin avoided his family as much as possible because he was ashamed of them. He hadn't shown Abby any pictures of his family, and Abby hadn't asked. She wished she had. She pictured his mother as a short, dumpy, gray-haired woman; his father a bald, squat man who could barely get around; his brother as an older version of Kevin with a beer belly and greasy coveralls. In fact, his earlier descriptions conjured up visions of rednecks in Abby's mind, although he'd never used that term.

She shuddered. "Do you really think we can get away with this, Kevin?" Each time he told her about his family, doubt nagged at her. What if she couldn't convince them she was Kevin's fiancée?

"Piece of cake," he said.

He obviously knew his family better than she did, so why didn't his confidence put her at ease?

"When was the last time you were home for a visit?" she asked.

"Let's see...Christmas, four years ago. I arrived the day before Christmas and left Christmas Day."

Abby stared at him. "That's all? Two days in the last four years? Why?"

"Actually, it was a little over a day. Ten at night to five the next afternoon. I get bored real easy. Nothing to do. I can tolerate only so much visiting, and then there's nothing left to say. I call every now and then. Lately, Jake's been after me to spend a little more time with the folks. Says they miss me. Mom especially. This seemed like a good time. I think Jake's a little worried about Dad, although he hasn't mentioned anything specific. After being gone from home for ten years, I guess I owe them a couple of weeks. I figured with Gail along, there would be more distraction and someone I could relate to." Kevin smiled. "I can handle it."

"That's big of you."

"What's that supposed to mean?"

"You live only 250 miles away. Surely you could visit more often."

"When you meet my folks and see North Fork, you'll understand."

"Maybe."

Little more was said between them. Abby settled back and enjoyed the scenery. McClure Pass proudly displayed the vivid greens of quaking aspen, pine, and fir, and splashes of yellow, red, and blue wildflowers that signaled early summer. The rugged mountains that bordered the pass were still crowned with snow. At Abby's prompting, Kevin put names to the mountains and rivers.

Her first impression of North Fork was of a peaceful mountain town nestled on the valley floor, surrounded on two sides by high peaks and accompanying foothills. Beautiful lawns, shaded by cottonwood, maple, elm, and ash trees showcased the houses. Rose gardens of various sizes decorated nearly every home. Petunias, daisies, alyssum, and marigolds bordered lawns and bloomed in storefront window boxes.

At the south edge of town, Kevin steered the rented BMW up a narrow and crudely paved road that wound into the foothills beneath two imposing peaks connected by a saddle. The higher peak still sported a small patch of snow at the top and along the north face. Fenced fields of alfalfa and fruit orchards bordered the sides of the road. After traveling about two miles, Kevin turned onto an unpaved road and drove another mile before turning down a graveled driveway. He slowed as they approached a white two-story Victorian-style house with blue trim.

A sizeable lawn flanked one side of the walk leading to the house. Lilac and spirea bushes, their blossoms long gone, bordered the lawn. Bloom-laden honeysuckle vines climbed trellises near the house, and petunias and alyssum grew along the walk.

Beyond the lawn, Abby noticed a woman, probably Kevin's mother, working in a garden. She looked toward the BMW as Kevin parked beneath a towering maple tree. He lowered the windows halfway. A strong, acrid odor of manure and another smell Abby couldn't identify stung her nostrils, causing her eyes to water.

"Smells like home," Kevin muttered.

"They're here, Leonard," Kevin's mother shouted toward the house. "The kids are here!"

Abby took a deep breath, nearly choked on the smell, and opened the car door. *Too late to turn back now.* She forced a smile and readied herself for the role she would play for the next two and a half weeks.

Kevin's mother, a tall, thin woman, embraced him as he stepped out of the car. Abby's heart ached. She missed the feel of her own mother's arms.

"Kevin, it's so good to have you home." Pat Karlson stepped back and cradled his face. "You look wonderful. Gail must be treating you right." She turned to Abby with outstretched arms. "And this must be Gail."

Before Abby could react, she found herself enfolded in Pat's arms. She smelled of fresh-baked bread, cinnamon, and tilled soil.

"And who else would I be bringing?" Kevin said.

Before she released Abby, Pat said, "Welcome to our home." She circled Kevin's and Abby's waists with her arms. "Come in the house. I've made fresh cinnamon rolls and iced tea."

Kevin's father met them at the door and embraced Kevin with his right arm when they stepped inside. "Welcome home, son." Abby detected a bit of discomfort on Kevin's part.

Leonard Karlson was tall—only an inch or two shorter than Kevin—and handsome. His left arm, bent at the elbow, rested across his mid-section. He was muscular and broad chested. Abby didn't see him as crippled at all.

Kevin turned toward Abby. "Dad, I'd like you to meet Abby."

"Abby? Don't you mean Gail?" He winked at Abby, then smiled and shook her hand. "Happy to meet you, whichever one you are. Name's Leonard and you've met Pat."

Abby didn't know what to say. She planned to answer to Gail for the next three weeks. But Kevin unwittingly called her Abby. Now what was she supposed to do?

"Oh, did I call her Abby?" Kevin said. "I do that all the time. She prefers Gail as her professional name, but those close to her call her Abby."

A deep voice came from the doorway. "So, what should

we call her?"

Abby turned and faced a man about Kevin's age, an inch or two shorter and slightly heavier and more muscular than Kevin, with light brown hair.

"Jake." The two men shook hands and embraced quickly, then Kevin turned to Abby. "Jake, this is my fiancée."

Jake nodded toward Abby. "Nice to finally meet you, Gail. Or is it Abby?"

She smiled. Kevin covered his mistake well, and Abby saw no reason not to play along, since she had never been called Gail. "It's Abby for family and friends. My full name is Abigail."

"Abby it is, then. Welcome to North Fork and the Karlson Dairy Farm." Jake extended his hand to Abby.

"Thank you." Jake's handshake was warm and firm.

"Hey, Mom, did you say something about cinnamon rolls?" Kevin asked.

"I did. Everyone sit down at the table where we can talk. I'll get the rolls."

Over warm cinnamon rolls and iced tea, questions punctuated the air around the table as each of them caught up on family news.

Abby studied the four of them and took note of the striking resemblance between Leonard and Jake. Kevin resembled his mother—tall and thin, with blond hair and blue eyes. Their faces were narrow and long. Abby noticed Leonard's eyes were dark green, but she wasn't close enough to Jake to distinguish the color of his, although they appeared a bit unusual. She assumed they were either blue or green.

Though most of the conversation covered family news, occasionally someone asked Abby a question. But as the four talked, Abby's unease increased. Kevin's family wasn't what she expected and not at all like Kevin—at least the Kevin she knew. They came across as genuine, honest people. When had Kevin changed? Though his business was public relations and advertising—Kevin referred to it as "telling lies for a living"—he sometimes seemed a little too slick even for that tongue-in-cheek description of his profession. Had she made a mistake in agreeing to Kevin's charade?

"So, Abby, how'd you get mixed up with this reprobate, anyway?"

Jake's question caught her by surprise. For some reason he rattled her. From the way he studied the two of them, she suspected he knew she and Kevin were lying.

She shifted on her chair. "Oh, well—"

"She couldn't resist my natural charm, could you, honey?"

Abby smiled and regained her composure. "He paid me."

K. L. McKee

26

Chapter 3

*F*rom Kevin's glare, Abby knew her comment hit its
intended mark. She met his eyes for a moment, then
said, "Actually, he just swept me off my feet. One date and
he had me. We've been together ever since."

In spite of her smooth transition from the truth, her
stomach churned. She asked for the bathroom and excused
herself when Pat pointed the way.

Abby splashed cold water on her face, hoping to rinse
away the sweat that had popped out on her forehead. She
studied herself in the mirror. She had lied more in the last
ten minutes than she had her entire life, and she half expected
to see "liar" written in bold letters across her forehead.

She wiped a smudge of mascara from under her eye, and
glared at the ring on her left hand. The huge and, in Abby's

estimation, gaudy multi-faceted diamond ring glinted on her finger. When Kevin had given it to her, she feared she'd walk leaning to one side. She hated wearing it.

The confused face in the mirror asked, "What have you gotten yourself into?"

"Kevin's parents are wonderful," she whispered. Pat reminded Abby of her own mother, and Leonard, well, he treated his sons the way Abby wished her own father had treated her. His pride and love for them shone in his eyes.

Jake watched Abby and Kevin with a wariness that left her flustered and apprehensive. "You should march right out there and tell them all the truth right now," she told her reflection. "Let Kevin squirm."

Abby closed her eyes and sighed. She was caught between the proverbial rock and hard spot. She gave her word to lie for Kevin for a few weeks. If she hadn't already spent the money paying her father's debts, she would give it back and call the whole deal off. *Too late. I'll have to see it through, like it or not.*

"Abby are you all right?"

Abby flinched at the sound of Pat's voice.

"I'm fine." She opened the door and smiled. "Sorry I've taken so long."

"That's all right. I was a little concerned. You looked a bit pale when you asked for the bathroom."

"I'm just tired, I guess. And I've been a bit nervous about meeting all of you."

"Well, that's understandable. Let's get you settled in your room. You can lie down for a while before supper."

Pat ushered Abby toward the stairs. "First bedroom on your right at the top of the stairs. Jake's room. You just lie down, and I'll have the boys bring up your luggage. I'm looking forward to getting to know you better." Pat turned toward the kitchen, and on her way Abby heard her say, "Kevin, you and Jake get your luggage out of the car and bring it in. Abby's a little tired. She's going to lie down for a while."

Abby trudged up the stairs and found Jake's room. She collapsed on the bed and closed her eyes. She could hardly wait until she was back home in Denver and this charade was over.

~

Abby awoke to sounds of laughter. She glanced at her watch and groaned. She had slept nearly two hours. While she slept, someone had set her luggage inside the door and covered her with a light blanket. The windows on either side of the bed were open.

Abby breathed in the smell of line-dried linens. Even the cotton bedspread smelled of sunshine. Pink, green, and white floral print curtains billowed into the room. Honeysuckle scent, sweet and heavy, floated on the late afternoon breeze. The pungent, eye-watering odor she'd encountered earlier from the dairy had vanished.

The bedroom barely accommodated a double bed, dresser and nightstand. A wooden rocking chair and floor lamp occupied one corner. Throw rugs covered a worn vinyl floor.

Abby rose and placed her suitcase on the bed. She unpacked, touched up her makeup, and tried to tame her unruly curls into some sort of order. As she set the brush on the dresser, a light knock sounded at the door.

She opened it to find Kevin frowning.

"I see you finally decided to get up."

Abby gritted her teeth and glared. "Is there a problem?"

"You're supposed to help me endure all the small talk with my family. They're about to drive me nuts."

Abby grinned and patted Kevin's cheek, reveling in his misery. "You'll survive. Besides, it'll probably get worse before it gets better."

"What's that supposed to mean?"

"I'll bet your Mom drags out your high school annuals and pictures from when you were a baby. I'm sure there will be stories to go with every one of them."

Kevin groaned as Abby stepped past him into the hallway.

"You don't really think she'll do that, do you?"

"Mothers usually do when fiancées are involved. I can hardly wait."

Kevin leaned against the doorframe and let his head fall back with a thud. "This was a big mistake. I'm not sure I can handle three days of sitting around in misery, let alone three weeks."

Abby laughed. "I'm sure there's plenty of work to do. Jake could probably use some help with the dairy. That should keep you occupied for part of the day."

Kevin pushed away from the doorframe. His eyes

narrowed. "Jake doesn't need my help. Besides, I don't do that stuff anymore."

Abby frowned. "Too good for manual labor?"

"Something like that." Kevin gripped Abby's arm and guided her toward the stairs. "Whatever you do, *don't* encourage my mother."

"You want me to act like your fiancée, don't you? By the way," she added before Kevin could answer, "thanks for opening the windows and putting a blanket over me."

"Wasn't me." Kevin stopped.

"Someone did when you brought up my suitcases."

"That must have been Jake's doing. He's the one who brought your suitcases in."

"Oh." Abby shrugged. "Anyway, it was a nice gesture." She should have known Kevin had nothing to do with something so thoughtful.

When Abby and Kevin stepped into the kitchen, Pat was busy preparing the evening meal. Jake and Leonard were gone.

"Where'd Dad and Jake go?" Kevin asked.

Pat set down a potato and peeler and wiped her hands on a hand towel thrown over her shoulder. "They're at the barn. Go on. Supper will be ready in about an hour. Take Abby with you."

"You go ahead, Kevin. I'll help your mother with supper."

"You sure?"

Abby nodded. Kevin kissed Abby on the cheek, then whispered in her ear, "If you so much as mention baby pictures, I *will* get even."

Abby grinned and shoved him toward the door and turned toward Pat. "Is there something I can do to help?"

Pat smiled. "If you don't mind finishing up the potatoes, I'll get started on the carrots. Then we'll pop them in the oven with the roast and get better acquainted."

Abby accepted a peeler from Pat and picked up a potato. "Were you able to rest? Is the bed comfortable?"

"It's fine. I didn't mean to sleep so long." Abby rinsed the skinned potato under the faucet.

"Evidently you needed it." Pat took the potato, quartered it, and placed it in a bowl, then cut a carrot into several sections. "We hope you'll be comfortable in Jake's room. Kevin's room is a bit bigger, but he seems to be territorial about it."

"That sounds like Kevin." She remembered the pink floral curtains in her room and tried to picture Jake sleeping there. Somehow the picture didn't work. "Where will Jake sleep?"

"Oh, didn't Kevin tell you? Jake has his own house at the other end of the property. If you had followed the road before you turned in our driveway, you would have seen Jake's lane about a half mile farther. The milking barn, equipment sheds, and corrals are halfway between the houses, so it works out pretty well. Jake has his evening meal here and sometimes lunch, but he hasn't lived here since he built the house five years ago. He started building it when he and Sondra became engaged. I wasn't sure he'd finish it after she jilted him. I should have known better. Jake always follows through on anything he starts."

Great, Kevin didn't tell me any of that. "Kevin just said Jake wasn't married. What happened?" Abby's curiosity always got the better of her, and she often stuck her nose in where it didn't belong. "Actually, you don't have to tell me. It's none of my business."

"No, it's all right. You're family, so you should know the story. I'm surprised Kevin didn't tell you."

Abby's heart flip-flopped when Pat said she was family. Her family died with her mother, and she missed being a part of something special. She was perpetuating a lie and wished she could slither into the sink and disappear down the drain.

Abby finished peeling and quartering the potatoes as Pat related Jake's story.

"Jake was engaged to marry Sondra, a local girl about five years younger than him. She stayed around after high school and worked at the bank. That's where Jake met her. She came from a good family, but she seemed too unsettled to me. I was a little concerned when Jake announced they were engaged. But Jake loved her, so that was good enough for me. Jake was devastated when she called off the wedding. Just two weeks' warning. Took him a long time to get over that one."

Pat opened the oven door and placed the carrots and potatoes in a Dutch oven with the roast. Abby's mouth watered at the smell.

"Did Sondra say why she changed her mind?" Abby asked. "Or did Jake keep that to himself?"

"After they started dating, Sondra talked Jake into

33

joining the local theater group. She was already a member and wanted to share it with Jake. Whenever he has time, JD MacCord directs some of their plays."

"JD MacCord? The movie star?"

"Yes, he lives here, you know."

"Really?"

Pat nodded. "Well, anyway, JD was looking for extras for a movie he was filming here, and Sondra jumped at the chance. Then, when an opportunity came up for a small part in another of JD's movies, she auditioned and got the part without Jake's knowledge. JD thought Jake knew about Sondra trying for the part."

Pat shook her head. "When she was through filming, Sondra announced she was moving to California and wanted to delay the wedding until she tried her luck in Hollywood. Never discussed it with Jake."

Pat sighed. "JD felt partly responsible when Sondra broke off with Jake, but it wasn't his fault. Seems to me she shouldn't have led Jake on or accepted his proposal if she had such a longing to leave North Fork and head to Hollywood. She shouldn't have accepted the part behind Jake's back."

Abby saw in Pat's eyes a tigress needing to protect her cubs from harm and felt the resentment in Pat that someone had hurt Jake. She pitied any woman that hurt Pat's boys. Pain stabbed at her heart as she realized that Pat would eventually feel the same toward her once Kevin broke their "engagement." Abby had no doubt Kevin would make her look bad in order to save face.

"I take it the wedding was more than delayed."

"As far as Jake was concerned, it was over between them. He said he couldn't marry someone who couldn't be honest with him and was too selfish to take into consideration someone else's needs and feelings."

Abby cringed inwardly at Pat's comment. She couldn't help but ask. "Has she been successful?"

"She's had bit parts in some television shows. Her mother tells me often enough about her small roles, whether I want to hear about them or not. I suppose that doesn't sound very nice, but I don't care much for people who hurt other people for purely selfish reasons and without a second thought. That's what Sondra did to Jake. I'm just glad it happened before they married."

"It sounds like Jake is better off without her."

"That's true, but he was like a lost little boy for a year. He kept hoping she'd come back. And I couldn't help him, except to pray for him. He had to work it out for himself. He's happy now, but he's lonely. He'd like to marry and have a family, but I think he's a little gun shy. Can't blame him. And the prospects in North Fork get slimmer the older he gets."

"I'm sure the right girl will come along one of these days."

"I keep praying for that. But only God knows the answer." Pat smiled at Abby. "He's answered my prayers for Kevin, though. He's found himself a wonderful girl, and we're so happy for both of you."

Pat hugged Abby, and Abby fought back the tears stinging her eyes. Pat didn't deserve Kevin's deceit, and

Abby was caught in the same lie.

~

"Oh look, Kev," Abby exclaimed. "You're so cute in this one. That fish you're holding is almost big enough to see."

After supper Pat had produced a stack of photo albums, just as Abby predicted, and settled on the couch with Abby and Kevin to browse through them.

Kevin groaned. "Gee, Mom, do you have to drag out all my old pictures? I think I've been tortured enough for one evening."

"Oh relax," Pat admonished. "Abby's getting a kick out of seeing what you were like when you were little. That was his very first fish," Pat said to Abby. "He was really proud of it."

"Until I caught a bigger one," Jake said. "Then he cried."

"Oh, poor baby," Abby said in mock sympathy and grinned at Kevin.

"Oh, thanks a lot. First you guys embarrass me by showing my baby pictures, then you call me a crybaby. And you're no help." He glared at Abby, and she shrugged her shoulders. "I don't have to take this anymore. I'm going to bed." He stalked from the room and took the stairs two at a time.

Abby waited until she heard Kevin slam the door to his room before she spoke. "I suppose I should go up and try to appease him a little. If I'd known teasing would upset him so much—"

"Let him sulk for a while by himself," Jake said. "He never could take teasing. He always got his hackles up, and the more upset he became, the more I teased him. He never did catch on."

"Just the same, I shouldn't add to his temper by taking part," Abby said. "I'll let him cool down for a while, then go up and talk to him."

"I suppose I shouldn't have drug out all his old pictures, but I thought you'd enjoy seeing them," Pat said to Abby.

Abby shrugged. "He'll get over it, and I am enjoying them."

"If you want to go on up, go ahead. We can look at the rest another time."

"No, I'd like to see more. It'll give Kevin time to simmer down."

Jake stood and stretched. "You two enjoy yourselves. Four-thirty comes real early in the morning." He crossed to where Pat and Abby sat on the couch and kissed his mother on the cheek. "Night, Ma."

"Night, Jake."

"Dad."

"Jake."

Jake smiled at Abby. "Nice meeting you, Abby."

"Nice meeting you, too, Jake. Maybe tomorrow I can get Kevin to give me a tour of the dairy."

"Maybe." Jake's eyebrows lifted slightly, then he turned and walked away.

As Abby watched Jake's back, she had the distinct

feeling that Jake doubted Kevin would give Abby that tour.

~

Jake stared at his computer screen, trying to concentrate on the columns of numbers, but all he could think about was Abby. In frustration, he hit save and exited the accounting program. The books would have to wait until he could give them his full attention.

He climbed into bed, but sleep hovered out of reach. Twenty minutes passed. He rose, slipped on a T-shirt and sweats, and stepped onto the second-story deck outside his bedroom. Leaning on the rail, he stared across the field at the house he had grown up in. The light in his old bedroom filtered through the closed curtains. He caught a glimpse of a shadow, then the light flicked off.

Crickets chirped in stereo, while the stars blinked, beautiful but indifferent. A cool breeze ruffled his hair. He gripped the rail and shoved away from it.

What was it Humphrey Bogart said in *Casablanca? "Of all the gin joints in all the world, she had to walk into mine."* That's not quite right, he thought, but close enough. He hadn't expected to like Abby, but he did the minute he saw her. When Kevin had talked to him about Gail, he'd pictured someone more sophisticated, less teasing. Gail—Abby—whoever she was, didn't seem like Kevin's type, or for that matter, the girl Kevin had described to him. She wasn't snobbish enough.

Jake shook his head and returned to the bedroom. That wasn't very nice, he thought. But Abby is the kind of girl I might fall for, not Kevin. Not that I would fall for her. After all, she's engaged to Kevin.

Jake liked his women a bit playful. Not so serious. Kevin always dated serious, sophisticated women. *Maybe Kevin's changed.*

Jake hoped so. Abby certainly was an indication of that possibility. Still, something about their relationship bothered him. Kevin and Abby didn't act like they were madly in love. They hardly touched. There was no spark between them. No love in their eyes. Tolerance better described the looks between them.

"Maybe that's what sophisticated love is all about," he mumbled, "but if that's the case, it's too boring for me." He shed the T-shirt and sweats and climbed into bed.

Chapter 4

*A*bby set her book on the dresser and rose from the rocker. She turned out the light and slipped into bed. Images of the day replayed in her mind like a B movie. Her innocent charade was quickly becoming a nightmare. What should she do? Kevin acted like a spoiled child, although she didn't know why that surprised her.

She could understand his discomfort over the pictures, but his tantrum came out of nowhere. Fifteen minutes after he stomped from the room, she had followed him upstairs. When she knocked at his door, he nearly bit her head off.

"*What?*"

"It's Abby. May I come in?"

Kevin flung open the door and glared. "What do you want?"

She stood her ground but didn't answer.

He jerked his head, giving Abby permission to enter. She stopped in the middle of the room and faced him.

"I'm sorry if looking at your childhood pictures made you uncomfortable. You were cute when you were little. I'll bet you had lots of little girls interested even then." She grinned and received a scowl in return.

Kevin closed the gap between them, grabbed Abby's shoulders and kissed her, hard and quick. When he finished, he held her at arm's length, the scowl still firmly in place.

Abby scowled back. "What was *that* all about?"

"A reminder that you're my fiancée, just in case you've forgotten."

Abby stared at him, then shook her head. "Believe me, Kevin, I haven't forgotten. But I wish I could. This is not going to work. You have a wonderful family, and I hate lying to them."

"To them, or just Jake?"

"What in the world are you talking about?"

"You and Jake seem to be hitting it off pretty good."

Abby was dumbfounded. She hadn't visited with Jake any more than she had Pat or Leonard. She tried to think what she had done to make him think...and then it hit her.

"You're jealous of Jake. That's it, isn't it? You think you have to be better, smarter, more successful than your big brother, and you'll do anything you think bests him."

Kevin turned around and stuffed his hands in his designer jeans' pockets. "*Seriously*? He's a *dairy* farmer, and I'm president of a nationally successful PR and advertising firm." His comment was laced with sarcasm and anger. He turned to face Abby. "It's Jake that's jealous. Always has wanted what I had, or had to do it bigger and better. But I've finally gotten the best of him. The point is, I don't like looking bad to my family, and I don't like being made fun of, especially by my fiancée."

"Nobody was making fun of you, Kevin. Teasing a little, but all in good fun. And for the record, I'm technically *not* your fiancée." Abby seethed inside. She struggled to keep her voice calm. Kevin sounded just like her father. Everyone was against him, or trying to put him down, or causing him to fail. They were both worse than a spoiled child.

"For the record, Abby, I paid you $50,000, *after* taxes, to pose as my fiancée, so I suggest you start acting like one."

"For the record, Kevin, I will when you start treating me like your fiancée. Then you'll get your money's worth." Abby stalked past Kevin to the door. "You don't act like I'm even around. You spent most of dinner bragging about how successful you are. After a while, I found your bragging boring, but your family was genuinely interested and happy for you. Not once did Jake brag about anything. He just listened politely while you went on and on, and then said how proud he was of what you've accomplished. You never once asked him about the dairy and how it's doing."

"Why should I? It's a dairy. You milk cows morning and night. It's no big deal. I did it for more years than I care to remember while I was growing up. It doesn't take any brains to milk cows."

Abby shook her head at Kevin. "I feel sorry for you. You can't see beyond yourself and what you want. Good night, Kevin."

Abby left Kevin's room disgusted with his attitude and self-centeredness. Retreating to her own room, she read for a while, trying to forget the way the evening ended. She finally gave up and hoped for sleep, which came in the early morning.

~

Morning didn't bring any relief for Jake. The minute he woke up he found himself thinking of Abby and looking forward to seeing her again. Her riotous gold-red curls, tentative smile, and emerald green eyes that snapped with impishness, drew him to her. But he saw something else in her eyes, if only for a moment. Something troubling. He would love to be able to read her mind; find out what thoughts swirled around inside that pretty head of hers. *What are you hiding Abby? What secret resides behind those captivating eyes?*

One thing in her favor was that Abby didn't seem to take Kevin too seriously. He took himself seriously enough. Jake could still hear Abby's throaty laugh as he trudged toward the milking barn.

Jake's musing turned to Kevin. His brother had accomplished a lot in his young life. He'd worked hard for it, and Jake didn't begrudge him his success. In fact, he'd never envied his brother. On occasion, he'd been disappointed in Kevin, proud of him more often than not, but he never wanted what Kevin had. Until now. Jake shook his head and wished there were more women like Abby. At least one more.

Inside the barn, he poured himself a cup of coffee, thankful he'd purchased a coffeepot with a timer for early mornings. He gulped half the cup. By the time he readied everything to start the milking, all thoughts of Abby were shoved aside.

Jake realized that with Kevin home his mom would probably make Kevin's favorite breakfast. The picture of whole wheat buttermilk pancakes dripping in homemade syrup spurred him on. He would have to finagle an invitation to breakfast. His usual zapped blueberry muffin, even a large one, didn't stick with him for long.

He hit the button for the automatic gate and waited as the metal barrier ushered the first bunch of cows into the milking barn. Each heifer backed into a stall, some stomping, others mooing, all wanting relief from the weight of milk in their udders.

Jake sprayed each udder and teats with an iodine solution, then wiped them clean. "Nothing like routine and a pretty lady to take a man's mind off another pretty lady," Jake said to the first heifer as he attached the automatic milking machine's inflations to her teats.

"You say something, son?"

Jake hadn't heard his father enter the barn, although he should have expected it. Leonard arrived at the barn the same time every weekday morning, so Jake should have expected him on Sunday, too, since Carlos was unavailable for his normal Sunday morning shift.

"Just telling number 84 here how purty she is."

Leonard grinned. "About time you got yourself a woman, Jake. I worry about you."

Jake smiled. "I'll stick with the four-legged ladies for now. They understand me, and none of them has ever let me down."

"Careful there," Leonard warned. "Somebody hears you talking like that, and they'll drag you away to the funny farm."

Jake laughed. Nothing like a bit of lighthearted banter with his dad to cheer him up. "Sounds like a good idea. I could use the rest. Just so you don't worry, though, I haven't asked any of these pretty ladies out. Yet."

Father and son chuckled together and set about doing the morning milking.

~

Abby sat at the kitchen table nursing a cup of coffee. Kevin came downstairs looking as tired as she felt, giving her some satisfaction. She didn't want to be the only one who hadn't slept well.

"Morning, sweetheart," Kevin said and kissed her on the cheek.

Okay, time to earn my pay. "Good morning, darling. Did you sleep well?" she purred.

"I did. How about you?"

"Fine," she lied. Odd, she thought, how much harder the truth was. If she admitted to not sleeping well, she would have to explain. Lying, in this case, was easier, but it still rankled. *I'm not lying, I'm pretending. I'm not lying, I'm pretending.* She kept repeating the phrase over and over in her mind, but the mantra didn't set well. If Kevin's family found out, it would still be a lie. That's the kind of people they were. That was a truth she knew without a doubt.

"Morning, Kevin," Pat said.

"Morning. Where's Dad?"

"Helping Jake with the milking. Carlos usually does it on Sundays, but he had to go to Montrose last night for a family wedding and reunion. Jake offered to do the morning milking. Leonard's helping so they can be through in time for church."

"How is Carlos?" Kevin asked.

"He's fine. Has another baby on the way."

"Why am I not surprised?"

Pat frowned at Kevin's sarcastic remark. "Are you two going to church with us this morning?" she asked as she set a cup of coffee in front of Kevin.

"I think maybe we'll take a drive," Kevin answered. "Abby would like to see some of the country around here."

"You'll have plenty of time for that while you're here. It would be nice for all of us to go to church together."

"Maybe next week. So what's for breakfast?"

"Your favorite—whole wheat buttermilk pancakes."

"With that kind of breakfast, I'm going to lose my sleek muscular build."

Pat laughed. "I doubt there's much danger in that."

The three of them ate in relative silence, concentrating

on the mouth-watering pancakes, with only a few words exchanged between them. Abby had never tasted pancakes so light, and she ate four before she forced herself to stop.

Abby saw Pat's disappointment when Kevin declined the invitation to attend church. For once, Abby was grateful for Kevin's refusal. She wasn't much for attending church herself. As a little girl, her parents insisted she go to Sunday school and church, but as she got older, she enjoyed it less and less. She still believed in God, but in her opinion, churches were filled with too many hypocrites like her father.

As she savored her last bite of pancake, Leonard entered the kitchen. He wore coveralls, a long-sleeved work shirt, the sleeves rolled up to his elbows, and work boots. Abby detected light scents of manure, milk, and something antiseptic.

"Mornin' all," Leonard said. He poured himself a cup of coffee and headed for the stairs. "Jake'll be here for breakfast, Hon," he said to Pat. "Heard you were fixing pancakes. He went home to shower and change for church first. I'll be down in fifteen minutes."

"I'll have your pancakes ready," Pat said.

Abby's curiosity got the better of her again, and before she could stop herself, she asked, "Are pancakes Jake's favorite breakfast, too?"

"Yes. Same as Kevin's," Pat answered. "He has the recipe, but insists they taste better when I make them." She picked up her plate and Kevin's and carried them to the sink.

Kevin leaned over and whispered in Abby's ear. "A little

curious about Jake, aren't you?"

Abby grinned and whispered back, "Just a little curious period. A bad habit I've always had. Surely you're not jealous."

"Nope, but watch it," Kevin said. "Some people might misinterpret."

"I'll try to control myself. Want more coffee?" Abby asked. Kevin nodded and handed her his cup.

While she filled both cups, Jake walked in the back door.

"Mornin' everyone."

Abby turned and caught her breath. Jake was dressed in tan slacks, an aqua short-sleeved shirt, and a tan tie. A tan suit jacket was slung over his shoulder. Polished maroon western dress boots finished the ensemble. He slipped the jacket over the back of a chair and moved to the counter. Abby froze. He smelled of musky aftershave, and her legs weakened in response.

"Got any extra coffee?" he asked Abby and lifted a cup off a peg on the side of the cupboard.

"What? Oh, sure." Abby filled Jake's mug and hoped her unsteady hand wouldn't spill any hot coffee on him.

"Thanks," he said when she finished, and she dared a glance at his face. In that moment, Abby caught a closer look at Jake's eyes and realized what made them so unusual. His right eye was a soft green, the left grayish blue. The difference was subtle, but they were definitely two different colors.

Jake sat at the table next to Kevin, and Pat set a plate of

pancakes in front of him. He assessed Kevin's attire. "Not going to church?" he asked.

"Abby and I have other plans this morning." Kevin raised his eyebrows a couple of times and smiled at Abby as she set his cup in front of him.

"Kevin's going to show me around North Fork this morning," Abby explained.

"Plenty of daylight for that," Jake said.

Kevin shoved away from the table. "What is it with you people? What we do and when we do it is our business. You going in that," he frowned at Abby, "or are you going to get dressed?"

Abby, still wearing her robe, glared at Kevin. "I'll go get ready. Shouldn't take me very long. Don't leave without me, sweetheart," she said and kissed Kevin on the cheek. As she headed for the stairs, the heat of embarrassment and anger spread through her. It was going to be a long three weeks.

~

Borrowing Leonard's red late-model Chevy pickup for the day, Kevin drove Abby around North Fork, showing her the schools he attended from grade school through high school. They passed by the city park with its enormous shade trees and expansive lawn. Swing sets, a jungle gym, and slides stood at the far end of the park. The football field bordered the park on the east, and beyond that a baseball field. He told her about all his touchdowns and homeruns and how his athletic prowess garnered him a football scholarship to the University of Colorado. Abby feigned interest.

When he finished the grand tour of North Fork, Kevin headed the pickup toward Kebler Pass. Abby absorbed the beauty of the North Fork of the Gunnison River winding along the valley floor. Kebler Pass was nature at its finest. Rugged mountain peaks pierced the skyline, and thick stands of quaking aspen, or quakies, as Kevin called them, bordered the gravel road. Profuse wildflowers of bright yellows, varied shades of orange and red, lavender, blue, and white added their own hues to the landscape, reaffirming this was God's country. She envied Kevin growing up in such a picturesque pristine area.

They picnicked at Lost Lake Slough, eating a lunch Pat had packed. Nestled beneath a glaciered craggy peak, the lake reflected beauty and tranquility. The ridged granite peak and basin of snow and ice below the summit resembled a photograph from a coffee table book. To experience a mountain so spectacular and up close was something Abby never expected. The mountains west of Denver were beautiful, but she had always observed them from a distance.

Scattered along the shore, fishermen cast their lines out on the mirrored surface. Two children played near the water's edge under the watchful eye of their mother. Kevin talked about the times he spent fishing the lake with his parents and Jake, and pointed toward a trail that led to a second, more isolated Lost Lake, about a mile away. As she listened to Kevin talk, Abby could see he had wonderful memories of growing up in North Fork. She wondered when, or why, he had turned his back on his heritage.

Chapter 5

"*K*evin Karlson, you sure are a sight for sore eyes."

Kevin grimaced, then turned and smiled at the older woman approaching their table. "Wanda. How are you?"

"Shoot, I'm doin' okay. But you. You look like you're doin' more'n okay. This pretty little thing your fiancée?" She smiled at Abby.

"She is. Abby, I'd like you to meet Wanda, owner of this disreputable joint. My fiancée, Abby."

Abby greeted Wanda and listened as Kevin answered, or artfully dodged, Wanda's torrent of questions. When Wanda turned her back and walked away, Kevin rolled his eyes, then crossed them. Abby laughed.

"I knew this would happen if we came here. Too bad Granny's Café has the best food in town. You see what I mean about a small town? Everybody knows everybody and their business. She already knew I was bringing my fiancée home. Now you know why I asked you to fill in for Gail. Easier than explaining."

"Easier than admitting something didn't work out, you mean."

Kevin frowned. "Just easier than explaining everything. This is exactly why I hate coming home. I'm bored to tears and have to put up with continual interrogation about my life, most of which they already know from my mom."

"I take it Wanda's been around awhile."

"She started waiting tables in here when she was in high school. About fifteen years ago she bought the place. She and Mom and Dad all went to school together. Just one big happy family."

Abby frowned at Kevin's sarcasm. How could he not like North Fork and the people who lived here? Wanda's interest in Kevin and his life appeared genuine.

Abby's father had moved his family so often she barely had time to make friends, let alone feel like she was a part of anywhere. Kevin's sour grapes attitude about his home was getting old. She had enjoyed the day until they stopped at the café. Over supper, Abby listened patiently to Kevin's diatribe about North Fork and its residents, until his complaining grew tiresome.

"You know, Kevin," she set her empty plate aside, "I'm tired of hearing how much you hate this place." She kept her voice low so the diners sitting near them wouldn't hear. "I'd give my eye teeth to have grown up the way you did. I never stayed in one place long enough to have any long-lasting friends, nor have anyone know me well enough to care what happened to me. We lived in cities where my father could remain anonymous enough to slip out of town without too much fuss.

"You have a father who loves you and takes pride in you and everything you do. I'll bet he attended every ball game and school function you were involved in, and I'll bet he went to all your back-to-school nights, too. How lucky you are."

Abby fought back tears but managed to keep her voice even. "I can count on one hand the number of times my father attended anything I was involved in. In fact, I don't even need one hand, because he never attended anything. He couldn't have cared less. My mother always came alone, and after a while I quit asking my father if he'd come. I knew he wouldn't. Oh, he promised, but something always came up at the last minute." Abby took a drink of water to wash away the lump in her throat.

Kevin placed his napkin on his empty plate and glared at Abby. "Are you through?" he asked.

She put the glass down. "Yes. I see you aren't interested in my life. Yours is so much more important."

"I was talking about the meal." He picked up the check. "Let's go. Time to make the family happy by showing up." He dropped a few bills on the table for a tip and scraped back his chair. "Women," he said under his breath and headed for the cashier.

55

~

Abby totaled the final bridge hand. "That's two rubbers to one," she declared.

"You two owe us a rematch," Jake said. "No way Dad and I are going to let you get the best of us."

Abby scooted her chair back from the kitchen table. "What do you think, Pat? You ready to take these guys in a rematch?" She placed the two decks in their box.

"Anytime."

"You're on, then. Just say when." Abby grinned at Jake. "Now, if you don't mind, I'd better see what Kevin is up to."

When she entered the living room, Kevin was absorbed in reading a trade journal. He had turned down the suggestion he play bridge in Leonard's place and spent the evening in the living room reading.

Abby sat beside him on the couch. "All work," she said and kissed him on the cheek.

Kevin frowned. "What's that supposed to mean?"

"Never mind. I think I'll go to bed."

"Good night."

For the second night in a row, Abby had trouble falling asleep. Kevin could actually be fun and interesting when he set his mind to it. She enjoyed spending the day with him touring the valley and surrounding mountains.

With such a spectacular setting, how could anyone not enjoy growing up in North Fork, let alone not want to visit occasionally? Abby had always wanted to live in a small town. She longed for the intimacy and the sense of belonging that seemed a part of smaller communities. She'd discovered that longing when she visited the small hometown of her friend and co-worker, Meg. She found that same longing here with Kevin's family.

"Why can't Kevin see how special all of this is?" she whispered. "Why doesn't he appreciate his family?"

~

What does she *want?*

Kevin studied the missed call on his cell phone. He entered the number, but stopped short of completing the call.

When he had finally set aside his reading and made his way upstairs to the privacy of his room, he checked his cell phone. Earlier that day he had turned off his phone, knowing there was little cell service in the higher mountain areas. He'd returned the message from his secretary, leaving extensive instructions on her work phone. It was the second call that upset him. He stood staring out his bedroom window into the dark, debating about whether to respond to Gail's message.

"Call me, Kevin. It's important. Please."

He might have ignored the message except for the "please." A week ago she had blown him off, said she didn't want to be engaged to him. Had she changed her mind? And if she had, did he really care?

Kevin's temper flared, and he resisted the urge to fling the phone out the window. Gail's timing couldn't be worse. She had the gall to dump him right before their planned trip to North Fork, and now she had the nerve to beg him to return her call.

Kevin disconnected the phone, undressed, and climbed into bed. He closed his eyes and thought about Abby. He actually enjoyed spending the day with her, until they stopped in town to eat supper. *How dare Abby lecture me about not appreciating my hometown and family. Gail would understand; or better yet, not care.* He grabbed his cell phone from the nightstand and punched in Gail's number.

~

Abby slept late the following morning. By the time she made her way downstairs, Pat was washing the last of the breakfast dishes. Kevin sat at the kitchen table reading the newspaper and sipping coffee. He smiled at Abby when she sat down beside him.

"What would you like for breakfast, Abby?" Pat asked.

"Just some coffee, I think. It's a little late for breakfast."

Kevin grinned at her. "'Bout time you got up."

"Sorry, this fresh mountain air helps me sleep." Pat set a cup of coffee in front of Abby just as the phone rang.

"It's for you, Kevin." Pat handed the phone to her son.

Kevin looked surprised as he took the phone, but something about his demeanor made Abby suspicious. He was just a little too animated, like he actually expected the call.

"Evelyn, this is a surprise," Kevin said after his initial hello. Kevin listened for a minute then said, "Can't Liz handle it? She's familiar with the account. I'm not ready to cut my vacation short just to appease a client." He paused again for Evelyn's response.

"That serious, huh?" He frowned. "I'll see what I can do. Tell Robert I'll call him as soon as I can." Another pause. "No, it's all right. You did the right thing. I'll check with you as soon as I get in."

Kevin clicked the phone off and set it on the table.

"Is there a problem?" Pat frowned, and the question in her eyes made Abby want to cry.

Abby knew Liz was on vacation in Europe and not available to handle anything. And Evelyn would have called his cell phone, not Karlson's home phone. Kevin put business above everything, so his reluctance to cut his vacation short for a crisis didn't make sense. Everything pointed to a set up. She was sure Kevin had just come up with an excuse to leave. She smiled. His lie meant she didn't have to pretend anymore. She could leave with him.

"I'm sorry, Mom," Kevin said. "A crisis with one of my biggest clients has come up, and I have to go fix it. He won't talk to anyone but me."

"What about your class reunion and the award dinner? That's the reason you came home."

"I'll be back in time. It's a little over two weeks away. This should take me only a few days to straighten out." He folded the newspaper and stood. "Guess I'd better get packed."

Abby set her cup on the table. "I'll need to get packed, too." She slipped out of her chair to follow Kevin.

"Oh, Abby, do you need to go, too?" Pat asked. "I feel like we're just getting to know you."

Before Abby could reply, Kevin said, "Mom's right, Abby. There's no need for you to leave. I'll be tied up in business meetings and who knows what else? You may as well stay and get better acquainted with my family."

Abby didn't know what to say. She hadn't planned on this development. "I'll help you pack," she said and followed Kevin upstairs.

"What do you think you're doing?" Abby asked as the bedroom door closed behind her. "There's no reason for me to stay if you're not here."

Kevin smiled. "There's every reason. My fiancée would jump at the chance to get to know my family better. It's a perfect solution. With you staying here, my family is appeased, and I can take care of business without feeling guilty."

Abby had never known Kevin to feel guilty about anything, and she was quite certain that included his family. Abby's temper flared, and she could feel the heat creep up her neck and into her cheeks.

"You planned this, didn't you? There's not really a crisis. You just want a good excuse to get out of here and leave me stranded to lie for you. I have a notion to march downstairs and tell your mother the truth."

"Whoa!" Kevin grabbed Abby's arm before she could make a move for the door. "Take a deep breath, Abby. What's the problem?"

Abby glared at him. "The problem is you're lying. I happen to know Liz is on vacation."

"So Evelyn reminded me." Kevin brushed Abby's

cheek with his knuckles. His look and voice softened. "Look, Abby, you appear to like my family. You should enjoy staying here. Besides, you have that $50,000 to earn, unless, of course, you're prepared to pay all of the money back."

The last of Abby's patience slipped. "When this is over, Kevin, you can find yourself a new business manager, because I quit!"

"We'll see. In the meantime, you can keep my family happy while I save my business. But if I don't take care of this crisis, I may not have a business, so quitting would be a moot point, wouldn't it?"

Abby seethed. He almost sounded convincing, but her gut instinct knew better.

"As soon as I get packed, we'll go downstairs together, arm in arm, just like a couple of lovebirds. Then you'll give me a big sexy good-bye kiss. Tears would be nice if you can conjure some up." Kevin released Abby's arm, picked up his suitcase, and dropped it on the bed. With his back to Abby, he began moving his shirts from the closet to his suitcase.

Abby looked around for a blunt object to clobber Kevin but found nothing handy. She clenched and unclenched her hands and took deep breaths. Her greatest acting challenge faced her in a few short minutes. The only thing stopping her from telling Pat the truth was that she couldn't pay Kevin back. It was that simple.

The $50,000 was already spent. She'd sent the checks the day before they left Denver for North Fork. She should never have taken the money up front, but she was stuck. She would have to make the best of the situation. Respite from

Kevin's moods for a few days seemed a welcome thought at the moment.

She shouldn't have been so anxious to rid herself of her father's debts. If only she'd taken more time to think things through....If only her father had been more responsible in his dealings....If only her father had been a man like Leonard....If only....

~

The trunk lid closed on Abby's last chance for escape.

"Are you sure you have to go?" she asked.

Kevin opened the driver's side door and turned to Abby. Cradling her face in his hands he said, "I'll be back before you know it. I promise."

He bent his head and touched his lips to hers, then gathered her in his arms as he deepened the kiss. Abby leaned into him, gave back as best she could, and counted silently until the kiss ended. Kevin kissed the tip of her nose, smiled, and winked at her. "Don't have too much fun while I'm gone," he said.

At Kevin's remark, Abby's temper flared, and as usual, when her temper flared, tears surfaced. Through a forced smile and clenched teeth, Abby said, "I'll get even with you for this."

"It was my turn, remember?" Kevin said through his own false smile.

"You've used your turn and then some."

Kevin gave Abby a quick kiss, slid behind the steering wheel, and started the BMW.

"See you in a few days, sweetheart." He closed the door and drove away.

~

Jake rounded the corner of the garage in time to witness the kiss. He stopped short and fought, to his surprise, the jealousy that surfaced at the sight of Abby melting in Kevin's arms. He sauntered across the grass as the BMW disappeared in a cloud of dust.

"Kev headed somewhere?" he asked.

Abby jumped at Jake's question and turned toward him.

Jake grinned. "Sorry, didn't mean to startle you."

Abby wiped a tear from her cheek. "That's okay." She smiled, and Jake's heart lurched. Was there trouble in paradise? "Everything okay? Where's Kevin going?"

"Back to Denver. Client crisis, and Kevin's the only one the client will deal with. He should be back in a few days."

"I see you decided not to go with him."

Abby shrugged her shoulders, sternness settling on her face. "Didn't see any reason to. He'll be in meetings with little time for me, if it's the kind of crisis he thinks it is." Abby moved toward the house and wiped another tear from her cheek. "He thought I'd have more fun here getting to know my future family better."

Jake watched her stiff back. Something wasn't quite right, but he couldn't put his finger on it. Abby appeared more angry than disappointed, but that didn't make sense. Maybe he just read her wrong. After all, he'd only known her a couple of days. He followed her into the house.

Abby stood at the sink, filling a glass with water. Jake could hear his mother start the washing machine in the laundry room just off the kitchen. He walked to the refrigerator and pulled out a pitcher.

"Could you hand me a glass from the cupboard to your left?" he asked Abby.

"Sure." Abby reached into the cupboard and grabbed a small glass.

"No. One of the big plastic ones, please. One shelf up."

Abby handed Jake a red opaque glass.

"Thanks. Would you like some iced tea?"

"I have a headache. I think I'll lie down for a while."

"Anything I can do for you?" he asked as Abby moved toward the stairs.

She turned and smiled at him. "I'll be fine after I rest a while."

Jake watched Abby climb the stairs and shook his head. If he were Kevin, Abby would be in the car beside him, and in spite of his meetings, he'd find time for her. "You're a fool, Kev," he muttered under his breath.

Pat entered the kitchen. "You say something, Jake?"

"What? Oh. Just mumbling to myself. So, what's up with Kev?"

"He had some kind of crisis that couldn't wait until after his vacation. Where's Abby?"

"She went upstairs to lie down. Said she had a headache."

"She was disappointed Kevin had to leave. It breaks my heart that he got called away. We don't get to see him often enough. I thought this time would be different since Abby came with him. But I guess not."

Jake slipped his arm across Pat's shoulders. "Look at the bright side, Ma. At least we have a chance to get better acquainted with Abby."

Pat smiled. "You're right. Isn't she a lovely girl? But she is a surprise. Not at all what I expected in Kevin's fiancée." She sighed. "I'm not sure what I expected, but it wasn't Abby."

"I know what you mean. We can hope Kevin's tastes have changed."

Jake chugged half the iced tea, refilled the glass, and headed for the door. "When Dad gets back from town buzz me. I'll be in the barn."

Chapter 6

"Now what?"

Abby flopped onto the bed, stared at the ceiling, and growled. She wished she had put her hands around Kevin's neck and squeezed. She smiled. On second thought, let him leave. For the next few days she wouldn't have to keep him happy. She could relax and enjoy his family.

Abby closed her eyes. Her heart fluttered at the image of Jake in his coveralls, work boots, and black baseball cap—"Karlson Dairy" embroidered in white script across the front. Between the brothers, she preferred Jake's down-to-earth knee-buckling looks to Kevin's Pierce Brosnan pretty-boy features. Jake's warm smile and the spark of mischief in his eyes added to the attraction. She couldn't get

Jake out of her head. Abby realized she wanted to get to know him better.

And what good will that do me? Once Kevin announces the breakup, Jake won't make a move. Too awkward, and something tells me Jake puts family first. And what makes me think he's interested in the first place?

Abby squelched a scream and sighed. Even if, by some miracle, Jake admitted he was interested in Abby after her "breakup" with Kevin, she would have to tell him the truth, and once he knew the truth, she'd look like an extortionist. She didn't believe in keeping secrets, period. Lies had a nasty habit of surfacing when you least wanted them to, and then trust took a permanent holiday.

Why did I agree to this?

A tear trickled across her temple and onto the pillow. No matter the outcome, she decided to enjoy herself the next few days and get to know the Karlsons better. They were the kind of family she always dreamed about, and she intended to make the most of it.

Abby awoke an hour later, her headache gone. The day had turned hot, and she changed from her jeans and blouse into denim shorts, an aqua tank top, and Birkenstocks.

The house was deserted, but Pat had left a note on the counter. Following her instructions, Abby made herself a sandwich and washed it down with iced tea. Her hunger sated, she wandered outside.

As her note stated, Pat was in the garden. Abby watched the stately woman for a moment and memories of her own mother tugged at her heart. Pat sported the same type of straw hat Abby's mother used when she gardened. Although her mother had been a nurse by profession, she loved plants and gardening was her hobby. Some type of houseplant filled every room in the house, and with Abby's help, her mother planted a garden whenever she could.

"Would you like some help?" Abby asked as she approached.

"I can always use help staying ahead of these weeds, but you'd better get a hat and some sun screen. You're much too fair to be without either. You'll find both in the kitchen. The sun screen is on the counter, and there's a hat hanging by the door."

Abby returned a few minutes later wearing a floppy straw hat and smelling of sunscreen. She worked with Pat weeding and tying up the tomatoes. A myriad of yellow blooms covered the vines, and a few small green tomatoes nestled among the foliage.

"It won't be long before you'll have some ripe ones."

"I got a good start on my garden this year. I started seeds in the house in March, and no hard freezes after May 1st this year."

Abby held a vine up while Pat tied strips of plastic shopping bags around the vine and a wooden stake.

"There, that ought to do it for a few weeks, anyway. Do you have a garden at home?"

Abby shook her head. "I wish. I live in a high-rise apartment. But my mother loved to garden, and I used to help."

Pat gave Abby an odd look. "Oh, I was under the

impression that you still lived with your parents on a large estate."

Abby panicked. What had Kevin told them about Gail that didn't apply to her? *Think. Think.* She hoped Kevin had been his usual self and not told them a lot about Gail. She would have to bluff and hope it worked. If not, then everything would be out in the open, and she would no longer have to lie. Time to start telling some of the truth.

"I moved out a short time ago. I needed more privacy. And since I work for Kevin, I have my own money, so I can do as I please."

"I didn't know you worked for Kevin. I never could keep Kevin's life straight. I thought he said you were glad you didn't have to work." Pat glanced at Abby. "Forgive me, Abby. I shouldn't pry. It's none of my business."

"No, you have every right to know. I have a trust fund, so I don't have to work," Abby bit her lip at the lie, then forged ahead, "but I was tired of not using the degree I worked so hard to achieve. It's been a bit awkward working for Kevin and being engaged to him, but we try to keep the two relationships separate. We're very careful about what we say or do at work, and keep the personal part of our relationship outside the office. So far it's working." Abby held her breath, waiting for Pat's reaction.

"I think it's wonderful you want to work for a while. You'll have to forgive my confusion. I'm afraid Kevin's dated so many girls that I get them mixed up." Pat blushed. "Oh, I think I've said too much."

"It's all right." Abby smiled. "I'm well aware that Kevin

was quite a ladies' man before he dated me. But I don't mind. I'm the one who gets him in the end." *If there's any justice at all.*

Pat stood and stretched, digging her fingers into her lower back to massage her tired muscles.

"If you want to sit down, I'll finish the tomatoes," Abby offered.

"Actually," Pat glanced at her watch, "it's time I took some iced tea and cookies up to the barn. I imagine Jake and Leonard are ready for a bit of a break." Pat removed her gardening gloves. "Would you like to go along?"

"I'd love to." Abby wiped beads of sweat from her brow. "I think I've had enough sun for a while." She removed the straw hat, and fanned herself with it.

"It's going to be a hot one. Time to find a cooler spot."

Abby followed Pat to the house and helped her collect the iced tea, large plastic glasses, and homemade chocolate chip cookies. They put everything in a basket that Abby insisted she carry.

Abby and Pat walked toward the milking barn on a wide worn track that edged an alfalfa field. A barbed wire fence bordered both sides. Thick, woody bushes grew along the other side of the path, a few feet separating each bush. Abby noticed tiny green fruits on the bushes.

"What kind of bushes are these?" she asked.

"Wild plums. They make the best jam. Won't be long before they're ripe, and I'm elbow deep in them."

Abby's mouth watered at the thought of fresh jam. She hadn't had homemade jam since her mother became ill.

"So, you work for Kevin? He did say you preferred Gail for your professional name. What do you do?"

Pat's comment took her by surprise. "I'm business and office manager for the firm. I have been for about three years."

"That's quite a responsibility."

"Kevin promoted me when he took over the firm. The previous owner's wife was my predecessor. I worked directly under her, so it was a natural transition."

"Isn't that a coincidence? The firm was run by a husband and wife and will be again." Pat sidestepped a rock in the path. "Will you continue to work after the babies come?"

Abby nearly dropped the basket she carried. She and Kevin hadn't discussed children. She didn't know if he wanted any or not. Most men wanted at least one child. She searched for a neutral answer.

"We'll see when the time comes. We're not in any hurry."

"Don't wait too long." Pat winked.

They arrived at the milking barn, and Abby stopped dead in her tracks, her heart leaping into her throat. If Pat said anything more, Abby didn't hear her. A mass of black, white, and gray fur greeted them with menacing barks. Abby's mouth went dry and her vision blurred. She felt Pat's hand on her arm.

"Abby, what's wrong? It's okay. Spur won't hurt you."

Abby realized the dog had stopped barking and sat only a few feet away, staring at her, wagging his tail.

"I-I'm not very good with dogs," she croaked.

"You don't have to be afraid of Spur. He only gets upset if you try to take something that doesn't belong to you, or do something that's harmful to one of us."

Pat took the basket from Abby's hand. "He barked to warn Jake someone was coming. Let him sniff the back of your hand and talk to him. Tell him you're part of the family."

"I-I can't."

"Sure you can. He's Jake's dog. Just another member of the family," Pat said as she nudged Abby forward.

Abby didn't want to upset Pat, who seemed so sure of Spur's good nature, so she willed her feet to move, extending the back of her shaking hand toward Spur. Abby stopped when Spur moved toward her. She forced herself not to withdraw her hand and hoped she'd still have most of her fingers left. Spur smelled her hand, then sat in front of her, his tail sweeping dirt from side to side.

Abby sucked in a deep breath and backed away, pleased she'd let a dog close enough to sniff her hand. Spur whimpered and cocked his head to the side as Abby inched backward. She bumped into something tall and solid and let out a small yelp.

"Let him taste you," Jake said near her right ear.

"T-taste me?" She glanced over her shoulder at him.

Jake put his hands on her shoulders and pressed down. "Kneel and extend the back of your hand again. Let Spur lick it."

Closing her eyes, she knelt and extended her hand. At the feel of Spur's soft tongue, Abby's eyes flew open; she flinched and pulled her hand back.

"I think he likes you."

Abby jerked her head up at Jake's comment. "How can you tell?"

"He's smiling."

Abby assessed the sneer on Spur's face. "That's a smile?"

"He wants you to pet him," Jake said, moving toward Spur, "like this." Jake scratched Spur behind his ears and under his chin.

Spur groaned and whimpered in pleasure. Abby couldn't take her eyes off Jake's hands. They were wide and strong. She couldn't help but wonder what they would feel like touching her.

"Go ahead," Jake urged.

"What? Oh." Abby realized Jake wanted her to pet Spur. Cautiously, she mimicked Jake's treatment of Spur, and the dog rewarded her with the same whimpers of appreciation Jake had received.

"What kind of dog is he?"

"He's a mutt, but don't tell him." Jake lifted an eyebrow. "He thinks he's special. He has some Australian Shepherd, some Border Collie. He's a duke's mixture, but we love him just the same, don't we, boy?"

Spur barked once; Abby flinched. Instead of moving, which her instincts told her to do, she continued to rub Spur behind his ears, surprised at how comforting the action was. But when Spur tried to lick Abby's face, she jumped up and back, the fear returning.

"No Spur. Bad boy," Jake scolded. Spur dropped his head and lay down. "Sorry, he doesn't understand that some people don't like dog kisses."

Abby willed her racing heart to slow. "I-it's okay. He just startled me. This is the closest I've been to a dog since I was five."

"Well, I think you've made a friend." Jake moved to a door at the side of the barn. "Come on in. I'll give you the grand tour of a milking barn."

As she followed Jake, Abby noticed a small corral close by with about six to seven cows milling around. "What's that for?" She pointed toward the enclosure.

"That's the maternity ward." He winked. "Those mamas are going to have babies."

"Oh." Abby felt the heat of embarrassment rise to her face. "What kind of cows?"

"Holsteins." Jake opened the barn door and Abby stepped through. Pat had taken the food basket in while Abby and Spur got acquainted.

A mixture of manure, antiseptic, milk, and something Abby couldn't identify assaulted her nostrils. The odor was stronger than what she experienced her first few days here. She had almost gotten used to the smell of the barnyard from a distance. She swallowed and wondered how anyone could work with this constant smell. The odor didn't seem to affect Jake at all.

～

Jake couldn't take his eyes off Abby's long, shapely legs.

He noticed several jagged scars from her knee to her ankle on her left leg, and the scars along her left arm seemed more prominent than when he first met her. He wondered, again, what kind of accident caused them. Not that it mattered. They certainly didn't detract from her beauty.

Abby stepped inside the barn and turned toward Jake. Caught staring, he shifted his eyes away from Abby's legs to her face. "Well, this is the milking barn. This is where we spend several hours morning and evening and sometimes a good part of our day, when we're not irrigating, haying, cutting silage, calving, feeding—well, you get the picture."

Abby smiled. "It's bigger than I expected."

"We built it last fall and have been gradually increasing the herd since. We're milking about 300 cows twice a day, but we're going to increase that to about 500 a day, plus start milking three times a day instead of two. That will boost our milk production by quite a bit."

Jake showed Abby how the milk traveled from the milking stalls through a two-inch stainless steel pipe to a cooler where cold water cooled the milk in the pipe before it went into one of two 4000-gallon stainless steel tanks.

"Here, put your hand on this pipe," Jake instructed Abby.

"It's very warm," Abby said.

Jake smiled. "That's the temperature of the milk when it comes out of the cow. Now touch this one." He indicated the pipe that exited the cooling unit.

Abby touched it and jerked her hand back. "It's really cold."

"That's the temperature of the milk when the trucks pick it up and haul it to market." Jake ushered Abby through a door into the milking area.

"Why three times a day?"

"What?"

"Why would you want to milk three times a day? Isn't that hard on the cows?"

Jake smiled, suppressing a chuckle. "Milking three times a day will increase our production about fifteen per cent. We'll have to hire more people, but we'll still make more profit. As for the cows, just makes them work a little harder."

"How many people do you employ?"

"Besides Dad and me, five. As the herd and work load increase, we'll add more hired help."

Jake couldn't help being proud as he talked about the dairy and how it worked. He led Abby down a cement aisle. Chest high on either side were milking stanchions, all cement. Attached to the aisle-side of each stanchion was a rectangular box.

Jake pointed to one of the boxes. "These are computers that tell how many pounds of milk a cow has given, how long it took to milk her, and if she gave more or less than the last time she was milked." He punched a button and the computer lit up with numbers. "The last cow was milked for eight minutes, gave 1.3 pounds of milk more than she usually does." He punched another button. "Now we're looking at cow #165, and she gave 35.1 pounds of milk or about 4 gallons last milking."

77

"How does the computer know which cow is being milked?"

"Each cow has a necklace with a red tag hanging from it. When they come into the barn, they walk through that archway..."

Abby followed Jake the length of the aisle and saw an archway on each side where the cows entered the barn from the corral.

"...and the computer reads the number on the tag and knows the order in which they entered. Just below us, in the basement, are the meters that keep track of the amount of milk, which travels through the pipes to the holding tanks."

"Amazing. I didn't think it would be so automated."

Jake smiled. Abby was genuinely interested in how a milking barn worked. "You thought we were still milking by hand?"

Abby's neck and face colored. "I guess I did."

"Isn't modern technology wonderful?" Jake winked. "I think I can hear Mom's cookies calling. Let's go snag a couple before Dad eats them all."

Jake led the way out of the milking area along a narrow hall and up carpeted steps. The top of the stairs opened into a large carpeted office with a window overlooking the milking area. A lone desk with a computer sat in front of the window. Leonard and Pat were talking in a smaller room partitioned off from the main room. The cookies and tea sat on a small table between them. Both waved, and Abby returned the greeting.

Pointing to the computer, Jake said, "That's what

controls all the mechanisms in the barn. It keeps track of everything here and then sends it to the computer in my home office."

"What happens if you have a power outage?"

"We have a backup gas generator that takes over until power is restored." He smiled at Abby. "So, what do you think of our operation?"

"I think it's wonderful." Abby pointed to a large round vat-like metal container with a gauge on the lid. "What's that?"

"That's semen. We keep it in liquid nitrogen until we're ready to use it." Jake opened the container and pulled out a long metal tube. "We call this a straw, which contains the semen and has the name of the bull on it. There's a cotton plunger inside and you cut the end with a razor blade, put a long clear plastic tube or sleeve over the plunger, put on long plastic gloves and impregnate the cow." Jake grinned, and Abby blushed again. "Works better than keeping a bull."

"Oh."

"You're welcome to watch the next time—"

"No, that's all right. I get the picture." Abby took a deep breath. "I'd like to come to the barn while you're milking and see how you do it."

"You're welcome anytime, Abby. Now, about those cookies you brought with you...."

Chapter 7

"Why don't we play some bridge?" Pat suggested as she cleared the supper dishes. Abby gathered up her plate and carried it to the dishwasher.

"Much as I want to get even," Jake said, "I need to relieve Carlos and finish up the milking. Then I've got accounts to go over. I'm several weeks behind on the books. And I can't get the last bank statement to come out right. Probably a mistake on my part, but I need to find it so the books balance."

"You should hire someone to do the books," Leonard said. "I know you don't like that part of this business anymore than I did. I'd help out, but you know me and computers." He shook his head and downed the last of his coffee.

"Accountants cost money, Dad."

Abby picked up Jake's and Leonard's plates. "A good accountant is well worth the money. I should know." She smiled.

Jake shot her a questioning glance.

Pat wiped the countertop. "Abby is business manager for Kevin's firm."

"Really?" Jake frowned. "I didn't know you worked." Jake's scrutiny bored through Abby.

She swallowed and concentrated on making her voice steady. "You must be thinking about Kevin's previous girlfriend. I've been Kevin's office manager and chief accountant for three years. I have a business degree, and I'm a CPA. I'd be happy to help you." She stacked the plates in the dishwasher.

"I'm sure I'll figure it out. No need to bother you."

"It's no bother. Really. I love crunching numbers and can spot a problem in no time at all. And I don't charge family. You can't beat a deal like that."

"I don't take charity," Jake grumbled. He stood and grabbed his cap from the hook on the wall.

Abby's eyes narrowed. "I wasn't offering charity. I was offering help."

Jake turned and stared at her for what seemed to Abby minutes instead of seconds. She returned his stare, refusing to back down or turn away.

He gave Abby a slight nod. "I'll be through at the barn in about an hour. If you're sure you don't mind, you can join me there. We'll walk to the house together."

"I don't mind at all."

Jake paused at the door. "Better change to long pants and bring a jacket. Nights get a bit cool around here this time of year, and the mosquitoes are thick as flies."

~

"Go ahead and go home, Carlos. I can finish up tonight."

"You sure, Jake?"

"Yeah. You need to be home with your family."

"Okay. See you tomorrow."

Jake methodically started milking on the newest bunch of cows, working down the line, attaching the milking inflations to each cow in turn. He heard the door squeak closed as Carlos exited.

He'd enjoyed showing Abby around the milking barn. She acted genuinely interested and fascinated with the process. That's a city girl, for you, he thought. Farm life is different from anything city people know, so they think it's fascinating and romantic, but after they experience the long hours and hard work, the enchantment wears off.

He'd been doing the same routine for too many years. The trouble with routine was it became so automatic he forgot to see the uniqueness in the process. Showing the operation to Abby gave him a new sense of pride in what he'd accomplished. It hadn't been easy to convince his dad to computerize the operation, but time and the efficiency provided by automation had proven Jake right.

Some things never changed, however, no matter how modern the operation. They no longer named the cows, but

Jake could still distinguish each cow in the herd and give a rundown on the difference of each one. Like humans, God never made two animals the same. That alone, Jake reflected, made life interesting and worthwhile.

His thoughts turned to Abby and her comment about working for Kevin. He was sure Kevin told him Gail came from a wealthy family and that she didn't work. Abby fit the physical description Kevin had given him of Gail—green eyes, red hair, and beautiful. Something about Abby's body language, though, told him things weren't as they seemed. It was too much of a stretch to believe that Kevin would know, or date, two women fitting the same description, and yet.... He wished he could figure out what was going on, but one thing was certain—something wasn't right.

"You're sure deep in thought."

Jake's head came up fast and hit the metal bar of the milking stanchion. He muttered a choice word or two as he grabbed his head and turned around. He was met by Abby's smiling emerald eyes and a throaty chuckle.

"I didn't mean to startle you. Are you okay?"

Jake removed his cap and rubbed his head. "I'm fine. How long have you been here?"

"A couple of minutes. You sure your head's okay?"

"Yeah, fine." He grinned. "My hard head probably dented the bar." Jake secured the cap on his head. "I didn't hear the door, and it squeaks really loud. How'd you do that?"

"I came in as Carlos was leaving. I introduced myself."

"Oh." Jake turned and sprayed an iodine solution on a

cow's teats, then wiped them clean. "I'll be darned. Would you look at that?"

"What?"

"Come here. We don't see these very often."

Abby moved next to Jake and looked at the cow's udder. "I don't see anything."

"Teat lice. They're pretty rare and hard to see, especially if you've never seen one. Get a little closer, and I'll see if I can point it out."

Abby moved her head closer. A stream of warm milk hit her square in the face. She jumped back, sputtering. Jake's laughter filled the barn.

"I can't believe you did that!" She wiped the sticky liquid off her face with her hand.

"Hold still," Jake said, a leftover chuckle escaping. He took her chin in one hand and wiped the remainder of the milk off her face with a dry cloth. Abby opened her eyes and looked at him. His heart flipped at the spark he saw flash from the emerald pools. He squelched the desire to kiss her.

"Oooooh, are you in for it. I can't believe I fell for that!" She grinned. "You are so gonna get it."

"Whoa! I was only getting even for the knot on my head." Letting go of her chin, he tapped her nose with his finger. "You might want to use a wet paper towel on your face. Milk can be a little sticky." He pointed toward the bathroom.

Jake whistled along with a country ballad playing in the background while he waited for Abby to return. That old trick worked every time, and he enjoyed getting the best of

Abby. She was a good sport. He'd never forgotten when he was a young boy and his dad pulled it on him. They both had a good laugh. Kevin had run crying to their mom when it happened to him. Kevin still wasn't good at dealing with teasing of any kind.

"Is there something I can do to help, providing it doesn't have anything to do with teat lice?"

Jake turned toward Abby's smiling face, and his heart did another flip-flop. "Naw, I'm about through. Just relax." *Kevin better get his business taken care of and come back quick. I don't know how much time I can safely spend with Abby. She's too tempting, and I haven't got any right to feel that way about her.*

Jake moved to the next stanchion, sprayed and cleaned the cow's teats.

"I could do that, if you'd like to show me how. Then you could do whatever else needs doing." Abby moved next to Jake, watching intently.

"All right, if you want to." Jake explained the process. "We spray an iodine solution on the teats before and after the cows are milked. Keeps bacteria at bay. Then we wipe them off with a damp cloth."

Jake showed Abby a long nozzled sprayer at the end of a spiraled tube attached below the stanchions at the halfway mark of the milking area on each side. The nozzle reached both ends of the milking stanchions. After treating the cows' teats with the iodine solution, then wiping them clean with a wet soapy cloth, Jake attached long narrow bell-shaped stainless steel cups, or milking inflations, to each teat, and the compressor began the milking.

By the time he hooked up the second row of cows to milk, the first row was finished milking and the inflations automatically dropped off the cows, one by one. Jake treated each cow again with the iodine solution, repeating the process as the second row of cows finished milking.

He then pressed a button on the wall and the metal gate that kept the cows in their stanchions moved forward and up, allowing the cows to saunter into the corral at the open end of the barn. Jake pressed a second button and another metal gate at the same end moved the next bunch of cows forward and into the empty stanchions.

When the cows had settled into their places and the gate was in place, Abby went to work with the iodine solution. Jake watched her closely on the first two cows, squeezed her shoulder and said, "You learn fast," then set about working the opposite row of sixteen cows.

Jake kept an eye on Abby as she worked the opposite side from him. He noticed she guarded the tennis shoes she'd changed into, carefully sidestepping puddles of water, dirt, and animal waste that might get them dirty.

As the last cows left the barn, Jake went down each side and pulled down a square-shaped holder set about a third of the way down on the cement wall below each stanchion. Each holder had four circular rings for housing the four milking inflations at each stanchion.

"What's that for?" Abby asked.

"Once we're done with one complete milking, we set the inflations here to get a good cleaning with hot water, soap, and a disinfectant. All I have to do once they're in place is flip a switch, and it's done automatically."

"Isn't automation wonderful?"

"Sure is."

Jake thanked Abby for helping. When he finished hosing down the milking area, he guided Abby to a back door. "Shorter this way," he explained.

~

They angled to the fence where Abby and Pat had walked earlier in the day and followed the path toward Jake's house at the opposite end of the property. The long summer day was still light enough to see the path that now edged the corrals. Spur, who was waiting when they came out of the barn, led the way, running off to chase after something only he could see.

A truck inched along the outside of the far corral fence, dispensing feed as it went. Cows milled about, some eating at the feeding troughs, some lying down, and others standing, chewing their cud. They took little notice as Jake and Abby passed by.

"I like your house," Abby said as they climbed the steps of a front porch as wide as the house. "It's an unusual design. Is it Prairie style or Cottage?"

"A little of both, I guess. I've always liked large, covered porches where you can sit and enjoy the outside. It's especially nice during a thunderstorm."

"I can imagine." Thoughts of watching a thunderstorm on the porch with Jake sent sparks coursing through Abby.

Down girl, it will never happen. Not in this lifetime.

Jake opened the door and ushered her inside. He slipped his boots off, set them next to the door, and hung his cap on a peg. Abby followed suit and removed her tennis shoes.

"You can hang your jacket here." Jake indicated a peg next to his cap. "My office is the first door to your right. Would you like something to drink? Iced tea, coffee?"

"Iced tea would be nice." Abby gazed around the interior of the house. To her left was a formal dining room. The entryway opened into a living room and kitchen, divided by a breakfast counter. A few steps ahead of her at the far end of the office were stairs to the second story.

Jake moved toward the kitchen. "Go on in the office. I'll be right there."

Abby hesitated. Jake had built a beautiful home, comfortable and warm. At least what she'd seen so far. She closed her eyes and imagined herself living there with Jake. *Fat chance!* Abby took a deep breath and entered Jake's office, setting aside her impossible daydream.

Chapter 8

*A*bby wandered into the office, shook her head and smiled. Jake was meticulous about the milking barn and how it looked. Everything in its place and as clean as you could get a barn.

His office was a different story. Papers and books cluttered the desk, chairs, and the top of the file cabinet. Books on veterinary medicine, crop management, and various agricultural subjects also filled a floor-to-ceiling bookcase. A *Stockman's Handbook* occupied the top of a pile on the desk corner.

Abby sat down and turned on the computer. While she waited for it to boot up, she studied framed pictures of Leonard, Pat, and Kevin on the desk. Next to the pictures sat a framed poem. She chuckled as she read the ode.

They walked up the lane together,
the moon was shining down.
He opened the gate before her,
as they returned from town.
She didn't even thank him;
she did not know how.
For he was just a farmer's boy,
and she a Jersey cow.

Unknown

Jake stepped into the office as the computer finished booting up. He handed Abby a glass of iced tea. "Unsweetened, right?"

"Right. Thanks." Abby took a sip as Jake cleaned a stack of books off a chair, placed them on the floor, and moved the chair next to her.

"Sorry about the mess. I've been meaning to clean all this up. Unfortunately, I'd rather hay and irrigate, or work outside. *Anything* but organize my files or do books. I do the basics in order to keep the dairy running. I'd make a terrible desk jockey."

"That's understandable." Abby reached for the mouse. "Okay, let's pull up your accounting program and see what we've got. Where's your checkbook, or do you generate checks from the computer?"

"From the computer."

"Good."

Jake pointed to the accounting icon. Abby moved the mouse and clicked on it.

"This is a good program. What made you decide to use it?""

"Kevin recommended it. Said it's what his office uses."

"That will make things easy, since I'm already familiar with the program."

Jake guided her through the accounts, explaining each one as they went. He kept detailed accounts of each heifer, how much milk she yielded daily, and when she'd last been bred.

Total milk production was documented, along with shipment days and market prices. Prices of grain and feed supplements were also carefully tracked. Payments for milk production, expenses, employee records, and employer expenses and taxes finished up the entries. Jake employed five people besides himself and his father. Contrary to Kevin's comment, Abby could see it did take brains to run a dairy.

"This is quite an operation," Abby remarked after Jake had explained most everything. "I'm impressed."

When she clicked on accounts payable, a Brian Murcheson Fund, Inc. showed some regular large debits. "What's the Brian Murcheson Fund, Inc.? You have large payments going to them."

"That's a fund set up by the MacCords to help local people. The fund provides very low interest rates on money borrowed for college, new business ventures, expanding old businesses, that sort of thing. It helped pay for my college education, plus Kevin's, financed the building of my house, and helped me expand the dairy operation. The payments are for the barn and computer system.

"I'm putting together a new business plan for the dairy but haven't had a lot of time to work on it. Once we're milking 500 cows three times a day, I'd like to process and bottle most of our milk, then sell it either from here or a location in town. If that's successful, then expand to delivering to grocery stores in North Fork and other towns in the area. Any excess milk we'd still sell through the co-op. I'd like to merge the old loan with what I'll need for the new venture."

Abby smiled at Jake. "That sounds very ambitious. I'd like to look at your plan. After studying your books, and checking out a few figures nationally, maybe I could help with the numbers."

Jake studied her for a moment. "You don't need to trouble yourself, Abby. I'll eventually get it worked out."

"It's no trouble. I need something to do while I'm here."

"Kev will be back in a couple of days, and then you'll want to spend the time with him."

Abby stared at the computer screen and fidgeted with her engagement ring. "Maybe Kevin can help, too. He could come up with a great marketing plan."

Jake shook his head. "I wouldn't want to trouble him."

Something in his comment made Abby wary. She decided to avoid Kevin's involvement for the moment. "What do your folks think of the plan?"

Jake shrugged. "I haven't approached them about it yet. Mom's the reason I've been mulling it over. She cooks at the school cafeteria during the school year. It's hard work, and I think it's time she had things a little easier. She could run the store with a little part-time help so she could still garden in the summer and do other things. Dad could help out a little, too, when he's not busy here."

Abby glanced at Jake. "Do you think she'd be happy doing that?"

Jake nodded. "She's great with people, and running the store would be ideal for her. She would still be able to do things around here and watch the store, too."

"So, you're thinking of refinancing the loan you already have to cover the new venture?"

"That's the plan. I'd be crazy not to take advantage of such incredibly low interest rates."

"How low?"

"Two per cent right now."

Abby choked on the drink of tea she'd taken. Jake patted her back.

"You okay?"

Abby coughed, then took a deep breath. She set her glass down and stared at Jake. "How in the world can they get away with only charging two per cent?"

"Well, JD MacCord donated the original—"

"JD MacCord, the movie star?"

"Yep. They have a ranch not too far from here. The fund's named after Mrs. MacCord's first husband. He died in Vietnam. Anyway, JD said he didn't want to make any money off it, just wanted to help people out. So the bank that administers the fund gets one half per cent, and the rest goes into the fund so others can use it. Qualifications are pretty rigid, and penalties for defaulting are plain stiff, but that's what makes the fund work so well. The MacCords and three other volunteer board members have final say on who borrows."

"We'd better come up with a solid business plan, then. Let's look at your bank statement."

Abby found Jake's error and corrected it in no time. In the process of working through the accounts, Jake's and Abby's hands touched occasionally and each time she melted a little inside. She liked his touch. She liked his company. She liked Jake so much better than Kevin. The two hardly seemed like brothers at all.

When they finished with the bank statement, Abby stretched and yawned.

Jake stood. "I've kept you too long. I'll walk you back."

"Thanks. Knowing me I'd probably get lost." She rose and found herself only inches from Jake.

"Thanks for helping me out, Abby. I really appreciate it." He smiled, and Abby's knees nearly buckled.

She found her voice and tried to sound nonchalant. "I enjoyed it, and I meant what I said about helping you. If you don't mind me coming here during the day while you're working, I'd love to work on that business plan. I think I can find what I need, and if I can't, I'll ask."

"If you're crazy enough to want to do it, then I'm happy to let you. You're welcome anytime. Door's never locked."

~

Before leaving the house, Jake handed Abby a

flashlight, and followed her down the porch steps. Spur was nowhere in sight. At the bottom of the steps, she stopped, sucked in a breath, and stared at the night sky. With no moon, the stars were brilliant, like a thick carpet of diamonds.

"I didn't know there were so many," she said. "I've always lived in cities. The stars never looked like this."

"We're a little over 6,000 feet here, so they're pretty bright, particularly on a night like this. Makes you wonder how God did it."

"Yes, it does."

Jake smiled as Abby started down the path toward his parents' house. He tried not to watch the cute little swing to her walk, without success. They were halfway to the barn when Abby stopped abruptly. Jake nearly ran into her.

"W-what was that?"

"What?" Jake looked around, but didn't see anything.

"That noise." She shivered.

Jake listened. A distant chorus of yipping floated on the night air. "Coyotes."

"Coyotes?" She turned toward Jake. "Are they dangerous?"

Jake chuckled. "Don't worry. They're miles away."

"Y-you're sure?"

"I'm sure."

Abby turned and resumed walking, a bit more tentative than before. Instead of following, Jake watched her for a moment. He heard Spur's paws beating the ground behind him and smiled. Spur had decided to join them. In his exuberance to join Jake and Abbey, Spur brushed against

Abby's legs. She screamed and dropped the flashlight.

Jake's laughter filled the quiet that followed Abby's short, high-pitched scream. When she remained still, Jake moved to her side, ignoring the flashlight lying on the path.

"Abby?" He could feel her fear. "What's wrong?"

"A-a c-coyote."

"A coyote? That wasn't a coyote. That was Spur." He whistled and Spur returned to the path from the adjoining field. "I told you the coyotes wouldn't bother us. They're too far away." A chuckle found its way out before he could stop it.

"I-it's not funny! I was scared to death!" Sobs surfaced in short gasps.

Jake pulled her against him and held her. Tears soaked his shoulder. She felt good in his arms. He was sorry he'd made her cry, but he liked holding her. More than he should. He liked the softness of her hair against his neck.

When her sobs ceased, Jake apologized. "I'm sorry I laughed, Abby."

"I-I'm deathly afraid of dogs," she said, still leaning against Jake's shoulder. "Spur's the first dog I've been able to get close to for years." She swallowed and rubbed her fingers across her lips. "When I was five, a neighbor's pit bull attacked me for no reason." She took a deep breath and shuddered. "He crashed through a wooden fence as I walked by."

"The scars on your leg and arm?"

She nodded her head. "A neighbor pulled him off, but it took me a long time to heal—physically and emotionally.

I've been afraid of dogs ever since. When I heard the coyotes...." She shuddered again. "Then Spur jumped out."

"He didn't mean to frighten you. He was just playing." Jake tightened his arms around Abby. He felt her sigh and relax.

Pushing away from Jake, she wiped the tears from her face and pulled a tissue from her jacket pocket. Spur trotted up. Abby flinched.

"Sit, Spur," Jake commanded. "Abby, Spur will protect you. Always. As long as he's with you, you'll be safe. He's *not* going to hurt you."

Abby looked down at Spur. He cocked his head to one side and whimpered.

"See, he's apologizing." Jake grinned at Abby.

Abby reached out and patted Spur on the head. "You're forgiven. Just don't scare me like that again." Spur licked her hand. This time she didn't flinch.

Jake put his hand under her chin and lifted her face to look at him.

"Are you going to be all right now?"

"I-I think so."

Jake would never be able to completely explain what he did next. Forces he'd never felt before intervened. He pulled Abby against him, bent his head, and tasted her lips with his.

Chapter 9

"*D*on't." Abby's hands pressed against Jake's chest and shoved him away. She stared at him. "W-why?"

Shaken, Jake took a moment to collect his thoughts. *Idiot!* What excuse did he have? That he was attracted to his brother's fiancée? That would stick about as well as a dry cow pie to the side of a barn.

"*Well?*"

"Just testing you." *Now where had that come from?*

"Testing me?"

"Yeah. Making sure you really do care about my brother and not his money. Things just haven't added up."

Her hand connected with his face. His eyes watered from the sting, but he stood his ground.

"How *dare* you. You have no right to question my feelings for Kevin."

Jake looked away, the dark night masking the shame he felt.

Abby bent down and retrieved the flashlight from where she'd dropped it. "I think I can manage the rest of the way on my own." She brushed past Jake.

"Spur, go with her."

Spur obeyed, positioning himself beside Abby on the path.

Jake spoke to Abby's retreating back. "Just send him home when you get there."

Abby didn't answer. The flashlight generated enough light that Jake noticed the stiffness to her stride. He closed his eyes and wished he could take back the last few minutes. He'd really screwed up. The slap to his face didn't sting nearly as bad as the guilt for what he had done. Stepping over the line by trying to kiss his brother's fiancée was bad enough, but trying to shame her to cover up his mistake was inexcusable.

He'd have to find a way to apologize to Abby. And he'd have to find a way to tell Kevin what he'd done before Abby did. He could handle Kevin's wrath; he wasn't sure he could handle Abby's. Coming clean wasn't going to be easy, but it was honest, and the right thing to do.

~

Abby eased onto the bottom step of the porch, clicked off the flashlight, and set it beside her. She wrapped her arms around her legs. Anger had kept the tears at bay until she reached the house, but when she sat down, the tears broke free and flowed down her cheeks. She buried her face in her hands and wept.

She'd never had anything hurt as much as Jake's accusation. He didn't believe she loved Kevin, and he was right. She didn't. But he believed the worst of her. He believed she was interested in Kevin only for his money, when she wasn't interested in Kevin at all.

Even worse, the touch of Jake's lips to hers left her wanting more. She'd reacted a little too late—enough to make him suspicious. The slap had surprised her. His comment lit a fire in her, and she reacted without thinking. How was she going to apologize?

Spur nudged her hand and whimpered. She'd forgotten about him. She lifted her head and winced slightly when Spur laid his head on her lap. She rubbed behind his ears and wiped the tears from her face with her free hand.

"What have I done, Spur? I've really made a mess of things, and I don't know how to fix it."

Spur looked up at her, then laid his head down again. She continued scratching behind his ears. He groaned.

Abby flinched at the sound of the door opening behind her.

"Is everything all right, Abby?" Pat asked.

"Fine." Abby didn't turn, afraid Pat would see her tears. "I thought I'd sit out here a few minutes and enjoy the stars."

"They are beautiful, aren't they? I'll turn out the porch and kitchen lights so you can enjoy them better. I'm going on up to bed. Good night, Abby."

"Good night. Do you want me to lock the door when I come in?"

"No, we never lock it when we're home."

The door clicked shut, and she sighed. Spur licked her hand, then settled his head on her lap again.

I can't go on like this. Whatever the consequences, I've got to tell the truth. New tears trickled down her face. She expected Kevin home tomorrow or the next day at the latest. As soon as he arrived she would inform him that the charade was over, at least for his family. No more lies. Enough was enough.

Abby laid her head on Spur's, surprised at how quickly she had bonded with him. "You're a good dog, Spur, giving me comfort like this." His whimper sounded more like a question—*Are you all right?* Of course, dogs couldn't talk, but she could swear Spur was trying to communicate with her.

Abby lifted her head. "You'd better go home before Jake gets worried and comes looking for you." Spur blinked his eyes, but kept his head on Abby's lap.

She smiled. "I'll be all right. Go home, Spur."

Spur moved away from Abby toward the path. He stopped where the path began and turned to look at Abby, as if making sure she would be all right.

"Go home, Spur. Jake's waiting."

Spur uttered a low woof and trotted toward home.

~

Jake sat on his porch swing and waited for Spur. When Spur didn't return right away, Jake paced. What was taking him so long? He was sure Abby had made it the rest of the way with no problems, so what was Spur doing? *Probably chasing a rabbit or skunk between here and there. Quit worrying.*

Jake tried to plan what he would say to Abby the next time he saw her. He had to apologize, but he didn't know how. The reason he gave for trying to kiss her was callous and not easily forgiven. How would he explain the tension between them to his folks? One thing was certain—there would be tension.

Spur barked and bounded up onto the porch. Jake knelt and petted him. "Thanks, Spur, for seeing Abby home. Good boy." Spur barked and moved toward the steps. "What's wrong, boy?" Spur stopped and looked at Jake, then toward the other house, then back at Jake.

"She did get home all right, didn't she?"

Spur barked at Jake, then returned to his side. Jake ruffled his fur and let Spur lick him on the cheek.

"Are you trying to tell me she's upset, and I should go apologize?" Spur barked again and moved to the steps. Jake walked over and sat down. Spur lay down beside him.

"I think we'd better let her Irish temper cool down a little, don't you?" Spur groaned, ending with a guttural woof. "Yeah, I think so, too. Of course, she has every right to be mad. I really screwed up." Spur let out a high-pitched whimper, and laid his head on his paws.

Jake scratched behind Spur's ears. "I sure did like the

way her lips felt. If she hadn't pushed me away....That makes me pretty sick—my own brother's fiancée." He shook his head. "How in the world am I going to face her? I can't exactly send flowers to apologize. Guess I'll just have to use my natural charm."

Spur sat up, let out a yip, and bounded off the porch. Jake laughed. "You're right. I'd better walk softly, keep a wide margin between us, and hope for the best. I don't think I can charm my way out of this one."

~

Abby awoke with a renewed resolve to put an end to her deceit. She would help Pat with whatever needed doing in the house or garden. After lunch, she intended to walk to Jake's and work on his business plan. She was still upset over the kiss and Jake's accusation, but she promised him she would help him gather figures and information for his proposal. She didn't agree to do something and then back out.

As soon as Kevin arrived, all the deceit would be put to rest. Abby could lick her wounds and get on with her life. She had no delusions that the truth would endear her to Jake. But the lies would be in the open and for the moment, that was the important thing.

After breakfast, Abby helped Pat clean house in spite of Pat's insistence that Abby was company and didn't need to help. Later, as they worked together in the garden, Pat talked about Kevin and Jake and some of their escapades when they were young.

"I'll never forget the time Jake challenged Kevin to a

106

bull riding contest." Pat hoed and pulled several weeds. "Of course, the bull was a calf and the boys were eight and five." She wiped the sweat from her forehead.

"Kevin never could back down from one of Jake's challenges. Working together, they caught the calf and put a makeshift halter on him. Kevin was first to climb aboard." Pat chuckled. "Well, that calf took exception to having Kevin on his back. Two stiff-legged jumps and Kevin found himself in a fresh pile of manure."

Abby laughed at the picture in her head. At the moment, it fit what she had in mind for Kevin. "Did you see it happen?"

"I'd gone to the barn looking for the boys and witnessed the whole thing. Kevin was furious, Jake was laughing, and the calf was bawling. Before I could do anything, Jake caught the calf, climbed aboard and rode him for eight or ten seconds, then jumped off.

"Unfortunately, Jake taunted Kevin, saying he couldn't ride a fence rail, let alone a calf. Kevin charged Jake, knocking him down. When I intervened, they were both covered in manure. Talk about smell!"

Abby couldn't stop the laugh bubbling up inside her. By the time she stopped, she had tears streaming down her cheeks. "How in the world did you survive having two such rambunctious boys?"

Pat smiled. "I'm not sure. Patience, a lot of love, and a *lot* of discipline."

"Did they get in trouble for trying to ride the calf?"

"More for making such a mess of their clothes. Leonard

doubled their chores for two weeks. I made them wash their clothes by hand in an old wash tub in the barn. Jake took it all in stride; Kevin didn't speak to Jake for two weeks."

"No spanking?"

"I didn't want to get all that manure on my hands, and I figured they had enough bruises from the calf and each other." Pat tossed a handful of weeds on the pile she and Abby had accumulated. "I think we'd better stop and get some lunch. Jake and Leonard will be ready for some nourishment any time."

Abby helped Pat fix lunch, all the while dreading seeing Jake for the first time since she'd slapped him. She didn't know what to expect.

When Jake and Leonard stepped into the kitchen, Abby busied herself filling glasses with tea. As she sat at the table, she avoided looking at Jake. He didn't speak to her, and she didn't speak to him. The one time she stole a glance at him, he was talking to Leonard about the yield they could expect from the second cutting of alfalfa.

When lunch was over, Jake left without a word. Abby should have felt relief, but instead her heart ached. She hated that a wall of anger and distrust had risen between them; a wall she didn't know how to breach.

As the screen door slammed behind Jake, the phone rang. Pat answered it.

"Kevin!" Pat listened a moment. "She's right here." She handed the phone to Abby.

Abby took a deep breath and pasted a smile on her face. "Kevin, hi."

Pat ushered Leonard out the door, leaving Abby alone in the kitchen.

"Where are you?" Abby hissed.

"Careful, Abby, you don't want the folks to think there's trouble between us," Kevin said.

"No problem. I'm alone in the kitchen, so I don't have to put up a front. When are you coming back?"

"Why, is there a problem?"

"Yes, there's a problem. I can't keep this charade up much longer. Your family's getting suspicious. We need to tell them the truth. The sooner the better."

Kevin's voice turned cold. "I suggest you squelch that notion right away. Unless, of course, you're prepared to pay back the $50,000 plus taxes."

"You'll get your money back, no matter how long it takes. I just can't do this anymore."

"Well, you're going to have to, Abby. I called to tell you the problem with the client is worse than I thought. I'm going to be tied up another week and a half at least."

"Kevin, you can't—"

"Shut up and listen, Abby. I expect you to hold up your end of the bargain or else."

Abby closed her eyes and squelched a scream. She clenched and unclenched her free hand. If Kevin were here, she'd wring his neck.

"Abby?"

"If you're not here, there's no need for me to be here, either. I'll just pack up and take the bus home."

"No bus service in North Fork. Besides, I need you there

to keep the folks happy."

"No. I've had it. I'll find a way back to Denver."

"Leave and you'll regret it the rest of your life."

Abby sat down on a kitchen chair and rested her elbow on the table, the phone still to her ear. "Is that a threat, Kevin? If you're going to tell me I'm fired, you're too late. I already quit, remember?"

"I remember."

She heard him take a deep breath.

"Now, listen very carefully, Abby, because I'm only going to say this once. If you *ever* want to work in accounting again, you'll keep your end of the bargain. I have enough connections to make finding a decent job nearly impossible, and I'll sue you for breach of promise. Is that clear? And yes, it *is* a threat."

The following silence threatened to engulf her. She gripped the phone and waited, unsure what to say.

"Don't push me, Abby," Kevin snarled.

Tears stung her eyes. "Why is this so important to you? Why does it matter so much?"

"I have my reasons, none of which should concern you. So, what's it going to be?"

Abby stared at the floor. She wanted to start her own accounting business as soon as she was free of Kevin. She didn't doubt for one minute that Kevin could ruin that dream for her. She'd already alienated Jake, as if he were a possibility anyway. *Dream on.*

"Abby?"

A tear slithered down her cheek. "All right, I'll stay, and

I'll do my part, but I don't have to like it. Just don't get too smug, because one of these days your way of doing things will catch up to you. I feel sorry for you when that happens, because you won't know how to handle it." Abby disconnected before Kevin could respond.

She silently counted the seconds until the phone rang again. "Karlsons'."

"Don't *ever* hang up on me again."

"Don't *ever* threaten me again," Abby said and disconnected. The persistent ringing of the phone echoed through the empty kitchen.

Chapter 10

*A*bby sat at the kitchen table long after the phone stopped ringing. Tears slithered down her cheeks. She hated Kevin. She rubbed her eyes, trying to staunch the flow of tears. She hated herself even more.

"Abby, honey, what's wrong?"

Abby's head jerked up at Pat's question. She wiped at the tears and accepted the tissue Pat handed her.

"Kevin's going to be tied up for another two weeks." New tears escaped.

Pat put her arm around Abby and pulled her close. "Oh, honey, I'm so sorry. I know how much you miss him."

Abby sobbed harder into Pat's midriff. She didn't miss Kevin; she wanted to strangle him for threatening her future. She didn't deserve Pat's sympathy but accepted it anyway.

New tears slid down her cheeks at the memory of her own mother's comforting embrace.

Abby sniffed and took a deep breath. "I-I'm sorry. I shouldn't let it upset me so much. I know how demanding the business is. I was just hoping he'd be able to get away from it for a while." She blew her nose.

Pat sat down on the nearest chair. "I'm afraid this is all our fault. Leonard and I taught our boys to have a strong work ethic, and they took the lesson to heart." Pat squeezed Abby's hand.

Abby nearly burst out laughing at Pat's comment. At least it made her stop crying. Kevin hadn't taken any of his childhood lessons to heart. Maybe Jake had hogged them all and there were none left for Kevin. As for Kevin's work ethic, he let his employees do the hard work, while Kevin played.

"Do you want to go back to Denver? We could find a way to get you there," Pat offered.

Abby managed a smile. "Do you mind if I stay here? I wouldn't see much of Kevin, and I am enjoying myself."

"We'd love to have you stay." Pat rose. "I have a church meeting in town this afternoon. I'd love to have you go with me."

"Thanks, Pat, but I think I'll go work on Jake's books. I promised I'd help him. I'm afraid I wouldn't be good company, anyway. Is there something I can do to help with supper?"

"Heavens no. I'll be home in plenty of time for that."

"Then I'll see you later." Abby rose and hugged Pat.

"Thanks."

Pat returned the hug. "Anytime, Abby. Anytime."

~

Halfway to Jake's house, Spur joined Abby. She stopped long enough to pet him, realizing her usual fear hadn't surfaced, and continued up the path, comfortable with the dog by her side. She didn't see Jake anywhere and assumed he was in the barn.

She fought her tears all the way to the house. She didn't understand what was going on with Kevin. His excuses made no sense. But what made less sense was his threat. Why was it so important for Kevin that Abby follow through without him?

When Abby reached the house, she sat on the porch swing, inhaled deeply, and gritted her teeth. Before she'd left for Jake's, she'd washed her face and stuffed her cell phone in her pocket. She pulled it out. Kevin had insisted she get a cell phone so he could get in touch with her at any time. Although she hadn't wanted one, at the moment, she was thankful he'd insisted. No one would overhear her conservation, except Spur. She punched in Meg's number, her friend and assistant.

"Meg. It's Abby. I have something I want you to do. You'll have to be discreet, but it's very important."

~

Jake knew Abby was at the house the minute he spotted

Spur lying on the porch near the door. He'd never seen Spur take to someone so quickly. On the other hand, he'd never taken to someone so quickly, either. Not that it mattered.

Jake stopped at the bottom of the porch steps and patted his leg. Spur trotted down the steps to Jake's side, and he knelt to pet the dog.

"So, she's inside, huh?" Spur licked Jake's face. "I guess it's time I faced the music. I don't think I can take much more of the silent treatment." Jake rose. "Wish me luck, boy."

Inside, Jake hung his hat on its peg and looked at the closed office door. He knocked twice and opened it. Abby looked up as the door swung open. Jake leaned his shoulder against the doorjamb.

"I didn't expect to see you here," he said.

Abby turned her attention back to the computer. "I promised I'd help you put a business plan together. I don't go back on my promises."

Jake bit the inside of his lip. *It's now or never.* "Abby, I'm sorry about last night. I was *way* out of line." He held his breath. Abby slowly turned her gaze toward him. He tried to read in her eyes what she was thinking, without success.

"Yes, you were," she said. "You had no right questioning my feelings for Kevin. Or accusing me of loving Kevin for his money."

Jake shifted his position, leaned his back against the doorjamb and stuffed his hands in his front pockets. *This is going to be harder than I thought.* He didn't like having Abby take him to task. He felt guilty enough. His defenses kicked in.

"I don't normally go around doing things like that. It's just that things haven't completely added up. When Kevin told me about his fiancée...well, I was under the impression he was engaged to a very rich girl named Gail who didn't work. Suddenly I'm confronted with someone named Abby who works as Kevin's business manager. Surely you can understand my confusion."

Abby turned away, moved and clicked the computer's mouse. The printer hummed and produced several printed pages. Abby gathered the copies and tamped them together before she looked at Jake.

"It's not my problem you can't keep Kevin's girlfriends straight. However, I *am* engaged to him, and I'm *not* after his money. Money has never been that important to me. My work has."

Jake pushed away from the door and stood next to the desk. His eyes narrowed. "I'm trying to apologize, Abby, but you're not cutting me any slack. You're right, however, that I can't keep Kevin's girlfriends straight. So shoot me." Jake turned to leave.

"Jake wait."

He paused.

"I'm sorry, too. I'm sorry I slapped you. I've never slapped anyone before."

"I deserved it."

"Maybe. Look, why don't we put this behind us and try to be friends, for Kevin's sake."

"I can if you can."

"Good." Abby smiled and turned her attention to the

papers in front of her.

Jake cleared his throat. "As soon as Kevin gets here, I'll tell him what happened and that it was all my fault."

Abby's head jerked up. "You're planning on telling Kevin what happened? Why?"

"It's the right thing to do."

Abby stared at Jake, and he thought he saw panic in her eyes.

"It's not necessary to tell him. You were concerned about your brother, however misguided. Let's leave it at that. Besides, by the time he gets back it will be old news."

Jake frowned. "What's that supposed to mean?"

Abby shrugged. "He's going to be tied up; won't be back until just before the awards banquet. I don't expect him until the first or second."

"You're kidding."

"Nope. He called after lunch. The problem is evidently bigger than he anticipated."

"Is this usual?"

"Advertising is very unpredictable. I think that's why he likes it so much."

"Are you staying?" Jake didn't know whether to hope she was staying or not.

"No reason for me to return to Denver. I would only be a distraction when Kevin needs to concentrate on the job at hand. Now, if you have time, I'd like to go over some things with you. Or would you rather wait until after supper?"

"Now would be fine. I have a little time I can spare." Jake sat in a chair next to Abby. Things still didn't add up.

Abby looked upset, but he couldn't tell if she was upset at him, Kevin, or the circumstances. She almost acted mad at Kevin for something that was beyond his control.

He closed his eyes for a moment. He could smell her soft perfume and hated the feelings that came alive inside him. He wasn't sure he could handle another couple of weeks with Abby and no Kevin.

"Jake?"

He opened his eyes and realized Abby was holding a set of papers for him to take. "Sorry. I've got a bit of a headache." A little white lie wouldn't hurt anything.

"Do you need something for it?"

"I'll be fine."

"Okay. I came up with some figures based on information you already had, plus I found some additional statistics I think will be helpful."

~

Abby concentrated on explaining what she'd put together for Jake, but her mind kept wandering back to her conversation with Meg. She was thankful when Jake asked for a minute or two to look over the papers.

Abby turned her chair to stare out the window. She marveled at the mountain that towered above the farm. A grayish-white patch of slide rock off to the side began to take on a distinct shape. She finally understood why the mountain was named Mt. Lamborn. The slide didn't exactly look like a lamb, but close enough she could understand the name.

Taking in the majesty of the mountain, she

contemplated the information Meg had managed to get for her. Meg had returned Abby's call about five minutes before Jake showed up, so Abby hadn't had time to think about it. She fought back her temper, hoping Jake wouldn't notice. *Client, my foot! Kevin, you are so in trouble. If I could get in touch with you right now—*

"This is really good, Abby."

Jake's comment startled her. She swung her chair around so she could see his face, as she worked to erase the anger from hers.

"Thanks. You did most of the work. I just put it together. But I think your idea is a very viable one. You should discuss it with your folks before too long. If they like the idea, then we can get real serious about making it a reality."

Jake smiled and gave her a slight nod. "Good idea. Are you sure you want to continue to work on this?"

"Absolutely. As I told you before, I need something to keep me busy while Kevin's away." She wanted nothing more than to help Jake see his idea take shape and share as much with him as she could. Here was a man with a tangible idea; one that would not only work but provide jobs for others, not just his mother. Unlike Jake, Abby's father's ideas were pie-in-the-sky that ended up costing others their investments. She wouldn't be a part of Jake's future, but she could help with a small part of it.

Jake handed the papers to Abby. "Thanks again. It doesn't look like we need much more information to start writing a business plan."

"I have a few more figures I'd like to research, then we

can put it all together."

Jake rose. "I'd better get back to work. Stay as long as you want. I'll see you at supper."

"Jake?"

He paused at the door and turned.

Abby smiled. "Apology accepted."

He grinned, nodded once, and left.

~

Abby lay awake, unable to set aside the unsettling day. After Jake returned to work, Abby took Meg's information, made a second call and confirmed her suspicions. Kevin was lying and making her suffer for it. Well, she wasn't going to suffer, at least not while she was in North Fork. She was spending time with three wonderful people, and she intended to make the most of it.

The danger was in becoming too close to them, especially Jake. She was beginning to care for him more than she should. It didn't matter that she'd only known him a few days. She had seen what kind of man he was, and she liked what she saw. She couldn't understand why Kevin had turned out the way he had.

Abby hadn't prayed much in recent years, but she felt a nudge to do so. *God, what am I supposed to do? I can't stop these feelings for Jake growing stronger inside me. I know I won't ever see him again after the Fourth. What will I do then?* She shouldn't let herself get so close, but she couldn't help it.

She fell asleep without any answers and dreamed of

kissing Jake.

~

Jake sat in his office until after midnight, studying the information Abby had put together. Once again, he wondered what was going on between her and Kevin. Things still didn't make sense. She had accepted his apology. He was thankful for that. What he couldn't come to terms with was his continued attraction to Abby.

He and Kevin never liked the same kind of girls, so why this attraction to a girl Kevin loved? That was the problem. Abby was someone Jake would pick. She wasn't Kevin's type, and Jake doubted Kevin had changed overnight.

The other thing that didn't make sense was Kevin staying away for so long, or Abby not returning to Denver. She said she'd just be in the way, but wouldn't Kevin need her expertise as business manager for the firm? And her name...what was up with her name? Was she Gail or was she Abby?

Jake rubbed his eyes and swiveled his chair to gaze at the night sky. He didn't know much about Kevin's business, so it was entirely possible that Abby wasn't needed to help solve a client problem. But if Jake had a problem, he'd want the woman he loved close by so he could bounce ideas off her, or if nothing else, just have her nearby for moral support.

No doubt about it, Jake definitely didn't understand their relationship. On the other hand, it wasn't his place to understand. It was his place to be happy for them. He had a duty to squelch his attraction to Abby. She belonged to

Kevin.

He placed the papers in a folder on his desk, shut the computer down, and climbed the stairs to his room. He would have to watch himself over the next couple of weeks. Every time he was around Abby, he wanted to touch her, hold her close, and kiss her. He settled into bed, unable to purge his troubled thoughts.

"God, I need your help. I need to look at Abby as my brother's fiancée, not as someone I might love. Please help me."

Chapter 11

*O*ver the next few days, Abby fell into a comfortable routine. In the mornings, she helped Pat; afternoons she spent at Jake's, working on the business plan; evenings, Abby helped Jake finish the day's work in the barn. She learned to ignore the stamping and mooing of the cows, and the sucking of the automatic milkers became background noise she barely noticed. Even the acrid odors of the barn no longer assaulted her. She was assimilating into the life of a dairy. While they worked, she and Jake talked.

"So, have you always wanted to be a dairyman?" Abby asked Jake one evening.

Jake was slipping the inflations onto the last cow. He answered without looking up. "Kevin didn't tell you?"

"Tell me what?" Abby sat on a high wooden stool Jake

had provided for her.

"That I wanted to be a veterinarian. Always did. Unfortunately, it didn't work out."

Abby detected a shadow of disappointment in Jake's voice. "What happened?"

Jake turned and leaned against the edge of the cement wall below the milking stanchions. "Well," he crossed his arms, "I had just graduated with my degree in agriculture and animal husbandry when Dad had his accident. His shirtsleeve got caught in a piece of machinery—smashed his elbow and injured his hand. He endured months of physical therapy."

Abby cringed. She could only imagine the horror of what Leonard went through.

Jake looked at the cement floor of the barn and scuffed his boot across it. "Anyway, his recovery was slow. The only way the doctors could set his elbow meant he would be unable to straighten his arm. With his arm permanently bent, he would be limited in what he could do.

"Kevin had just finished his freshman year at the University of Colorado. We sat down and discussed the options. If I went on to veterinary school, Kevin would have to quit college and run the dairy, since Dad wasn't able, at least for a while. Hiring someone to run the dairy wasn't a viable option, and selling was out of the question. We couldn't afford to have both of us in school, and I didn't want Kevin giving up his football scholarship or giving up his college education. I already had mine."

"You gave up veterinary school so Kevin could finish

college?"

"That made the most sense. I stayed home and Kevin finished his education. We made a pact that after Kevin was out of college, he'd come home and help run the dairy, and I'd go to veterinary school."

"What happened?" Knowing Kevin, Abby was pretty sure she knew the answer.

Jake uncrossed his arms and let them dangle at his side. "When Kevin graduated, he got an amazing offer from the firm he now owns. An offer he couldn't refuse. Too good an opportunity."

"So he broke his promise." Abby clenched her jaw. Another example of Kevin's selfishness.

Jake pushed away from the wall and sauntered over to the opposite row of cows as the milking inflations dropped off one by one. "What could I do? Kevin came home all excited about the offer. A chance not only to work in a prestigious advertising firm, but a chance to take it over in a few years. He had interned with them, and evidently the owner saw his potential."

"You could have reminded him of his promise."

Jake turned and looked at Abby. "Why?"

"Because you had a dream, too. Kevin made a promise. He had no right to back out of his promise or take away your dream. It wasn't fair." Abby slipped off the stool, grabbed a damp cloth, took the spray nozzle from Jake, and sprayed the teats of the first cow.

Jake smiled and placed the milking inflations on their cleaning rack. "Life's not fair, Abby. If it were, we'd all get what we think we want. There'd be no challenges. Or lessons."

"How can you be so...so magnanimous about Kevin's betrayal?"

Jake frowned. "Because sometimes you have to listen to what God wants for you, not what you want for yourself."

"And you think God didn't want you to become a veterinarian?"

He shrugged again. "I'm happy doing what I'm doing, Abby, and so is Kevin. It all worked out."

"Not if you had to give up your dream."

"If I had become a veterinarian, I'd have to spend a lot of time taking care of little old ladies' yipping lap dogs. It would have driven me crazy." He chuckled.

Abby smiled in spite of the anger she felt toward Kevin. She'd already known he was selfish, but robbing Jake of his dream went beyond selfish.

"As it is," Jake continued, "I do most of the doctoring on my dairy herd, and I don't have to put up with everyone's house pets. Besides, I'm proud of what I've done with the dairy, and what I plan to do. There's always a challenge. That's good enough for me. And it's good, honest, hard work. Keeps me out of trouble." He winked at Abby and her heart constricted. "Most of the time."

Why couldn't I have met you first, Jake? You've really screwed this one up, girl. You're lying for a guy who cheated his brother out of his life's dream. Good going.

Jake finished placing the inflations on the cleaning racks, grabbed the damp cloth from Abby, and wiped the cow's udders and teats clean as she worked her way down the line of cows with the iodine spray. Abby carefully guarded her tennis shoes, making sure she kept them as clean as possible. Not an easy task under the circumstances.

"I'm going to town tomorrow to pick up a few things," Jake said. "Would you like to go?"

"Sure. I need to get some personal items. What time?"

"Somewhere around eleven. I'll buy you lunch."

"Okay. I'd like that."

They finished up the night's work and parted company. She looked forward to the trip into town with Jake. Abby smiled as she climbed the stairs to her room.

~

Jake held the door open for Abby as they entered Wilson's Western Wear Tack & Boots. The oily smell of leather enveloped her as she stepped inside. She followed Jake to the back of the store where a variety of boots were displayed on shelves lining two walls.

Jake pointed to one of the seats used for trying on footwear. "Sit down."

"No thanks," Abby said. "I'll wander around and browse while you're trying on boots."

Jake smiled. "Sit."

"I'm not Spur."

"That's for sure. He minds better. Now do as you're told."

Before she could protest further, Jake grabbed her arm, guided her to a seat, and set her in it. He winked, then walked over to a row of boots. "What size do you wear?"

"I don't need boots, Jake."

"Yes, you do, so don't argue." He picked up a boot and eyed Abby's foot.

"Hey, Jake, what's up?" An older man wearing jeans, cowboy boots, and a western-style shirt walked past Abby to where Jake stood.

"Bert, how ya doin'?"

"Good. Didn't I just sell you a new pair of work boots a month ago? They haven't worn out already, have they?"

"Yep and nope. They aren't for me. They're for the little lady here." Jake grinned. Abby frowned.

Bert turned and nodded at Abby.

"Bert, I'd like you to meet Kevin's fiancée, Abby Stewart."

Bert smiled. "Howdy."

Abby couldn't help the smile that replaced her frown.

"Abby needs a pair of work boots," Jake said. "She's been helping me out in the milking barn, and I hate to see her good sneakers get ruined. I don't know her shoe size, so I'll let you take over while I go pick out a pair or two of your jeans."

Bert smiled, sat down in front of Abby and removed her right tennis shoe. "Well, now, let's see what size we need."

"Don't I have a say in this?" Abby asked.

The older man sitting in front of her grinned. "Knowing Jake, probably not." Once he'd measured her foot, Bert disappeared for a minute or two, then returned with two large boxes.

Fifteen minutes later, Abby found a pair of lace-up work boots that felt comfortable. She was about to say she'd take them, until her eyes focused on the price. She nearly swallowed her tongue and her teeth.

Jake dropped onto the seat next to her. "So, what do you think? You like those?"

"They're nice, but I think I'll pass."

"What's wrong? Don't they fit?"

"They fit fine. I just think I'll wear my tennis shoes. If they get ruined, I'll buy a new pair." Abby could buy three or four pairs of tennis shoes for the price of the boots.

"We'll take them, Bert."

"Jake, I can't—"

"Here, take these back and try them on." Jake handed Abby two pairs of jeans. "I had to guess on size. Let me know if you need something different."

Abby remained in her seat. "Jake, I have a very tight budget. I can't afford to buy stuff I'll seldom use."

Jake stood and pulled Abby to her feet. "The boots and jeans are on me. Now, go try on the jeans."

The heat of anger warmed Abby's neck and crept toward her face. "If you think I'm going to let you buy me such expensive boots, you have another think coming." She heard Bert snicker and squelched the urge to clobber him. "I can work just fine in my tennis shoes."

"You can't work in sneakers. If you dropped something heavy on your foot or ran your toes into the cement wall, you could end up with a serious injury, and you're not on my workers' comp. Work boots will protect you, and they're a whole lot cheaper than a hospital bill. Now go try on the jeans with the boots so you can tell if the length is right." He pointed the way to the dressing room.

Abby glared at Jake. "This is ridiculous. I can't accept something this pricey."

Jake returned her glare. "Consider it payment for helping with my books and the business plan."

"I told you, I don't charge family."

"And I told you I don't take charity. Now go."

Abby stood her ground. When she refused to move, Jake took hold of her shoulders, turned her toward the dressing room, and gave her a slight shove.

Abby took a few steps and turned. "You are *so* stubborn."

"That makes two of us. And hurry up. I haven't got all day."

Abby left Wilson's carrying a boot box and a sack with two pairs of jeans and three T-shirts. She insisted on paying for the T-shirts and jeans herself.

Jake bought Abby lunch at Granny's Café. It was Abby's first encounter with Jake's popularity in the community. Throughout their lunch, people stopped by their table to chat. Abby met so many people that after a while the names and faces all blended together, but she loved every minute and longed to be a part of a community like North Fork.

~

After supper, Jake treated Abby's new boots with a water-resistant spray to protect the leather, and she wore them to the barn to do the evening chores. Jake noticed Abby took more care with her boots than she had with her tennis shoes.

"You don't have to be so careful," Jake remarked after watching Abby trying to avoid getting her boots wet or dirty. "They're called work boots for a reason." He grinned.

A sheepish look spread across her face. "Sorry. It's just that they're so expensive, I'm afraid I'll ruin them."

"They're made to last a long time. That's why they cost so much. Get them dirty. That's what they're for. Don't abuse them. Let them do their job."

"Old habits are hard to break. We didn't have much when I was growing up. Money was tight, so I took extra care with everything." Abby attached the milking inflations to one row of cows, while Jake worked the opposite row.

"It's all right to take care of things, but don't be obsessive about it."

"Hard to change what I had drummed into me as a child."

"Your mom was obsessive about things?" Jake didn't know why he asked, except he was curious about Abby and her background. He knew very little about her, except what Kevin had told him. And her earlier comment about not being able to afford the boots didn't make sense.

"My mother was careful; my dad was obsessive. I remember when I was about five or six my mother bought me a new pair of shoes for Easter. I was so proud of those white shoes I didn't want to take them off. I wore them all around my room without my parents knowing. Somehow I scuffed one of the shoes. I tried to hide the scuff mark, but when my dad saw it, he came unglued."

Jake noticed tears in Abby's eyes. He couldn't imagine making a big fuss about something so minor.

"He told me I was lucky to get the shoes in the first place. He carried on forever about me ruining the shoes, and how I'd never get another nice pair, since I wouldn't take care of them."

Abby wiped at a tear. Jake's heart ached for her. He wanted to hold her and chase away the hurtful memory.

"After that, I made sure I was extra careful with everything."

"I'm sure your dad didn't mean to make such an issue of the scuff mark. If times were tough, he was probably reacting out of worry."

Abby looked at Jake and shook her head. "My father didn't care about me or my shoes. I was a nuisance. He wanted a son, and got a daughter instead. Daddy either ignored me or took out his frustration on me verbally."

"Are you sure he felt that way?"

Abby finished hooking up the last cow and leaned against the cement wall. "Oh, I'm sure. He told me."

"Maybe you misunderstood him."

"No, Jake, I didn't misunderstand."

Abby pulled a tissue from her jeans' pocket and wiped her eyes.

"I'm sorry." Jake shoved his hands in his hip pockets. He didn't know what else to say.

"You and Kevin are very lucky to have a father like

Leonard. He loves you both, and I have no doubt that if you'd both been girls he'd have loved you just as much."

Jake smiled. "You're right, and I do know how lucky I am. Dad has always been someone I could look up to. I can't think of a better example of how to live my life."

"I wish I'd had a different father. My dad was a con man—good-looking and smooth-talking. He bilked people out of their money with fancy schemes that always failed. He never risked any of his own money, just everyone else's. And when things went wrong, we'd pack up and leave town."

Jake's suspicions about Abby and Kevin resurfaced. Abby's story didn't fit what Kevin had told Jake about his fiancée. But Jake knew, without a doubt, her story was true, which confused him even more.

"If he was that dishonest, what kept him out of jail?" I shouldn't ask, Jake thought, but I can't help myself.

"My mother would make arrangements with the people he cheated to pay back what was owed. Most of them were too embarrassed to press charges. My father never knew what my mother was doing. Or if he did, he chose to ignore it. She worked as a nurse, so she always had a job wherever we went. I never understood why she stuck with him."

"Maybe she loved him."

Abby looked at Jake. "That's what she always said. And she believed in commitment. But he made her life miserable and lonely. We never stayed anywhere long enough to make friends, until after he died."

"When was that?"

"Over ten years ago, when I was a junior in high school.

He died of a heart attack. No warning. My mother was devastated. To this day, I'll never understand why she loved him so much."

Jake walked over to Abby and put his hands at the side of her head, tipped it up, and looked into her eyes. "We can't always control who we fall in love with. We try not to fall for the wrong person, but sometimes we can't help ourselves. It sounds like your mother not only loved your father, but she believed in marriage, and she believed in him."

Abby closed her eyes and a tear trickled down her cheek. Jake wiped it away with his thumb. She opened her eyes and half smiled at Jake. He took his hands away before he was tempted to take things a step further.

"You're right about both things," Abby said. "Mother always had an excuse for Daddy's failures. When I was old enough to understand, I wasn't as sympathetic. Daddy and I never saw eye to eye. He treated me with indifference most of the time. He never attended activities I was involved in; he always had an excuse. He had an excuse for everything. We barely tolerated each other."

Stepping away from Jake, she moved to the opposite line of stanchions and grabbed the spray nozzle. After spraying and cleaning a couple of cows, she stopped and wiped her eyes on her sleeves. Without turning to look at Jake, she spoke.

"Even after Daddy died, Mother insisted on paying off his debts. When she died, she still owed several individuals a lot of money. Just before she died, she insisted I finish paying off the debts. In spite of my dislike for my father, I've honored her request."

Jake shoved his hands in his pockets. "I'm sorry Abby, but I admire you for following through. Your mother sounds like she was a very special woman."

"She was. She's been gone for eight years, but I still miss her very much." She turned toward Jake. "Both your parents are wonderful people. Treasure them."

"I do. Every day. I don't know what I'd do if—"

Jake reached for the buzzing pager attached to his belt. He rushed to a telephone mounted on the wall and punched in several numbers. "Jake here." As he listened, he felt sick and light-headed. He hung up and turned to Abby. "Will you call Dad and ask him to help you finish up?"

"Sure. What's wrong?"

"Mine accident. I have to go."

Chapter 12

*A*s Jake rushed from the barn, Abby wondered what he had to do with a mine accident. She heard the pickup spray loose gravel as he drove away. Abby moved to the phone and called the house.

When Leonard arrived at the barn, Abby asked, "Why was Jake called for a mine accident?"

"We have a number of coal mines here, and each one has rescue teams made up of miners. As head EMT of the fire department, Jake fills in if an EMT on one of the rescue teams is not available. He's had all the hazard training. I'm comforted knowing that he'll be accompanied by an experienced miner.

"Oh." Abby bit her lip.

As Leonard worked, he elaborated. "We don't have

many mine accidents, but when we do, it's a community disaster." He motioned to Abby. "Come here."

She followed him outside.

"Listen."

Abby could hear a distant whistle piercing the evening air.

"The wind's right tonight, so you can hear the town whistle blowing. One long steady blast means a mine accident." Leonard shook his head. "Never have gotten used to that sound."

They returned to the barn and went to work.

"Will Jake have to go into the mine?" Abby asked.

"Depends on which team reaches the trapped miners first. It's possible."

Abby's heart stopped. "Isn't that dangerous?"

"Can be." Leonard shut down the compressor to the milkers. "Jake won't take unnecessary chances, and the mining company takes every precaution." He took the water hose from Abby's hands. "I'll finish up here. Why don't you go to the house and help Pat put some food together. The rescuers and families will likely need something to eat before the night is over."

~

While Abby helped Pat make sandwiches and iced tea, Pat explained that local families helped by providing food, moral support, or whatever was needed for the victims' families. "The number of men required to rescue trapped miners depends on the extent of the accident and the time it will take to reach them," Pat expounded. "Rescuers are divided into eight- to ten-man teams and work in shifts. Survivors are transported to the hospital in Delta, thirty miles away. Those with life-threatening injuries are evacuated by helicopter to Grand Junction or Denver. Because of the danger with any rescue, members of the rescue team might require minor first aid."

Abby shuddered at the thought of men trapped underground. She visualized total darkness, maybe lack of oxygen, and injuries too frightening to consider. She couldn't help but worry about Jake and said a silent prayer for his safety.

When they finished making dozens of sandwiches and several gallons of iced tea and coffee, they loaded all the food into the pickup, and Leonard drove them to the mine. A sheriff's deputy stopped them as they turned onto the mine access road.

"How bad is it, Kale?" Leonard asked.

The deputy shook his head. "Not good, Leonard. We've got six guys trapped, and they haven't been able to make contact."

"Who?" Leonard asked.

"John Baker, Ted Wilson, Jim Price, Henry Dolinski, Albert Decker, and Rick Hirsch."

Pat sucked in a breath at the mention of the names. "Oh, no. Lord, please help them."

Abby laid a hand on Pat's arm. Pat gripped her hand.

"What was Rick doing there this time of night?" Leonard asked.

"They called Rick in earlier this evening to look at some problem areas," Kale replied. "They weren't sure how to proceed. The cave-in happened about an hour after he descended into the mine. Several miners did make it out, but they weren't very optimistic about the chances of the other six. Sure pray they're wrong." Kale held Pat's gaze. "Hope you brought lots of food. The rescue teams are definitely gonna need it." Kale waved them on.

"This isn't going to be easy for Jake." Pat turned to Abby. "Rick Hirsch is one of Jake's best friends. He has a wife and three great kids. As a mining engineer, he's called in to evaluate any problems."

"I'm so sorry," Abby said. She felt helpless, her comment inadequate.

When they arrived at the mine, the rescue operation was in full swing. Floodlights lit up the mine entrance, and rescue vehicles, pickups, and other cars crowded the area. At the edge of the parking lot, a makeshift control center had been set up under a large canopy. Another canopy covered long tables, and a third sheltered dozens of chairs.

Abby saw Jake's pickup but didn't see him anywhere. She recognized a couple of people she'd met in town, but she couldn't remember their names. Several people came over to help unload Leonard's pickup.

A beautiful, blond woman about Pat's age grabbed a box packed with cookies and sandwiches. "Pat, I swear you did this in record time. And none too soon. The first bunch of rescuers are due topside anytime, and I'm sure they'll be famished."

"I had help this time. Stacey, I'd like you to meet Kevin's fiancée, Abby Stewart. Abby, this is Stacey MacCord."

Stacey nodded toward Abby. "Nice to meet you. Thanks for helping."

"I'm glad to help, however I can."

"Stacey's son, BJ, Jake, Rick, and Kale's older brother, Cam, all ran around together from the time they were in grade school," Pat told Abby as they followed Stacey to the tables set up under the second canopy. The three women set out the food, Pat shook her head and smiled. "Those four boys were inseparable all through school. If they weren't at Stacey's, then they were at Rick's or Cam's or our house. Sometimes I thought I had five boys instead of two. But I loved having them."

Pat stood still for a moment, tears glistening in her eyes. "I hope Rick's all right. I hope they're *all* okay."

Stacey hugged Pat. "I hope so, too."

"How's BJ doing?" Pat asked Stacey as they unloaded more boxes. "I don't think Jake's talked to him for a while."

"Fine. He's on the road for a couple of weeks, then back in Denver for a few home games. We don't see much of him this time of year unless we go to a game. JD's trying to contact him to let him know what's happened. I just hope by the time he catches up to BJ, we'll have good news."

Pat turned to show Abby where to put the Styrofoam cups and must have noticed the bewildered look on her face. "BJ plays first base for the Colorado Rockies. He's leading the home run race right now."

"Oh." Abby realized not only who Stacey MacCord

was, but also who BJ was. She was a big fan of the Rockies, and loved watching BJ Murcheson play first base. At that moment, JD MacCord joined them.

"I left a message with the night clerk at the hotel," JD said to Stacey. "They'll give him the message to call first thing in the morning. I didn't ask them to wake him since we don't have any news yet. He can't do anything from Atlanta, anyway."

Abby was introduced to JD, and when he shook her hand she nearly fainted. She was actually standing in the same space with *the* JD MacCord—movie star extraordinaire. He was her favorite actor, and Abby, like most women, was completely enamored of him.

"Glad to meet you, Abby. Sorry it had to be under these circumstances." JD turned and kissed Stacey, then joined a group of men near the entrance to the mine.

The women continued to make small talk. Little by little people arrived, some bringing food, others bringing blankets, extra chairs, and various items needed to see everyone through what promised to be a long night ahead. Abby was amazed at how the town pulled together when disaster hit. She scanned the area looking for Jake every few minutes, hoping to catch sight of him, but to no avail.

Several women, some with toddlers and some with older children, arrived and sat in chairs under the canopy set up near the food tables. As more families of the trapped miners made their way to the staging area, they were warmly greeted by a volunteer. No family member was left alone at any time. When a pretty young woman with short blond hair arrived, Pat grabbed Abby's arm and together they walked over to her. Pat hugged the young woman and let her cry for a few minutes before urging her to sit down.

"I'm so sorry, Sarah. We don't know anything yet about Rick or the others. They're still trying to make contact, but haven't had any luck. We'll just have to wait and pray. Jake's here somewhere helping out."

Sarah forced a smile and nodded her head.

Pat introduced Abby to Sarah "Abby is Kevin's fiancée. Pat sat beside Sarah and nodded at Abby to join them. "Where are the kids?" Pat asked.

"Mrs. Jenkins is staying with them at the house. I would have been here sooner, but I had to wait for her. Didn't think it was a good idea for even Danny to be here." She fought back a sob. "The company has told me what little there is to know."

"I think it's wise you left the kids at home. It may be a very long night. Would you like something to eat or drink?" Sarah shook her head. Pat turned to Abby. "Abby, do you mind sitting with Sarah? There's more food coming, and I need to make sure it gets where it belongs."

"I don't mind at all. You go ahead."

Pat squeezed Sarah's hand and hurried off. Abby and Sarah sat in silence for a few minutes. Sarah wrung her hands and fought back tears.

"How many kids do you have?" Abby asked.

"Three," Sarah answered. A smile pricked at her mouth. "Danny's five, Courtney's three, and Tyler's eight months." Tears slid down her cheeks. "Rick has to be all right. He *has*

145

to be. The kids need him. *I* need him." Sarah's shoulders began to shake, and Abby slipped her arm around Sarah.

Abby was at a loss as to what to do. She couldn't give Sarah false hope, but she needed to comfort her in some way. She laid her head against Sarah's and whispered, "Go right ahead and cry. It's okay."

Abby tried to tune out the voices and the crying of others sitting nearby. She couldn't imagine what they were going through. Her stomach knotted when she thought about Jake putting himself in danger. After a few minutes, Sarah wiped her eyes and blew her nose.

"Why don't you tell me about Rick," Abby suggested. "I understand he's a good friend of Jake's."

Sarah smiled. "Good friend doesn't quite describe their relationship. More like blood brothers—Rick, Jake, Cam, and BJ. They used to call themselves the 'four butts.'" She giggled. "When we got married, all three stood up with Rick. Jake was best man. I was afraid Rick was going to invite them all on the honeymoon."

Abby laughed at that and urged Sarah to continue talking. Half an hour later, Abby had heard at least half of Rick's life story and, without ever having met him, knew she'd like him. As the minutes stretched into hours, Abby and Sarah grew closer. Sarah was the kind of person Abby would have picked as a friend. But Abby would never have the chance to cultivate that friendship. In fact, she would never have the opportunity to get close to anyone in North Fork, including Jake. Something she regretted more each day, thanks to Kevin and his scheme. She despised Kevin for his selfishness and his absence.

From time to time, others waiting to hear word would stop by and chat with Sarah and Abby. Pat and Stacey came by several times before moving on to other families caught in the agonizing game of waiting. At one point, Pat insisted Sarah try to get some sleep and urged her to lie down on a makeshift bed laid out in the back of Leonard's pickup. Abby stayed with Sarah and managed to get a little sleep.

Morning brought word that the rescue teams were still digging and trying to make contact. Progress was slow moving through the extensive roof fall, and the team strictly adhered to all safety precautions. Besides the chamber where the men were working, several hundred feet of passageway had collapsed and needed shoring up. Abby caught only glimpses of Jake. He stood vigil at the entrance where the excavation took place, and occasionally disappeared from sight.

Leonard left to oversee the morning milking and to make arrangements with Carlos and the other employees to carry the workload of feeding, irrigating, and milking. By the time he returned it was late afternoon. Everyone was tired and on edge, some pacing, some with slumped shoulders, and some crying silently. For all, the waiting was unbearable.

Sarah talked to her two older children several times by phone during the day. To pass the time, Abby and Sarah took walks up and down the mine access road. Walking helped their restlessness. Each time they neared the turnoff to the mine, Abby could see newshounds with cameras trying their best to gain access to the mine and the families awaiting word. Several sheriff's deputies monitored people coming and going, while maintaining a semblance of order.

At Abby's questioning look, Sarah explained the miners and their families had decided years ago that they didn't want the press to have access at such a difficult time. The company that operated the mine provided a single spokesperson who took care of keeping the press informed. That protected the families and rescuers from unwanted publicity and invasion of their privacy.

Five o'clock that evening, the families were informed that the rescuers were close to breaking through to the chamber where the men were trapped. Unspoken hopes and fears hung on the air. In a little while, they would know if there were survivors.

Abby held her breath as she watched Jake walk toward her and Sarah. Beads of sweat trickled through a layer of coal dust and over his grim expression. He nodded at Abby, then turned his attention to Sarah, kneeling in front of her and taking her hand.

"Sarah, they've about broken through to the chamber. Listening devices were inserted earlier through a small hole to try and make contact. We haven't heard any sounds, but that doesn't necessarily mean anything. They may just be unconscious and unable to respond. It won't be long before we know something. Keep positive thoughts."

"Thank you, Jake." Sarah touched his face with her hand and tears trickled down her cheeks. "Are you going in?"

"I don't know yet. I'm filling in for the vacationing

EMT on Dick Adler's team. If Dick's team goes in next, I'll be with them. "

"If you do, please take care of yourself. Don't do anything foolish. Rick wouldn't want that."

"I know." Jake rose and walked toward the mine entrance.

Abby followed. "Jake wait."

"Thanks, Abby, for helping out," Jake said when she caught up. "Sarah's going to need a lot of moral support right now. I'd appreciate it if you stayed with her."

"I will." She hesitated. "Is there something you're *not* telling us?"

He shrugged. "The fact there's no response on the listening device is troubling. We'll know shortly, but...." He shook his head. "Pray for the guys going in—for what they'll find and for their safety."

She clenched and unclenched her fists. "I will." She touched his arm. "Have you gotten any rest at all? You look exhausted."

Jake frowned. "Everyone is exhausted. We'll rest when we have those six men out."

"Please be careful."

"Pray for a miracle, Abby. We need one."

"I have already, over and over." She fought back tears and swallowed the lump in her throat.

"Thanks." Jake smiled. "Every prayer helps."

Abby's heart constricted as he strode toward the mine entrance. She closed her eyes and prayed—for the trapped miners, for the rescuers, for the families, and for Jake.

Chapter 13

*J*ake double-checked the light attached to his hard hat. Along with Dick Adler, leader of the rescue team, he climbed aboard the personnel carrier equipped with bench seats to carry the rescue team into the mine. Besides the medical supplies he carried, instrumentation for checking methane and oxygen levels was also part of his equipment. Although the passageway was approximately eight feet high and eighteen feet wide most of the way, traversing the ten miles into the mine and the site of the accident was slow. As they approached the area of the roof fall, Jake closed his eyes, said a quick prayer, and tightened his hand around the first aid supplies. The rescue team they were replacing climbed aboard their transport to exit the mine. Jake waited while Dick's team broke through the last of the debris.

Jake's initial survey of the cavern told him everything. He and Dick glanced at each other but said nothing. Tears pricked at Jake's eyes. *Why, God? Why?*

The roof fall covered a fairly wide area, five of the bodies visible in the same approximate space. The men appeared to have died instantly, but each would be checked to confirm what Jake already knew. The rescue team had secured new roof bolts in place, making the immediate space more stable, but they continued to work to stabilize the entire area. Jake and Dick moved from man to man double-checking for signs of life they didn't expect. Jake fought the bile rising in his throat. At least five families were now without husbands or fathers, brothers or sons. Rick wasn't one of them. *Maybe Rick's still alive.*

Dick strode to the closest mine telephone, gritted his teeth, and reported what they'd found. "So far no survivors," Dick reported. "We've examined five of the six. Still haven't found Rick, but not hopeful he survived. Let's not report this to the families yet." Dick listened, hung up, and returned to where Jake stood. "They're sending down body bags." He glanced above him. "Roof looks stable for now, but we need to move with caution."

"Right." Jake dreaded their next move. They had to find Rick. The last man who made it to safety said Rick shoved him out of the path of the roof fall. That left only one place to check—the large pile of shale debris near the entry to the cavern.

Jake's hands shook as he and Dick removed the smaller rubble, piece by painstaking piece. Another member of the rescue party went to work with a sledge hammer on the larger pieces of shale.

So many wasted lives. At the moment he was thankful his father was a dairyman and not a miner. He wondered if people understood the dangers miners faced daily to provide coal for heat and industry. He doubted people thought much about coal mining at all, except to complain.

Jake and Dick levered a slab of shale off the pile and stared in shock. Jake fell to his knees and threw up. Tears flowed down his face. He threw up again. Having taken the brunt of the cave-in, Rick was barely recognizable. Jake couldn't stop what became dry heaves.

"Jake, you okay?" Dick placed a hand on his shoulder.

"Give me a minute," Jake choked between stomach convulsions.

"Seen it before," Dick said. "Reacted the same way my first time. Never will get used to it." Dick squeezed Jake's shoulder.

The dry heaves stopped, but Jake couldn't stop the tears, and he couldn't stop shaking. He'd seen some terrible injuries and even death working as an EMT, but nothing like this, and nothing that had involved a close friend.

Dick helped Jake to his feet. "Let's get you out of here. There's nothing you can do. My crew will take over. You'll need to work topside with Doc to verify the cause and time of death. Not that there's any doubt."

Jake felt himself being guided toward the passageway and the personnel carrier. He waited while the rescue crew loaded the body bags, one by one. He couldn't stop shaking and he couldn't stop the tears. Why God? he asked again, silently.

Once they gained the surface, Dick described their findings to those in the control center. Jake leaned against one of the ambulances that would take the bodies to Crawford's Funeral Home instead of the hospital. Someone handed him a damp towel and a bottle of water. He wiped his face and inhaled a deep breath of clean air. The smell of death lingered in his nostrils. He blew his nose on the towel and wiped his face again, then took a drink, rinsed his mouth, and spit out the offensive taste of bile.

He glanced up at the sound of his name. Sarah ran toward him, Abby close behind. He prayed for courage. He didn't want this, didn't know what to say to Sarah. What could he say? Sarah stopped in front of him; hope drained from her face.

~

When Jake exited the mine, his demeanor told Abby something was wrong. Her heart ached for him, and she said a prayer of thanks that he was safe. When she saw his face, his eyes revealed everything; he was devastated by what he'd found.

Jake took Sarah's hands as new tears streamed down his face. "I'm sorry, Sarah. Rick didn't make it. None of them did."

"No!" Sarah's knees buckled. Abby grabbed her around the waist to hold her up. "*Why?*" She beat her fists against Jake's chest as sobs wracked her body.

Abby gave Sarah over to Jake. He held her in his arms, saying over and over, "I'm sorry, Sarah. I'm so sorry."

Abby rubbed Sarah's back, hoping to give some comfort. She didn't know what else to do. Tears flowed down her cheeks, and she tried to close off the sounds of others as they heard the news about their loved ones.

After a while, Sarah lifted her head and looked over Jake's shoulder. "I have to see him." She choked on the words. They watched as rescuers loaded a body bag into an ambulance.

Jake held tight to Sarah. "No. Not now."

Sarah struggled to loose herself from Jake's hold. "Let me go!"

Jake tightened his grip. "Sarah, listen very carefully. You don't want to see him this way. Trust me. *Please.*" Jake's stricken face paled at what he inferred. "Let Crawford's take care of him. You don't want to remember him this way."

Sarah pushed away from Jake and looked at him. "I have to—"

"Sarah, he died saving Ray Stark's life. He took the brunt of the roof fall. Don't do this to yourself. Go home to your kids. *Please.*"

"Oh God." Sarah's body shook with new sobs, and she leaned against Jake's shoulder.

Abby's own control faltered. Tears streamed down her face, and sobs escaped in spite of her fight to keep them at bay.

"Abby," Jake said, "get Mom and ask her to take Sarah home."

Abby nodded and searched the crowd for his mother. She spotted Pat and ran to her. When Pat saw the tears and anguish on Abby's face, she put her arms around Abby and cradled her head against her shoulder. Abby gently pushed away and took a deep, shuddering breath. "Jake wants you to take Sarah home. H-he doesn't want her to see.... Rick is..."

"It's okay, Abby. I'll be happy to see her home. Leonard can follow and pick me up. Can you catch a ride with Jake? I don't want him driving home alone."

"Yes, of course."

Pat walked toward Jake and Sarah. Leonard had joined them and had his arm around Jake's shoulders. Abby sank onto a chair. She thanked God again that Jake was safe and said a prayer for Sarah, her children, and the other families who had lost loved ones. She couldn't help but ask God why He had allowed this tragedy to happen. So many prayers had been said for the safety of the trapped miners. *Why didn't you answer our prayers, God?*

She wanted to hold Jake in her arms and comfort him. It wasn't just the tragedy of six deaths. She couldn't forget the look on his face when he'd emerged from the shaft, or the look in his eyes when he'd told Sarah she didn't want to see Rick. What he'd witnessed would haunt him for a long time. Maybe a lifetime. In spite of the warm evening, a chill shuddered through Abby's body.

Pat ushered Sarah to her car and drove away, Leonard following in his pickup. Jake talked to some of the other rescue workers as he shed his coveralls and gear. He dunked his head in a tub of water near the mine entrance, accepted a cup of coffee, and waited. When the last body was loaded into an ambulance, Jake trudged toward Abby.

He reached in his pocket, pulled out his keys, and tossed them in Abby's lap. "You drive. I don't think I can."

"Okay." She scooped up the keys and stood.

The minute Jake settled himself on the passenger's side, he reclined the seat, leaned his head back, and pulled his cap down over his eyes. Abby said nothing, knowing he needed peace and quiet.

As they drove away from the mine, dozens of reporters waited, hoping to talk to the families or the rescuers, camera bulbs flashing. The sheriff's department cleared the way so Abby, and everyone else, could drive through without stopping.

Once they'd gotten past the reporters, Jake straightened in his seat and stared out the passenger window. He didn't say anything during the ride home. Abby parked the pickup in front of his house.

"We're home," Abby said quietly.

Jake didn't budge. She waited. Finally, he turned toward her. He attempted to smile, but failed.

"Thanks for driving me home. You can take the pickup to the folks' house. I'll get it tomorrow." He opened the passenger door. Before exiting he looked at Abby again. "Thanks for being there for Sarah." His voice cracked a little. "I really appreciate it."

He exited the pickup and started up the steps to the house. At the top he sat down. Spur snuggled against him and laid his head on Jake's lap. New tears pricked at Abby's eyes. She pulled the key from the ignition and joined Jake. His eyes had a vacant, glazed look. He didn't seem to be aware of his surroundings as he absently rubbed Spur's head. Shock was setting in.

"You can't sit out here all night. You need a shower and something to eat. Then you can rest." When silence met Abby's comment, she stood, took hold of Jake's arm, and gently tugged on it.

At her nudging, Jake stood. "A shower would feel good. But I'm not hungry. You should go."

"I'll go when I've seen to your needs. While you're showering, I'll fix you something to eat."

"You don't need to do that, Abby."

"I know," she gently pulled him toward the front door, "but I want to, so don't argue."

~

Abby set a plate of scrambled eggs, toast, and bacon along with a glass of milk on the breakfast bar in front of Jake.

Jake stared at the food for a moment. Without looking up, he said, "I'd like some coffee."

"Coffee will keep you awake. You're going straight to bed as soon as you finish eating."

"You sound like my mother."

"I'll consider that a compliment. Now eat."

Abby forced a smile, but the weariness and pain in Jake's eyes distressed her. He'd dressed in clean Levi's, a

158

white T-shirt, socks and no shoes. She resisted the urge to wipe away a tiny smudge of grime near his ear.

"Speaking of my mother, I should call and see how Sarah's doing."

"Your dad phoned while you were showering. He's home, but your mom is going to stay with Sarah tonight. Your folks helped Sarah make calls to her parents and Rick's mom. They'll arrive sometime tomorrow night. Now eat, please."

Jake looked at Abby. "I should have taken Sarah home, but I just couldn't. She would have wanted too many details, and I wasn't prepared to deal with that." He rubbed his face with his hands, scrubbing away new tears.

Abby turned away, giving him a moment of privacy. She filled a glass with water and ice. When she turned back to the breakfast bar, she noticed Jake had taken a couple of bites. He swallowed some milk, set the glass down on the granite counter, and shoved the plate of food aside. He cradled his head in his hands.

"I've responded to a lot of accidents since I trained as an EMT," he said, "but I've always been able to handle the injuries without falling apart." He took a deep ragged breath. "This was different. I've never seen someone...Rick was crushed by the roof fall. Completely. The others were hit by pieces of shale, but Rick...." His voice caught.

Abby placed a hand on his arm. She kept silent, hoping he'd continue to talk about what he'd seen to help purge the memory.

Jake looked at Abby. "He was one of my best friends.

I've known him all my life. I was best man at his wedding. We go fishing, play softball...Abby, I hardly recognized him. His skull was crushed. Oh, God!"

Jake broke down, his chest heaving with sobs. Abby moved next to him, swiveled the stool he sat on, and put her arms around him. She didn't care what he or anyone might think. He needed comforting, and she was there. He laid his head against her shoulder as his whole body shook. Tears flowed down Abby's cheeks. She rubbed his back and held him. His arms circled her waist.

~

Minutes passed without either one moving. Even after his sobbing had ceased, Jake remained in Abby's arms. He didn't want to move from the comfort her presence gave him. Until he remembered she was his brother's fiancée; until he realized he had no right to cling to her for strength.

He gently pushed her away from him, slipped off the stool, and stepped to the center of the kitchen, his back to her. He scrubbed his hands over his face and dragged them through his hair. *What am I doing?*

He turned and looked at her. Remnants of tears stained her cheeks. She clenched her hands at her sides.

"Jake—"

He held up his hand to stop her. "Don't Abby. This is my doing. I'm sorry. I had no right to put you in this situation. I'm *way* out of line here. I should be able to control my emotions. I shouldn't have dumped on you or—"

"Jake, shut up."

"What?"

"You haven't done anything wrong. *We* haven't done anything wrong."

He stared at her and swore her eyes had turned a shade darker as they narrowed. A frown creased her forehead.

"You've just witnessed the death of your best friend. You have a right to let go and grieve for him. Your family's not here, but I am. It's the least I can do. For your folks. For Kevin. You shouldn't be alone while trying to deal with this tragedy. You *need* to talk about it. You need to let go. I'm here to listen and to understand."

He shook his head and almost smiled. "You're a treasure, Abby. Kevin's a lucky man."

Abby glanced at the floor and wiped her hands on her jeans. Jake looked around the kitchen, trying to figure a way out of the awkward situation. He couldn't deny he wanted to stay in Abby's arms. He couldn't deny he was falling in love with her. He didn't want her to leave. Not yet. But he didn't expect her to stay. Not after...

"Are you going to finish your eggs?"

He shrugged. "I'm sorry, Abby. They're good. Really. I just don't have an appetite. I couldn't eat another bite."

She picked up his plate and half-full glass of milk. "Sit down," she ordered and nodded toward the stool he'd vacated. She carried his plate to the sink, poured the milk into a cup she found hanging on the side of the cupboard, and placed the cup in the microwave.

Jake sat on the stool. Abby set the cup of warm milk in front of him.

"Drink. It'll help you sleep."

He half smiled and picked up the cup. "So, were you a drill sergeant in your previous life?" He took a sip.

Abby grinned. "Maybe." She sobered. "Jake, why didn't God answer our prayers? He seldom seems to answer prayers. Mine anyway."

Jake frowned at her. "What prayers hasn't he answered?"

"For one, bringing the trapped miners out safely. Healing my mother."

Jake paused for a moment. "God's timing isn't our timing. He sees and knows things we can't even fathom, let alone understand. He sees the world through eternity. Truth is, mining is a dangerous business, and those six men knew the risks. They were in the wrong place at the wrong time, but I believe God was there with them."

He closed his eyes for a moment. "Before I went into the mine...before I found...you said you'd pray for me. What did you pray?"

She frowned. "That God would protect you and the rescuers."

"Did He answer the way you expected?"

"Yes, but—"

"I don't pretend to understand why God saves one person while another dies. I wish I could. I wish with all my heart that He would have saved Rick and the others. Tragedy happens. That's life. We don't have control over everything or the outcomes that we'd like."

"Your faith is much stronger than mine."

"I've worked hard at it. I was really angry at God when Dad got hurt, especially when I had to give up veterinary school and stay home. But I finally realized that God can see the greater plan, and I have to have faith and trust Him. 'God is our refuge and strength, an ever present help in trouble. Therefore we will not fear, though the earth give way...'"

"That's beautiful."

"Psalm 46. One of my favorites."

"I'm not sure I know how to have that kind of unquestioning faith."

"It takes practice to trust, Abby. As for questioning, I don't think God minds. Makes us dig deeper for answers." Jake drained the cup of milk and set it on the counter.

"I need to go see Sarah tomorrow. It's important I go. Would you like to go along? The two of you seemed to hit it off."

"I don't want to intrude."

"I could use the moral support."

She sighed. "Okay. What time?"

He shrugged. "I want to check on the morning milking and make sure it's handled. I'll let you know. Now, if you don't mind, I'd like go to bed and get some rest before I talk to Sarah tomorrow. Won't do her any good if I'm too tired to make sense."

He rose and placed his hands on Abby's shoulders. "Thank you for being here tonight. I don't normally fall apart like this, and I'm really thankful my family, or anyone else, didn't see it. Take the truck to the folks' house. You can pick me up in the morning." He lowered his hands and turned toward the stairs.

"Spur can walk me back. You can pick *me* up in the morning."

He turned to look at her. "Are you sure?"

"I'm sure. Fresh air and the walk will do me good. I'll finish cleaning up and turn out the lights on my way out. Keys are on the counter."

He nodded and smiled. "Thanks, Abby. Good night."

"Good night, Jake."

As he climbed the stairs, he heard the clink of dishes and water running. Concentrating on putting one foot after the other on the steps, he prayed he would be able to sleep.

Chapter 14

*J*ake leaned against the frame of his open bedroom window and watched the night sky, waiting for Abby to leave. Though he knew it was wrong, he didn't want her to leave. He longed for the comfort of her presence and the warmth of her arms around him. Afraid to stay in the same room with her, he had reluctantly climbed the stairs to his room.

"What's wrong with me, God?" he prayed aloud. "I'm not supposed to be falling for my brother's fiancée. But I am, and I can't help myself." He closed his eyes. Damn Kevin for leaving. He should be here protecting his interests. Jake snorted. That Kevin needed to protect his fiancée from his own brother was a sad state of affairs.

The front door closed, and he heard Abby call Spur's

name. He leaned closer to the window, just to hear her voice.

"Hey, Spur," she said, "are you going to walk me home?" Spur barked. "Come on, then. Let's go."

In a moment, she was striding along the path, Spur at her side. Jake smiled. Spur had taken quite a liking to Abby. And Abby to Spur in spite of her fear of dogs.

Jake watched until all he could see was the bobbing flashlight. He shoved away from the window, eased onto his bed and closed his eyes. Every muscle in his body ached from clearing away the slabs covering Rick's body. Tears stung his eyes. The barely recognizable image of his friend plastered itself in his thoughts. His eyes flew open and he sat up.

"Lord, I don't want to remember Rick like that. I can't. Please, take away the image. I need something pleasant to think about." Even as he spoke, Abby's smiling face materialized in his mind. He fell back onto the pillow and closed his eyes. Thinking of her was the lesser of two evils, and he didn't have the strength to fight it. He'd deal with his feelings for her some other time. At the moment, her image provided comfort. A smile stole across his face as he pulled the sheet over him and gave in to exhaustion.

~

Abby sat on the porch step, Spur by her side. She absently stroked him and struggled with a myriad of conflicting emotions. She should try to contact Kevin and let him know what had happened. Though fairly certain she knew where he was, she didn't have access to the number.

It's probably unlisted, anyway.

She reached into her purse, pulled out her cell phone, called Kevin's home phone—just in case—and left a message about the mine accident in the hope he would check his messages. She then called his cell phone and left a message. Just like him not to answer. He'd wanted her to have a cell phone so he could get in touch with her at any time. He never afforded her the same courtesy. She stuffed the phone in her purse.

Kevin should be here. If he hadn't left, he would be here to help Jake work through what he'd seen. Anger surfaced. As usual, Kevin's self-interests always came first. Abby bit back an oath.

She couldn't get the pain and sadness she saw in Jake's eyes out of her head. And she couldn't forget the way she felt when he put his arms around her waist and accepted her comfort.

Abby leaned back and rested her arms on the step behind her. Spur laid his head on his paws and sighed. A quarter moon inched its way across the sky, and millions of stars winked at her, as if saying, "We know what's happening. You're falling in love with Jake."

Abby sighed. Tears pricked at her eyes but refused to spill. Her emotions, raw and confused, burned inside her. *You're wrong,* she corrected the stars. *I'm already in love with Jake.* She'd never felt this depth of need for anyone in her life. "Oh, God, what am I going to do?"

Spur raised his head and whimpered. Abby smiled down at him. "You know, don't you? You know how I feel about

Jake." Spur nudged her leg with his head and stood. "Sorry, fella, but he'll never know. I won't tell him and neither will you. Life's playing a cruel trick on me, but I guess I deserve it for lying."

Abby leaned forward and put her arms around Spur's neck. A tear slipped down her cheek. "Promise me you'll take good care of him after I leave. I'm depending on you." Spur answered with a soft woof. "Good. Now go home. He'll need you in the morning." Spur licked Abby's hand, then headed for the path.

Abby rose and stretched. One last look at the brilliant night sky left her feeling small and insignificant. "God," she whispered, "Jake says you have a greater plan than what we can see or understand. What was it he said? '...our refuge and our strength.' Help me remember that over the next two weeks. I'll need all Your strength to see this through."

~

Jake parked his pickup in the driveway of a yellow, split-level house with brown trim. Petunias edged the driveway, separating it from a lawn that needed cutting. He stared at the front door and leaned on the steering wheel.

"The longer you wait, the harder it will be," Abby said. "She's your friend, too. She'll be glad to see you."

Jake turned toward Abby. "You're right. Thanks for coming with me."

Leonard pulled his pickup in next to Jake's as the front door opened. Pat stepped out and waved at Leonard. Jake exited the pickup and Abby followed.

Pat hugged Jake and shook her head. "She had a rough night. I'm glad you're here. She needs a friend right now, not a mother telling her what needs to be done. Danny still thinks his daddy is coming home, and Courtney keeps asking about him."

"Thanks for staying with her last night. She needed a woman with her."

"I'll see you at home." Pat kissed Jake on the cheek, squeezed Abby's arm, and then joined Leonard for the ride home.

Jake climbed the steps to the front door, with Abby close behind. The door opened before he could knock, and Sarah fell into his arms, sobbing. Jake moved inside, still holding Sarah and guided her to the couch. They'd barely sat down when two blond-headed blurs rushed toward them, yelling, "Uncle Jake, Uncle Jake!"

Abby closed the door as pandemonium reigned. Five-year-old Danny threw himself into Jake's arms, forcing Jake back against the couch. Three-year-old Courtney climbed onto the couch, wedged herself next to Danny, and slipped her arms around Jake's neck chanting, "Unca Jake, Unca Jake."

Jake laughed, gathered both kids into his arms, and tickled them. Squealing and giggling filled the room until Sarah dried her eyes and put a halt to the wrestling match.

"Danny! Courtney! Enough! Uncle Jake's had a hard night. Now be quiet."

Big sighs and lingering giggles mingled with "Ah, Mom" and "But Mommy."

Jake peeled Danny and Courtney off him and set them on the couch beside him. He ruffled both kids' hair. Abby turned away and pushed back her tears. He'll make a wonderful father, she thought.

"Danny, where's Tyler?" Sarah asked.

"In the playroom."

As if hearing his cue, Tyler crawled into the front room as fast as his short legs and pudgy arms could propel him. Jake rose and scooped Tyler up and over his head. "Hey, Sport, how's things?" Tyler whooped with glee. Jake returned to the couch and set Tyler on his knee.

"You kids have been behaving yourselves, haven't you?" Jake raised his eyebrows several times at the kids. They laughed.

"Sure," Danny said. "We've been really good. Who's that lady?" He pointed at Abby.

Abby sat down in a chair opposite the couch. "Hi. I'm Abby. And you must be Danny. Your mom told me all about you."

"She did?"

"Yep. Said you were a really good baseball player, and could ride a bike, and that you help take care of your sister and brother."

"That's me all right." He grinned and dimples framed his mouth.

Abby turned to the little girl. "And you must be Courtney. You're as pretty as your mommy said you were."

Courtney buried her face in the couch next to Jake's side. He put a protective hand on her. "She's a bit shy," he said.

Abby smiled. "So I noticed."

"Did Daddy come home with you?" Danny asked.

Sarah gasped. Jake looked away. Abby clenched and unclenched her hands, the silence deafening.

Jake pulled Danny against him and held him. "What did your mom say about your dad coming home?"

"She said that he wasn't coming home. That he couldn't. That he's gone to live with God. But I thought maybe she was wrong. I thought maybe he went fishing with you."

Jake gritted his teeth. Abby wished she could spare him the next few moments.

"Danny," Jake said, "I'm sorry, but your mom is right. Your dad is with God. I wish he had gone fishing with me. He went to work instead, and there was an accident. He would come home if he could."

Abby swallowed the lump in her throat and waited. She watched as Jake's eyes clouded and darkened.

"It's not fair!" Danny cried. "He was going to take me to get a pizza after the game today."

Jake closed his eyes a moment, then said, "I don't think there's going to be a game today. All the games were canceled."

"But I was going to get to play first base."

"Next week, buddy. Next week."

"Will you come and watch me?"

"Uncle Jake's a busy man, Danny," Sarah said. "Besides he may have a game of his own next week."

"I'll be there. Wouldn't miss it."

"Cool."

Sarah rose from the couch and picked up Tyler from Jake's lap. "Danny, why don't you and Courtney go into the play room for a while? I'll bring Tyler. Uncle Jake and I need to talk."

Reluctantly, Danny took Courtney's hand and followed his mother. "Come on, Courtney, let's go play."

When Sarah returned to the living room, she hugged Abby. "I didn't mean to ignore you. Everything just happened so fast, and I—"

"*Mom*, Courtney won't do what I tell her." Danny stood at the living room door. "She says I'm not her boss."

Sarah sighed. "Just a minute. I'll be right there." She shrugged her shoulders. "I haven't had a minute's peace since they got up. I wish Rick..." She put her hand to her mouth and fought back a sob.

"Is there a park nearby?" Abby asked. "I could take the kids in Jake's pickup and come back later. That way the two of you could talk without interruptions from the kids."

"Oh, Abby, are you sure you want to take on three little hellions? They can be a handful."

Abby smiled at Sarah's description. "When I was in high school, I babysat for spending money. One family I sat for had five boys, ages 6 months to seven years. If I survived them, I'm sure I can survive your three for a couple of hours."

Jake rose from the couch. "Abby, that's a great idea. The city park is about two blocks away. You could walk, and I could pick you and the kids up later."

"Abby, are you sure?" Sarah asked.

"Absolutely. Help me put together a lunch, just in case,

172

any toys they may want, a diaper bag for Tyler, and we'll be on our way."

Chapter 15

*A*t the park, laughter and shrieks of delight filled
the early afternoon air as Jake exited his pickup.
He closed the door quietly, not wanting to call attention to
his arrival. He leaned against a tree to watch.

Quiet descended for only a moment. Abby held Tyler in
her arms and stood facing Danny and Courtney. She counted
off—"Hut one! Hut two! Hut three!" At the count of three
she sidestepped Courtney and ran, with Danny and Courtney
hot on her heels. Tyler squealed as their two pursuers yelled,
"Stop!"

Abby glanced behind her, slowed her steps, letting
Danny catch up. He grabbed her arm, and as he did, she
slowly crumpled to the ground, cradling Tyler as she went
down, landing first on her bottom, and then falling onto her

back, with baby Tyler on top of her. Danny sprawled on the ground beside Abby, and when Courtney caught up, she fell across Abby's legs.

"We got you, we got you!" Courtney yelled.

Abby's laughter mingled with that of the children. "We almost had a touchdown, Tyler!" Abby gasped. "One more down and we'll score."

Courtney and Danny scrambled to their feet, and Abby sat up. She set Tyler on the ground beside her and ruffled her gold-red curls, hoping she didn't look too disheveled. Courtney crawled onto Abby's lap and picked something out of Abby's hair. Abby hugged Courtney and fell back. Tyler crawled on both of them, and laughter filled the air again.

Jake chuckled and pushed away from the tree. He awoke that morning resolved to push aside his feelings for Abby. But seeing her with the children, his resolve vanished. She'd make a great mother, he thought. The irony was he wanted to be the father of her children. A pang of regret stabbed his heart when he acknowledged he would not be the father. Unfortunately, it was unlikely she'd ever have children if she married Kevin. Kevin had told Jake years ago he never wanted children. Jake doubted he'd changed his mind.

When the foursome lined up again to resume play, Jake strode toward them. "May I join in, or is this a closed game?"

Abby, holding Tyler again, turned and smiled at Jake. "Anyone's welcome, right kids? But you have to lose the boots. This is a barefoot game."

Jake glanced at everyone's feet. They were all barefoot.

Danny ran to Jake, grabbed his hand, and pulled.

"You're on our side, Uncle Jake."

"Hold on," Abby said. "If Jake's on your team, Tyler and I are outnumbered."

"Heck no," Danny said. "Now we're even."

Abby squinted and tried to hide the smile threatening to give her away. "Looks like it will be three against two, instead of two against two. And Jake's bigger than me. I think you have an unfair advantage."

Danny pondered the dilemma for a moment. "Okay, you can have Courtney. That'll make it even. Courtney, you're on Abby's team."

"I wanta be on Unca Jake's team."

"Tell you what." Jake winked at Abby as he sat down to remove his boots. "Why don't I take Tyler? He's pretty heavy and since I'm the biggest, that will give me a handicap. Courtney, you can be on Abby's team, making it the girls against the boys. What do you think?"

"Oh, Courtney, that's a wonderful idea. The girls can beat the boys, easy," Abby declared.

Courtney pursed her lips, a defiant look in her eyes. "Yeah, the girls can beat the boys."

Jake took Tyler from Abby, and along with Danny, lined up across from Abby and Courtney. Abby picked up a small foam football. She whispered something in Courtney's ear, faced the boys, and counted. On "Hut three" Abby pivoted toward Courtney, then sidestepped Jake and Tyler, dodged Danny, and took off with Courtney following. Jake, Tyler, and Danny ran after them. Without warning, Abby turned and grabbed Jake and Tyler in a bear hug while Courtney ran past her. Danny grabbed hold of Abby until he realized Courtney was running away from the group with the ball. He took after Courtney, and Abby released Jake and chased after Danny, with Jake and Tyler in pursuit.

"We won, we won!" Courtney jumped up and down as Danny caught up with her. She threw the ball in an attempt to spike it. It hit the ground, barely bounced once, and rolled.

Abby swept Courtney up and hugged her, spinning in a circle. "We beat the boys! We beat the boys! Yaaay!"

Courtney giggled and mimicked Abby. "Yaaay! We beat boys!"

"Man, I can't believe it." Danny sprawled on the grass.

Jake laughed. "They sure had me fooled." He winked at Abby. "Nice fake. Danny was sure you'd have the ball."

"We figured that's what you'd think. We're pretty smart cookies, aren't we, Courtney?"

"Yep." Courtney grinned and hugged Abby.

"It's our turn Uncle Jake. I bet we can fool them and make a touchdown, too," Danny said.

The five of them played their version of touch football another thirty minutes, until Abby declared, "That's it. I'm all done in. You guys will have to go on without Tyler and me."

"What? Chickening out now that the boys have you where we want you?" Jake challenged. "Besides, I kind of like my little handicap, here." Tyler squealed when Jake tickled him.

"Chickening out? *Never.* Quitting while we're ahead is more like it. Besides, your little handicap needs his diaper changed."

"That right, Tyler?" Jake sniffed and wrinkled his nose. "Guess I've been around barnyards too long."

Abby reached for Tyler, but Jake held him back. "I'll do it if you want me to," he offered.

Abby smiled and shook her head. "Thanks, but I don't mind. Besides, I think Danny and Courtney would like to play a little more."

Jake shifted Tyler into Abby's arms. Their gazes met and held for a moment. Jake smoothed his hand over Tyler's head without looking away from Abby. "Thanks, Abby." He turned and, in one movement, scooped Danny and Courtney up and swung them in a circle before falling down on the grass and engaging in a three-way wrestling match.

~

Abby spread a blanket in the shade of a giant maple tree and changed Tyler's diaper. Laughter and shouts of joy continued to fill the afternoon air. She noticed Tyler's eyes getting heavy, so she settled him against her shoulder and sang to him, rubbing his back as she did.

She watched Jake and the children, snuggled her cheek against Tyler's head, and wished that this were her family. Jake would make a wonderful father, and she wondered what it would feel like to be the mother of his children. She'd never wanted anything so much in her whole life. She bit the inside of her cheek to stem the threat of tears. Abby had always wanted things she could never have—a permanent home when growing up, her father's love, and Jake.

She'd used changing Tyler as an excuse to get out of the football game. She wanted to continue playing but was afraid if Jake touched her one more time, even in the fun of the game, she'd give away her feelings for him. She couldn't do that. Not until Kevin returned, and she convinced him to at least tell his family the truth. Maybe there was an outside chance Jake would forgive both of them and see Abby as someone he could love.

"Fat chance," she whispered and closed her eyes against the tears.

~

"Looks like our little handicap is all tuckered out."

Abby flinched and opened her eyes.

"Sorry," Jake apologized. "Didn't mean to startle you." He held Courtney in his arms. Jake knelt and set Courtney on the blanket near Abby, then sat beside her.

"Game over?" Abby asked.

"'Fraid so. Courtney says she's tired. Danny's going to play on the swings and slide for a while."

"I want some yemonade," Courtney said.

Jake found the jug of lemonade and gave Courtney a drink, then took one for himself.

"If you're hungry, I think there's a sandwich or two left from the lunch Sarah packed." Abby nodded toward the food basket.

"Thanks, but Sarah fixed lunch for us. Gave her something to do while we talked."

Courtney curled onto the blanket and closed her eyes.

Jake pulled down her shirt to cover her back and smoothed her hair out of her eyes.

"I still can't believe Rick is gone. He loved these kids so much. It's not right they've been left without a father. The sad part is that Courtney may not remember him, Tyler won't at all, and Danny will have only a few scattered memories."

"But they'll have their Uncle Jake." Abby smiled. "They're very lucky that way."

"Thanks." He took a breath, let it out slowly. "I appreciate you bringing the kids over to the park. As much as Sarah loves her kids, she needed a little time to herself. She's promised to rest this afternoon. I turned the ring off on the phone, set the answering machine, and put a "Do Not Disturb" note on her door. Her folks and Rick's mom will be in later this evening."

"Where do they live?"

"Sarah's folks are from Salt Lake City. Rick's mom lives in Phoenix with her sister—they're both widows." Jake cleared his throat. "I told Sarah I'd take the kids until after everyone arrives. She'll need a little time alone with family."

Abby touched Jake's arm. "You're a good friend, Jake."

Jake looked at Abby and smiled. "And you're a good sport for taking on these three. I'd best get you back home."

Abby shifted Tyler from her shoulder to her lap. He stirred slightly, but went right back to sleep. "I'm in no hurry, Jake. I'm having a great time. They're good kids. Easy to take care of. If you'd like help with them, I'm free for the day."

Jake studied Abby a moment. She and Kevin were complete opposites. How he wished they weren't engaged.

He should turn down Abby's offer. He could handle the kids by himself. The truth was, however, he wanted to spend the rest of the day with Abby. Right or not, that was what he desired, and he had a perfect excuse to make it happen.

"Are you sure you want to be saddled with the four of us?"

"Absolutely. This is the most fun I've had since I've been here. Why stop now? Besides, I can't imagine you changing Tyler's diaper."

"I beg your pardon." Jake tried to look insulted, yet couldn't help but smile. "I've changed Danny's, Courtney's and Tyler's diapers, more than once, I might add."

Abby chuckled. "If you say so..."

"If you weren't holding Tyler right now, I'd—

"You'd what?"

Jake shook his head. "I'd—"

"Uncle Jake! Watch me!"

Jake winked at Abby. "Saved by a five-year-old show-off. Must be your lucky day." Jake rose and sauntered toward the swings.

~

Abby sighed and eased Tyler off her lap and onto the blanket. "If it was my lucky day," she whispered, "I'd be able to tell you how I feel about you, Jake Karlson. If it was my lucky day, I'd be engaged to you instead of Kevin."

She lay back on the blanket and a tear slipped from her eye. She fingered the oversized diamond ring on her left hand and squelched the urge to throw it as far away from her as she could.

Tyler whimpered. Abby sat up and rubbed his back until he settled down. Courtney raised her head for a moment, then turned over without waking. A robin's song drifted across the park, and a light breeze ruffled Abby's hair. She watched as Jake pushed Danny higher and higher in the swing, and for a while she was content.

~

Silence filled Jake's pickup, where only a few minutes earlier two children and two adults sang *Old MacDonald Had a Farm, If You're Happy and You Know It,* and *The ABC Song* at the top of their lungs. Several times. Tyler slept through the entire repertoire.

After leaving the park, the five of them spent the remainder of the afternoon at Karlson Dairy. Jake took Abby and the children to see the week-old calves. Then they went to the barn to watch the milking. Jake gave Danny, Courtney, and Tyler each a ride on the tractor and then in the feed truck. He even teased Abby that he'd give her a tractor ride sometime before her visit was over.

For supper, Jake treated everyone to pizza at Tonio's Pizza Parlor. By the time they dropped Danny, Courtney, and Tyler at their home, all five of them were exhausted. Abby had never spent a more enjoyable day. She regretted it had come to an end.

Jake backed out of Sarah's driveway and settled in for the drive home. Abby leaned her head against the headrest and closed her eyes.

"Tired?" Jake asked.

"A little, but it's a good tired." Abby opened her eyes and smiled. "Kind of quiet, isn't it?"

"Just a tad." Jake chuckled. "Those kids sure have a lot of energy."

"Endless." Abby grinned. "But they're good kids. They mind, and that's half the battle when taking care of someone else's kids."

"You'd make a good mom, Abby. You're a natural with kids. It's a shame you won't have the chance to raise your own."

Abby sat up a little straighter and glanced at Jake. "What makes you think I won't have any of my own?"

Jake's jaw tightened. "Kevin always said he didn't want kids. You should know that."

Abby wanted to scream. She'd spent a perfectly wonderful day with Jake, and now he was not only reminding her of Kevin, but reminding her she knew very little about Kevin's desires. A part of her wanted Jake to figure things out. She wanted him to realize that she and Kevin had nothing between them.

"I know that right now Kevin's not too keen on having children, but I'm sure I can change his mind."

Jake frowned. "Don't count on it, Abby. It's one thing he's always been adamant about."

Abby bit her lip. "We'll see."

They rode the rest of the way in silence, while Abby's resentment of Kevin grew deeper. When Jake dropped Abby off at his parents' house, Abby broke the silence.

"I had a wonderful day, Jake. Thanks."

"I should be thanking you, Abby. You were great with the kids."

"I enjoyed every minute spent with them. And don't worry about Kevin and me. We can always spoil your kids if we don't have any of our own." She forced a smile and closed the pickup door.

Chapter 16

Sunday morning Abby attended the early church service with the Karlsons. She sat as far away from Jake as possible, putting both Pat and Leonard between them. She didn't dare go through an entire church service sitting next to Jake, afraid people might see how she felt about him.

The service came as a pleasant surprise for Abby. She enjoyed the music and the sermon, which was a tribute, in part, to the six men who died in the mine. Three of the men were members of the congregation. The sermon title was "Death to Life," and the minister talked about the hope and triumph in the resurrection of Christ. When the sermon ended, Abby felt reassured that there was hope, even for a liar like her.

During the fellowship between services, Abby was greeted by people she'd already met plus a few new ones. She felt genuinely welcomed by everyone, but as people expressed interest in her engagement to Kevin, the knot tightened in her stomach again. Abby's guilt increased tenfold. She half expected that before the day was out, lightning would strike her. She almost hoped for it. It would end her misery…and her lies.

At the house, Abby changed to shorts and a tank top. She took a minute to check her cell phone to see if Kevin had called. He hadn't. *So what did you expect? That Kevin would suddenly have a conscience? Fat chance*

The rich odor of Sunday dinner baking in the oven, drew Abby to the kitchen. Leonard and Pat sat at the table enjoying fresh brewed coffee. Jake joined them after going home and changing into jeans and work boots. Abby tried not to focus on Jake's muscular build, accentuated by his tight-fitting T-shirt. The rich green color darkened his green eye and enhanced the blue one. Abby fidgeted and tried to avoid his gaze. Every time she looked up, Jake's fascinating eyes settled on her.

"Ever been fishing, Abby?" Jake asked while sipping a cup of coffee.

Intent on not looking at him, the question startled her. "What?"

"Ever been fishing?"

"Uh, no."

"I was thinking about heading for Lost Lake this morning. Any takers?" Jake looked around the table.

Leonard shook his head. "I promised your mother I'd finish up that end table I've been working on. Don't have anything pushing at me today."

"I've got to coordinate the dinners for the families after the memorial services. Our church alone has three to do in the next week." Pat said.

"Do you need any help?" Abby asked. She wanted to go fishing with Jake, but knew it an unwise choice.

"It's mostly phone calls today," Pat said. "But come time for serving the dinners, I could definitely use your help."

"Then you'll have it."

"So what do you say, Abby?" Jake asked. "You game to try your hand at fishing? I'd never forgive myself if I didn't at least try to teach Kevin's fiancée how to fish."

"Kevin does like to fish, although I've never gone with him." Abby knew she was on solid ground concerning Kevin's fishing. He often took clients on fly fishing trips and seemed passionate about it. He occasionally shared his latest fishing adventure with his staff during coffee breaks and before staff meetings.

"Guess it's time I learned," she blurted. *So much for being wise.* "I can surprise him when he gets back," she added, justifying her decision more to herself than anyone.

"I'll get the gear loaded. You'll want to wear your boots and jeans. Be sure to bring a jacket. It gets chilly in the high country toward evening."

"Wait. Don't I need a license?"

Jake stopped on his way out. "We'll get you one on the way out of town."

"I'll put together some food for the day while you're changing, Abby," Pat offered.

"I won't be long. I'll be right back to help." Abby rushed upstairs to change.

~

Pat waved as Jake and Abby climbed into his pickup. Jake waved as he drove away. Pat returned to the kitchen and started the dishwasher as Leonard walked in. Grabbing a dishrag, she scrubbed at a spot on the stove.

"Something bothering you?" Leonard asked.

"No. Nothing." Pat continued to clean.

Leonard leaned against the counter and crossed his arms. "Out with it, woman. I know when something's bothering you."

Pat smiled at her husband's use of "woman." While it might be offensive to some, it was a term of endearment between them. He had used the term to tease her when they first dated. It became a habit. Pat stopped cleaning and looked at her husband.

"I'm worried about Jake."

"Any particular reason, or just worried in general?"

"I'm afraid he's going to get his heart broken again."

"Abby?"

"You've noticed it, too?"

"I've noticed they seem to be spending a lot of time together. They've become...close, I guess you'd say."

"I think they've become more than close."

Leonard frowned. "Maybe I should have gone with

them."

"It might have been a good idea."

"You think something's happened between them?"

"Nothing out in the open. It's more subtle. But I think he's falling for her, and I don't think she's doing anything to discourage it."

"You think she's encouraging it?"

"Not exactly. But with Kevin gone, she's bored. Jake provides relief from too much time on her hands. He is, after all, much closer in age to Abby than we are."

"So you think she's making a play for Jake while Kevin's gone? Doesn't seem the sort to me."

"No, of course not. But I'm afraid she's attracted to Jake."

"Heavens, woman, she's engaged to Kevin. I doubt—"

"That's just it. Didn't something seem a little, I don't know, not quite right between Kevin and Abby? They're newly engaged, but they don't act like they're head over heels in love. He acts irritated with her, and she seems to tolerate him. She also sounded a little angry with him when he left. If I'd been his fiancée, I'd have left with him. But he insisted she stay. Wouldn't he want her with him?"

"I can't answer that, honey. You know how Kevin is about things. He approaches everything different than we do. Sometimes I wonder who raised him."

"Still, I'm afraid both my boys are going to be hurt, and Abby will be the cause."

"I take it you don't like her."

Pat shook her head. "That's just it. I really do like her. If

I'd had a daughter, I'd want her to be like Abby. She's sweet, caring, interested in us and our way of life, and she's always willing to help. It's not an act. You can see that." Pat sighed and scrubbed at the spot on the stove. "What's really strange is she's much better suited to Jake than Kevin. Actually better suited than any girl Jake has ever dated. But she's engaged to Kevin." She wiped the clean stove one last time. "It doesn't make sense. *I'm* not making sense."

Tears pricked Pat's eyes. Leonard gathered her against his chest with his good arm. Pat put her arms around her husband and leaned her head against his. A few tears slipped from her eyes.

"I love both my boys, but Kevin seems to slough things off easier than Jake. Jake takes everything to heart. I'm afraid he's letting Abby get too close, and then he's going to get hurt far more than he was when Sondra left. I'm afraid both my boys have fallen for the same girl, and I don't know what to do about it."

Leonard rubbed Pat's back to soothe her. "You can't do anything about it, honey. Interfering will only cause more trouble. What if you're reading things wrong? Abby's trying to get to know us for Kevin's sake. She may not realize what's happening." Leonard kissed Pat's cheek. "I don't want to see Jake get hurt, either. He's sacrificed a lot for us and for Kevin. He deserves to be happy.

"I couldn't help him when Sondra left except to listen and understand. We can't live our boys' lives for them. Jake and Kevin are adults. They're responsible for their own actions. All we can do is be here for them when they need us."

Pat leaned back and looked at Leonard. "There must be *something* we can do."

"There is. Leave them in God's hands, including Abby. Let God work it out. Praying is the only thing we can do."

Pat's shoulders slumped, but she managed a small smile for her husband. "I know you're right. But it's so hard."

"If it's any help, I like Abby, too. And I agree she's much better suited to Jake, but it's not our decision. She's engaged to Kevin. We have to leave it at that."

"I know. I'll try. And I'll keep praying that God will make it right."

"That's the woman I married." Leonard tipped Pat's face up and kissed her. "How 'bout helping me stain that coffee table after you make those calls?"

~

Abby watched the scenery slip by as Jake drove the same route she and Kevin had taken her second day in North Fork. Spur lay sleeping at her feet. The two-lane highway followed the river as it wound its way through the valley.

Cedar, oak brush, pine, and piñon trees dotted the sandstone hillsides on one side of the river. Quaking aspen, or quakies, as Kevin had called them, and spruce trees covered the hillside on Abby's side of the road. Along the river, cottonwood trees grew in abundance. Interspersed along the road were fields and farm houses.

"You're awfully quiet," Jake commented. "Thinking about Kevin?"

"What? Oh, yes," Abby lied. She was thinking how nice it was to spend the afternoon with Jake. Yesterday played like a fairy tale that ended too soon. Today, right or wrong, she had a second chance at the fairy tale.

"Too bad he's not here. The three of us could have quite a day fishing. When we were little, Dad had a hired man who helped him out on Sundays so the entire family could go fishing and do other things together."

"I bet you had a lot of fun."

"Yep. Kev always made it a contest, though, to see who could catch the biggest fish."

"I can just imagine." Abby said the words with a little more sarcasm than she intended. She'd have to be more careful with her tone of voice.

Nothing was said for a while, a comfortable silence filling the pickup cab. When Jake broke the silence, Abby wasn't prepared for his comment.

"Call me crazy, but lately, when I mention Kevin, you seem a bit put out with him."

She swallowed and searched for a good answer. "Sorry. It's just that I think he should be here with his family right now, not off doing his thing." The words left a bad taste in her mouth.

"Maybe, but then Kevin always was an over-achiever. Can't stand to be second best. It's flowed over into his work ethic."

Abby squelched the need to scoff. Kevin's ethics weren't exactly what Jake thought they were. She wasn't, however, going to ruin Jake's perception of his little brother.

"Kevin needs to learn when work is important and when to take a few days off. Which, by the way, brings up a question for you." She was weary of discussing Kevin.

"Shoot."

"Don't you need to be home to do the milking tonight?"

"What makes you think we won't?"

"You said I'd need a jacket because the evenings get cold."

Jake grinned. "For the last four years I've made a point to take Friday night and all of Saturday and Sunday off. Carlos takes those three nights and two mornings. He's Catholic, so he goes to Saturday evening mass. One of the other guys starts the milking Saturday and leaves when Carlos arrives. That way he can cover the weekends. It works out real well. Then I give him Monday and Tuesday off. I covered last weekend because he had a family reunion."

"So what do you normally do with your free time?"

"Well, summer weekends I play on a co-ed fast-pitch softball team. I'm the catcher. So far this year we're unbeaten. JD and Stacey used to play regularly on the team. Now they only play if needed and serve as our coaches. They also sponsor the team."

"Sounds like fun. Mind if I tag along next weekend?"

Jake frowned. "You're welcome to come," he said. "The folks always do."

Abby bit her lip. "I've said something wrong."

"No. It just hit me that Rick won't be there to pitch. He was our best pitcher. It's going to be hard without him."

"Oh, Jake, I'm so sorry." She laid her hand on his arm.

He smiled at her. "Thanks. Our first few games are definitely going to be hard." A frown crossed his brow. "But we'll manage. Rick would be disappointed in us if we didn't play. Maybe we'll dedicate the rest of the season to him."

Jake slowed the pickup as the pavement ended and a gravel road began. They had passed a fork in the road a few miles back. A crystal clear stream flowed through the valley on Abby's side of the pickup. The pickup rattled over ruts in the road, and Jake became quiet, lost in thought.

At Lost Lake Slough, Abby helped Jake unload the pickup. Spur stretched his legs, sniffing at bushes and chasing birds. Jake loaded a couple of backpacks with fishing supplies, food and water.

When Jake indicated he wanted to put one of the backpacks on Abby, she planted her hands on her hips. "I thought you were going to teach me to fish, not take me on a backpacking trip. I think I've been had." She smiled.

"If you want to learn to fish, we have to go where the fishing's good. Now turn around. You have to carry your fair share."

Abby turned and let Jake help her into the straps of the backpack. She wavered slightly at its weight. "Hey, remember I'm a city girl."

Jake turned her around to face him and grinned as he fastened and adjusted the waist strap and shoulder straps of the backpack, making sure they were snug. "Quit complaining or I'll make you carry the heavy one."

"I thought this was the heavy one."

"Nope."

Jake finished checking Abby's backpack and swung the second one onto his back. When he had it secure, he whistled at Spur and headed toward a narrow trail that skirted the edge of the lake and disappeared toward the jagged snowcapped peak that towered above the clear water.

"Where are we going?" Abby fell into step behind Jake.

"That way," he said, pointing ahead of him. "Holler if you need to rest."

Chapter 17

*A*bby stared in awe at the mountain towering before her—a solid granite pointed peak with ragged scars along its face—a sentry over a mirror-smooth lake. A gouged basin below the peak proudly displayed the snow-covered glacier still at work. Slide rock circled the snow and ice, working its way toward water. The peak's majesty reflected back at Abby from the lake's surface, along with pines shading patches of snow, quakies, and wild flowers bordering the lake,

"Beautiful, isn't it?" Jake stood beside her.

"It takes my breath away," Abby replied.

"I thought that was from the hike." Jake grinned.

Abby appreciated that Jake had made the uphill trek to Lost Lake as easy as he could for her, making sure they stopped regularly to rest and drink water. While they rested, Jake named the flowers, bushes, and trees along the trail.

"It's the same mountain as the one where we parked, right?"

"Same one."

"It's so much closer here; so much more impressive."

"'You will go out in joy, and be led forth in peace; the mountains and hills will burst into song before you, and all the trees of the field will clap their hands.'"

"Is that a psalm?"

"Nope. Isaiah 55:12. But if you want something from the Psalms, 'Be still and know that I am God.' Psalm 46:10."

Abby smiled. On several occasions, Jake had, openly and with ease, shared his knowledge of the Bible. Abby envied the faith she saw in Jake. First thing on her list when she got home was to dig out her Bible and read it. The book of Psalms seemed to be one of Jake's favorites, but she liked the Isaiah verse, too. She'd have to start with those two books.

"You seem deep in thought," Jake said.

"Oh, just thinking about how God must have felt when he created all this."

"Very satisfied, I think."

"Yes. To create such beauty..."

"Since we're made in God's image, we all have the ability to create beauty, whether it's in something we build, paint, our words, or our deeds."

Abby looked at Jake. "You really believe that? With all the things going on in the world?"

Jake looked at Abby and smiled. "Yep. The potential is in all of us. We only have to choose to use it. God has planted the seed; it's up to us to make it grow."

"You're quite the optimist, Jake. I admire that."

"I'm blessed to live in an area and have a family that are constant reminders of how fortunate I am." Jake unbuckled his backpack and eased it onto the ground. "Let's get your pack off and do some serious fishing."

Jake helped Abby shed the load she carried, then handed her the water bladder. She took a drink and handed it back.

"You did all right on the hike up here. I hope it wasn't too hard."

Abby flexed her shoulders, happy to have the extra weight gone. "No, it was fine. You stopped often enough. I'm sure you'd have made it in half the time without me."

"Time isn't important. Enjoying the trip is. Hungry?"

"Not right now. I'm ready to learn how to fish."

Jake unpacked the fly rods, assembled them, and strung them with fishing line. Abby watched with interest as he threaded the line through each guide and tied a fly to the leader.

"One of my special flies," he said. "An elk hair caddie."

"Yours?"

"Yeah. I tie most of the flies I use. It's a way to relax."

"I'm impressed." Abby wondered if there was anything Jake couldn't do.

When he had Abby's rod ready, Jake explained to her how the reel worked, and then he took the rod and crept to the lake's edge. "You have to walk to the lake's edge very lightly," he said, "or the fish will feel the vibration of your steps. You don't necessarily have to be quiet, just light on your feet."

Jake cast his line out. "Casting is like a waltz," he said. "Timing is everything. Like this." His right arm moved to the count—lift 2, 3, back 2, 3, forward 2, 3, down. With his left hand he stripped more line from the reel, then let it out as he cast. His movements were fluid and graceful. He turned toward Abby and motioned to her.

"Let's see what you can do."

Jake stood behind Abby and rested his left hand on her back. He used his right hand to guide her through the casting strokes. Abby gripped the rod as she'd seen Jake do, concentrating extra hard to keep her mind off Jake and the feelings his touch stirred in her. Having him so close was unbearable, yet the thought of him moving away tore at her heart. She attempted a cast with his help, but the line fell far short of where Jake had cast it by himself.

"You're trying too hard," Jake counseled. "Relax. Let it flow. Think of the rod as an extension of your arm. Use your whole arm, not your wrist. It's a little like pounding a nail with a hammer. Your arm from the elbow to your hand should stay straight. Keep a firm wrist."

With Jake's help, Abby cast again. The fly at the end of the rod settled gently on the lake. He talked her through stripping more line from the reel, then helped her cast again.

"That's it. You're doing great. You're a natural, Abby." Jake stepped away from her. "Now try it again."

Abby regretted Jake moving. She wanted him next to

her, touching her. She gritted her teeth and tried a cast without Jake's help. She rushed the forward cast and the fly and line coiled at the edge of the lake instead of out on the water where it had landed the previous cast.

"Rats!"

Jake chuckled. "That's okay. Your timing was a little off. Remember the waltz. Pull in some line with your left hand and start again."

Abby did as she was instructed and tried again. With each cast she became more comfortable with the rhythm.

"Good. You're getting the hang of it. Just remember, don't rush your cast, but don't pause too long, either. Timing is everything."

"What happens if a fish takes the fly?"

"Lift the rod tip to set the hook and then follow his lead. Don't worry, I'll talk you through it."

Abby frowned at Jake. "Easy for you to say. I've never done this before."

"You get a fish on your line, just holler. I'll come running."

"Where are you going?" She tried to keep the panic from her voice.

Jake pointed behind him. "Over here under a pine tree."

"Aren't you going to fish?"

"Later. Right now I'm going to take a short nap. The last couple of days have caught up with me. Don't worry, I'll be close if you need help."

"Well, don't sleep too soundly."

"I won't. I promise."

~

Jake settled under a tall pine and watched Abby as she concentrated on her casting. He smiled as her rhythm became more natural. After a few minutes, confident she could handle the challenge, Jake lay back, closed his eyes, and fell asleep.

"Jake, help."

Jake felt someone nudge him. He opened his eyes. Abby hovered over him.

"What's wrong?" He sat up.

"The fly's caught in my hair. I can't get it out."

Abby offered her hand to help him up.

"Is it just in your hair, or did you hook your scalp, too?"

"No, just my hair, but it's tangled pretty good."

Jake looked where Abby pointed and smiled. "You did a good job of it, Ace."

"Thanks a lot for the sympathy. Just get it out."

"Okay, hold still." Jake took his time working the hook out of her hair, not because the hook was tangled that badly, but because he liked the feel of her hair, and he liked having her close. In spite of the insect repellent and sunscreen she'd applied, she smelled good...and soft. Abby's forehead rested against his shoulder as he worked the fly free.

"There, all done." He took the rod from her and leaned it against the tree.

She smiled. "Thanks."

"My pleasure." He noticed tears in her eyes. "You okay?"

"Yes."

"Abby?"

"I'm okay. Thanks for helping me." She kissed him on the cheek. That simple act was his undoing. He slipped his arms around her and pulled her against him.

"I love you, Abby," he declared. "I can't ignore my feelings for you anymore."

She raised her head and studied his face. Her momentary surprise softened into a smile. "I can't ignore my feelings anymore, either. I don't love Kevin. At least not the way I've come to love you."

"Do you really mean that, Abby?"

"Yes."

Jake touched his lips to hers, then deepened the kiss—

Jake! Help! Help me, Jake! Quick!"

Jake's eyes flew open and he scrambled to his feet. He could hear Spur barking.

"Jake! I think I have a fish! What do I do? Jake!"

"Coming!" he yelled and rubbed his face. He'd been dreaming, yet the kiss seemed so real.

"Jake!"

Jake hurried toward Abby. Spur stood with his back to Abby, barking at Jake, his tail moving at high speed.

"Just relax and let the fish have his way for a minute," he called. He could see the bend in the rod. She definitely had a fish. He grinned as he stepped to Abby's side. Spur stopped barking, but his tail continued to beat the air in excitement.

"About time you got here. I don't know what to do."

205

"Let him take some line."

"What?"

"Play him a little, let him run. Let him think he's getting away, then use the rod to turn his head."

"That doesn't seem fair."

"It'll tire him out, and he'll be easier to land."

"Oh." Abby chewed the inside of her bottom lip as the fish pulled the line farther out into the lake.

With Jake's patient instructions, Abby played the fish for a bit, then slowly reeled it near the shore. Jake guided a net under the fish and dragged the net close to the bank. He lifted the 12-inch trout from the net and cradled it in his wet hands. He carefully backed the hook from the fish's lip and grinned as he showed Abby her catch.

"Your first fish. I should have brought a camera. Sorry." He noticed tears in Abby's eyes. "Is something wrong?"

"Does it hurt them?"

"What?"

"The hook. Does it hurt them?"

Jake shrugged. "Why?"

"It was exciting catching it, but if it hurts—"

"Abby, it's okay. Do you want to keep it?"

"I don't know. What do you think?"

"If it was a Cutthroat, I wouldn't give you the option because they're natives. But since it's a Brookie, it's your choice."

"If I keep it we'll have to kill it, right?"

"Yep. What'll it be?"

"Can we put it back in the lake?"

"You sure that's what you want to do?"

"Hurry before it dies."

Jake knelt next to the lake, and still cradling the fish, gently held it under water until it revived. Moments later it darted away.

Jake stood and smiled at Abby. "He'll be fine."

She nodded.

"Does this mean you don't want to fish anymore?"

Abby shrugged. "Catching a fish was exciting, but I don't want to hurt them."

"The fly you're using is tied on a barbless hook. It lessens the possibility of the fish getting injured so you can return it to the lake if you want. It's called catch and release. You want to keep fishing?"

"As long as I can put them back."

"That's the plan."

Abby settled herself in the same spot and began casting out the line. Jake took his time tying a fly to his leader. He needed to settle his nerves.

The vivid dream he'd had about kissing Abby still lingered, too real to let it go, yet he had to. If he didn't get a grip on his feelings, he was headed for a mountain of hurt. Abby loved Kevin, not him. Even if the dream came true, there was no future in loving Abby. He could never marry someone who was once in love with and engaged to his brother. Family came first. He hoped Abby and Kevin would be happy together. Nothing else was possible.

~

Abby and Jake had settled on a shaded grassy spot near a pine tree to eat a late lunch. The site afforded a clear view of the lake and the mountain guarding it, with a cerulean sky providing an endless canopy. A bumblebee buzzed around them, and a chipmunk scolded them from a nearby rock.

"There's another sandwich if you want it, Abby."

"No thanks. One sandwich is plenty for me. You'd better eat it. You may need it for strength in case you have to carry me out of here."

"You wimping out on me?"

"Not on purpose. I think I've worn myself out fishing. It's so much fun. Do you fish up here a lot?"

"I fish a lot of places. Mostly streams and rivers rather than lakes. I came here today because I thought lake fishing would be easier for you to learn. Fishing a stream is a bit more of a challenge."

"I've had a great time today. It's so beautiful and peaceful up here."

Spur trotted up to Jake and settled next to him. Jake took the extra sandwich and fed it to Spur in quarters.

"This is one of my favorite places. I never tire of coming up here."

"I can see why." Abby sighed, leaned back on her elbows, and stared at a marshmallow cloud floating across the sky. "It sounds selfish, but it's been nice having it all to ourselves."

"Yes, it has," Jake agreed. "Unusual, but nice."

Jake watched Abby and gritted his teeth. He suggested they come fishing because he wanted to share this beautiful spot with her. He expected his folks to join them, and when they didn't he was actually relieved. Now he wished they weren't alone. He was dangerously close to feeling like this was the way things were supposed to be.

Jake cleared his throat. "Think I'll do a little more fishing." He looked at Abby. "You ready?

"I'll watch you for a while. Maybe take a short snooze."

Jake nodded, picked up his pole, and moved toward the lake. Spur followed. He smiled a while later when Abby joined him at the lake. They fished in silence.

Fishing helped Jake take his mind off Abby. As the sun began to sink in the west, he dismantled his pole. "It's going to get dark pretty soon. We'd better head out. I don't want you negotiating an unfamiliar trail in the dark when you're tired, especially with a heavy backpack on."

~

Jake heard Abby's boots slip on the graveled trail and turned to help her, but he was too late. She'd landed on her bottom and slid several feet before coming to a stop. He knelt beside her, his heart in his throat.

"You okay?"

She tried to smile, but he could see the moisture forming in her eyes.

"I'm fine. Just a scrape or two."

"Let me see."

She held up her right arm. A scrape the length of her forearm, plus the edge of her palm, were beginning to bleed a little.

"I'm sorry Abby. Sit tight." Jake shed his backpack and retrieved a small first aid kit. He cleaned the scrapes, applied medicated cream, and wrapped her arm and hand with gauze. She said nothing while Jake ministered to her.

"There, that should hold you till we get home." He looked at Abby. She smiled, and his dream begged to be true. He fought the desire.

"You're a good medic. Now help me get up."

He took her left hand and pulled her to her feet. "You want me to take your pack?"

"You can't carry two. I'll be fine. I just wasn't paying attention. I was too busy taking in the evening sky instead of watching the trail."

"I can manage two packs. It's not that much farther."

Spur backtracked on the trail to see what was wrong. He barked, encouraging them to follow him.

"Just get going. I'm not too tired to carry my fair share the rest of the way."

Jake looked at her a moment.

"Go," she insisted.

He turned and headed down the trail, regretting not kissing her; knowing he'd regret it more if he had.

Chapter 18

*A*bby lay in bed, staring at a ceiling she couldn't see in the darkened bedroom. Tears slid across her temples and onto her pillow. The afternoon and evening spent with Jake had been a dream come true, yet the memory of the outing left her miserable. Miserable because she loved a man who could never love her.

As soon as Kevin arrived, she intended to bail out. He didn't really need her, and she sure didn't need the misery she'd brought upon herself. She believed Kevin when he threatened to blackball her efforts to get another job. She'd have to convince him she didn't need to continue playing his fiancée, and that he no longer needed her in North Fork. Paying back the money he'd advanced to her would be a struggle and delay her future plans, but she would figure out a way to do it. After all, she'd been paying her father's debts for years.

She shivered at the memory of Jake's touch as he taught her to cast, and that same touch when he doctored her arm and hand. She stroked the gauze bandage. Jake had insisted he rebandage her arm after she showered. The scrapes weren't nearly as raw as the ache in her heart.

What am I going to do? But she knew. Pray. Jake had taught her that. *God, I don't deserve your help, but I need it. I need to stop loving Jake and get out of this mess I made.*

Abby closed her eyes and tried to swallow back the sobs. She turned over, buried her face in her pillow, and cried herself to sleep.

~

A meadowlark trilled a greeting as Abby negotiated the path to Jake's house. As she passed the milking barn, Spur joined her. At Jake's, she sat on the porch steps and petted her companion for a few minutes before going inside.

Abby hadn't had much time to work on Jake's business plan in the few days since the fishing trip. She had promised Pat help with the funeral dinners for the miners' families, which kept her busy the first three days of the week, as one memorial service followed another.

Jake had attended all the services, but Abby had little time to talk with him. The hardest for all of them was Rick's. Abby didn't know how Jake managed to get through the service, let alone help give the eulogy along with Cam Morgan and BJ Murcheson. They talked about how they called themselves the "Four Butts" and of the numerous adventures—planned and unplanned—that they experienced over the years.

All four played sports together from T-ball to varsity. On the high school football team, Rick was the quarterback, BJ a tight end, Cam a running back, and Jake the center. In basketball, Cam and Rick were forwards, BJ the center, and Jake a guard. Baseball had Rick pitching, BJ on first base, Cam third base, and Jake catching. All had college degrees, but only Rick had married. As the three men talked of their childhoods, their championship teams, and their brotherly bond, they'd openly laughed over memories and shed tears for their lost friend.

Abby could barely contain her own grief as she listened to Jake and the others. When they concluded their last salute to a fallen friend, Abby's tears flowed freely. She envied Jake his lifelong friendships. She'd had a few friends, but hadn't kept in touch with them. In spite of her envy, she was happy that Jake had such wonderful memories. Good memories could sustain a person for a lifetime.

Helping Pat and other women serve dinners to the families of the deceased gave Abby a sense of belonging. How often did the people of North Fork really take stock of how lucky they were?

After the last of the memorial services, life eased back into its normal routine, and Abby had finally found an afternoon to work on Jake's business plan.

In Jake's office, Abby pulled up the plan Jake had written, made a few adjustments, and then opened the spreadsheet that showed the figures and projections she'd worked on earlier. As she poured over the information and made changes, she found several discrepancies only Jake could answer. She printed out the data in question and saved her changes on both the hard drive and a disk. She put the papers into a manila envelope and headed for the barn, hoping to find Jake.

As she opened the front door, Spur jumped up from where he'd been sleeping. She'd barely put one foot on the porch when Spur laid back his ears, bared his teeth, and growled. Startled, Abby stepped back in the house, the screen door shutting behind her. In spite of the warm day, cold chills ran up her spine as she remembered the dog that attacked her when she was five. Her hands shook and sweat beaded on her forehead. She breathed deeply until her racing heart slowed. *What is wrong with Spur?* Abby wasn't sure what to make of Spur's aggression. He'd always been friendly to her.

Spur sat and watched the door.

"Spur, what's the matter?" Her voice shook, and she swallowed the fear building in her. "Y-you know me."

Spur's tail switched back and forth on the porch. The bared teeth were gone along with the growl. He seemed friendly enough. Perhaps she had misinterpreted his demeanor. She cautiously opened the door again. Spur laid his ears back, bared his teeth, and growled at her. Abby wasn't sure what to do. He'd been fine when she arrived. The only difference was the envelope she carried.

She laid the envelope on the floor and cautiously

stepped out on the porch, sweat trickling down her face. Spur wagged his tail and let her pet him. Odd, she thought. She stepped back in the house and picked up the envelope. Another menacing growl greeted her as she tried to leave.

Abby took the envelope to the office, retrieved the disk from the computer and stuck it in her back shorts' pocket. She didn't need the hardcopy. The disk would do, since the computer in the office above the milking stalls would be able to pull up the information. She thought that by taking a hardcopy, Jake could avoid quitting his work for a trip to the office.

Spur was waiting when Abby reached the door, his tail wagging. As she opened the door, he laid his ears back, bared his teeth, and growled.

This is crazy. "Spur, what's gotten into you?"

He stood his ground and uttered another deep guttural growl. Abby stepped back into the house and pulled the disk from her pocket, her hands shaking. She laid the disk on a bench near the door and stepped out onto the porch. Spur greeted her like a long lost friend. Abby tried several more times to exit with the disk, hiding it in various places on her body while out of Spur's sight, yet every time she tried to leave the house with the disk or the papers or both, Spur threatened her.

Finally giving up, Abby picked up the phone in the office and called the barn. She choked back a sob at the sound of Jake's voice. "Jake, thank goodness. I've been working on your business plan, but I had a couple of questions. I tried to come down to the barn to talk to you, but

Spur won't let me out of the house."

"Did you have anything from the house in your hands when you tried to leave?"

"I thought I'd bring some of the papers down. That didn't work, so I tried bringing just the disk. That didn't work either, even when I hid it on me."

"I should have warned you. Spur doesn't like people taking things from my house unless I'm there to approve."

"I hid it on me. He couldn't see it, and he still wouldn't let me leave."

"I guess he can smell it. At any rate, he senses it."

"You've taught him well."

"I didn't teach him that, Abby. That's something he's done on his own. Smartest dog I've ever had. Seems to have a second sense about everything. Put the disk in a padded envelope. There should be a small one in the desk. Give it to Spur and tell him to bring it to me. Then you can follow him."

"That'll work?"

"Should."

"I'll try it." Abby hung up, found a padded envelope and placed the disk inside. At the door, she knelt down and held the package out to Spur. "Here, Spur, take this to Jake."

Spur took the package from Abby, waited for her to leave the house, then took off for the barn. Abby followed, shaking her head. Every now and then Spur turned, making sure she still followed him.

"Afraid I'm going to go back to the house and steal something?" she asked. Spur twitched his ears. Abby was pretty sure that if she tried to go back to the house, Spur would go with her.

~

"This looks good, Abby." Jake sat in front of the computer screen. "What was your question?"

Abby sat in a chair next to him. "I'm not sure about the figures on page six. We discussed several different scenarios, but never settled on one. If you can decide which works best, then I'll be able to finish everything up."

Jake looked at her. "It's ready to go?"

"Except for those figures. There are a couple of things I need to finish once I have the information, but that will take thirty minutes at the most."

"I'm impressed. This would have taken me forever to get done. Thanks." He smiled, and Abby wanted to throw her arms around him and tell him how she felt. Instead, she straightened some papers on the desk in front of her.

"I've enjoyed doing it."

He narrowed his eyes at her.

"*Really.*"

"If you say so." He shifted his gaze to the computer screen. "Let me look at this later. Right now I need to start the milking."

"I'll be happy to do the milking while you go over it," Abby offered. "Unless you think I can't handle it."

Jake chuckled and shook his head. "Oh, you can handle it. I just don't like taking advantage of you. You've done way more than you need to."

"You're not taking advantage. At least I feel useful."

"Okay, I'll help you get the first bunch of cows in, then I'll come back up and see if I can fill in the numbers."

~

Jake stood at the office window overlooking the milking stalls as Abby worked. She was wearing short shorts, a sleeveless blouse, and her boots, which he'd sent her to the house to change into. She had beautiful legs—long and shapely—and she moved with the grace of a dancer, even in boots. He should have suggested she change into her jeans, but he couldn't bring himself to do it. *So shoot me, Lord. I like looking at her legs. And her face. And her hair. And her eyes.*

Abby must have sensed him watching, for she looked up at the window. Seeing him, she waved and smiled, and returned to work.

And her smile. Lord, why couldn't I have met her first? Kevin doesn't deserve her. He immediately felt guilty for coveting someone who didn't belong to him and never would. *Forgive me, Lord, and take away these feelings I have for Abby.*

Jake returned to the computer and played with several different scenarios until he was satisfied he had the right one. He saved the file and removed the disk, laying it on the desk.

A few minutes later, he entered the milking barn. Abby had her back to him, wiping down the teats of the last cow with a rag.

"How's it going?" he asked.

Abby turned, a frown on her face. "I'm not sure. I think there might be something wrong. Would you take a look?"

When Jake stood next to her, she pointed at one of the teats. "I think she may have a small cut."

Jake leaned toward the cow. "I don't see anything. Are you sure?"

"Well, I think so. It's right here."

Jake leaned a little closer. The warm milk in his face startled him. He backed away and wiped at the milk trickling down his face, embarrassed he'd been fooled so easily. He turned toward Abby with a menacing look.

Abby stepped back, fighting the grin creeping across her face. She lost the battle as the grin became a full-blown smile, reinforced with a giggle. Jake stepped toward her. She put out her hands to stop him.

"Now don't get mad, Jake. I'm just getting even for the milk bath you gave me. All's fair."

Jake continued moving slowly toward Abby. Abby backed away.

"If I recall, Miss Get-even, you startled me, and I bumped my head. The milk bath I gave you was supposed to even things out."

"I can't help it if you bumped your head. That wasn't my fault. Just admit we're even."

"I'm not going to admit something that isn't true. Stand still and take your medicine."

"I don't think so." Abby turned and hurried toward the door, but Jake grabbed her around the waist before she reached it. He captured her arms and held tight. Abby struggled to get away, her effort lost in her laughter.

"Now what would be a fitting punishment for the crime?" Jake teased.

"Letting me go for good behavior?" Abby gasped.

"Good behavior? What judge would buy that?"

"A fair one?" Tears streamed down Abby's face as her laughter continued. Jake accidentally tickled her as he tried to keep her arms contained.

"Stop struggling." Jake's laughter joined Abby's. "We're going to slip on this slick floor and both go down."

"Then let me go."

"Give me a good reason."

"I'll finish your business plan if you do, otherwise..."

"That sounds like blackmail."

Abby accidently stepped on Jake's foot, and he grunted.

"I need some kind of edge," Abby gasped. "You're stronger than me."

She tried to move her arms, but Jake held tight. Abby stilled. They stood, bodies molded together, her back against his chest. Jake took a deep breath.

"Okay, I give. Truce. I'll let you go, count of three. One, two, three."

The moment Jake released Abby she bolted for the door. Jake removed his cap and scratched his head, the urge to follow her fading as his conscience reared its head and whispered about the dangers of doing so. A movement above him caught his attention. Abby stood looking down, smiling.

Jake grinned, shook his head, and yelled, "You're not out of the woods yet, Abby. Not by a long shot."

She saluted him with the computer disk and disappeared.

Chapter 19

*A*bby focused on the computer in Jake's home office. The printer hummed as it spit out sheet after sheet. She gathered each one, tamping them together and adding them to the bottom of a stack on her left. Jake sat in a chair next to her, picking a page at a time from the pile, reading through each one. He'd taken a rare afternoon off in order to go over the final business plan with her.

Abby clenched and unclenched her hands as Jake read. The printer spit out the last page, and Abby slipped it under the papers she'd just straightened. Jake's expression failed to reveal whether or not he was pleased with the plan she'd finished from his research and ideas. Abby knew next to nothing about dairies and milk production, but she knew her way around business plans, marketing, and accounting.

She couldn't stand to sit there while he read through the proposal. "Would you like something to drink, Jake?"

"Huh?" Jake glanced at Abby.

"Would you like something to drink? Coffee? Iced tea?"

"Maybe later. But help yourself if you want."

"I'll wait." She continued to fidget until Jake finally set down the last page.

"Well, what do you think?" Abby asked.

Jake stared at the stack of papers. "You did a fantastic job of putting this together. I can't find anything wrong with it."

"Are you sure?"

He smiled at her. "I'm sure."

Abby breathed a sigh of relief. "Good. Now all you have to do is find time to go over it with your folks, and if they're game, present it to the...what was the name of that trust fund you said helped finance businesses and things?"

"The Brian Murcheson Fund."

"Right. Anyway, if they accept the plan, then you're on your way."

Jake gave a slight shake to his head. "You make it sound easy."

"You'll make it work."

"It still needs serious consideration and prayer before I present it for financing, but with your help I'm several months ahead of schedule. I'd like to pay you for your time."

Abby frowned. "I don't charge family. And don't insult me again by offering to pay me. Besides, you bought the boots for me. I'd say we're even."

"Just the same, I owe you. Somehow, some way, some day, I'll get even."

"For the milk bath or the business plan?"

Jake laughed. "*Both*. Now hand me that pad of sticky notes. I want to flag some places and jot down some thoughts before I present this to the folks."

As Abby handed Jake the pad, she heard Spur barking.

"Shall I check on Spur?"

Jake shuffled through the papers. "If you don't mind. Probably someone stopping by. Just tell Spur 'come' and 'sit.' That should take care of it."

Abby opened the front door and called Spur. A car door opened and a composite of Marilyn Monroe, Madonna, and Pamela Anderson emerged.

"Hi," the blonde said. "Is Jake home?"

Spur let out a guttural growl as he sat next to Abby.

"Jake? Uh, yes. May I tell him—"

"Don't bother. I'm Sondra. Where is he?"

"In his office."

Sondra stepped onto the porch and pushed past Abby into the house. "Which way is the office?"

Abby pointed and watched as Sondra entered the office and declared, "Surprise, Jake! I'm home."

When Abby stepped into the office a moment later, Sondra was in Jake's arms, kissing him. Or rather devouring him, in Abby's opinion. She swallowed and looked away, trying in vain to bury her jealousy. She turned to go, but Jake's voice stopped her.

"Abby. Don't run off. We still have work to do."

She turned and forced a smile. "It can wait."

With her back to Abby and her arms still wrapped around Jake's neck, Sondra said, "Let your poor secretary go, Jake. We have some serious catching up to do."

Jake peeled her arms from around his neck. "Abby's not my secretary, Sondra. She's Kevin's fiancée. Abby, this is Sondra Gardner, an old friend."

Jake didn't look happy to see Sondra. He'd referred to her as an old friend, but Abby recalled that Sondra was the name of his former fiancée. Abby could already see why Pat didn't like her.

"Kevin's fiancée, huh? Well, congratulations for landing the playboy of the family."

Abby accepted a limp handshake. Sondra looked Abby in the eyes and said, "Jake's holding back, Abby. I'm more than a friend. I'm Jake's fiancée. Looks like we'll be family."

Jake clamped a hand around Sondra's arm. "Let's go into the living room."

As he ushered Sondra from the office, she asked, "When did you get a dog?"

Jake ignored Sondra's question, turned toward Abby and pointed at her, his eyes narrowed. "Don't leave. I mean it."

Abby bit the inside of her lip. When Jake and Sondra were gone, she forced back the tears trying to escape. Sondra was beautiful. No wonder Jake had fallen in love with her. Pat had said Sondra had jilted Jake five years ago, but Sondra acted as though nothing had changed. On the other hand, Jake looked like he wanted to strangle the woman.

Abby's curiosity got the better of her. Against her better judgment, she tiptoed to the edge of the stairs bordering the living room and eavesdropped. She frowned as she listened to Jake's raised voice.

"I don't care what you think, Sondra. You have no right waltzing in here after five years and announcing you're my fiancée. We're no longer engaged, or don't you remember the part where you decided your career was more important than our getting married?"

"Jake, darling, I told you I'd be back. I know you're hurt—"

"*Hurt?* I don't think you've grasped what you did to me—to us."

"I saw things the way they really were. You'd resigned yourself to living here and working the dairy. I knew that deep down you really didn't want that. I did what I had to do. And it's paid off. I've been offered a starring role in a sitcom next fall and a healthy six-figure salary per episode."

"That's great, Sondra. I'm happy for you."

"I knew you would be." Her words dripped honey. "And I knew you'd wait for me."

Apparently Sondra hadn't detected the sarcasm in Jake's voice.

"I didn't wait for you," Jake said.

"Whatever. You haven't found anyone else. That's because you still love me. Don't you see? I'm giving you the chance to change things. I want to share my success with you. With this sitcom we can make our dreams come true. We're all set."

"*You're* set, Sondra. They're *your* dreams, not mine. Leave me out of it."

"Jake, don't let the past ruin what's between us. I've never stopped loving you. But I wanted more for us than a smelly old dairy farm and a life of struggling to keep ahead of the creditors. I knew I could do better if I had a chance. Now I can provide the perfect life for us."

"*You* wanted something more, Sondra. Not me. I like my life just the way it is. I *like* this 'smelly old dairy.'"

"You're just saying that, Jake. You're afraid to say what you really want."

"You think you're all set, Sondra, but consider this— what if the sitcom is canceled?"

"That won't happen. It's going to be a big hit. All the early testing has proven that. At any rate, I'm guaranteed six episodes. I'm on my way, and I want to share it with you."

"You still don't get it, do you? I don't want what you want. And I don't love you, Sondra. Not anymore. I got over you a long time ago. We *never* wanted the same things in life, although that wasn't obvious to me when I proposed."

"But we do want the same things. Love, a family, enough money to do as we please, and a house. I know you want a big house, Jake.

"I built you a house, and you didn't want anything to do with it."

There was a pause, and Abby held her breath.

"It's a nice house, Jake, but we can have so much more. We can have a house twice, three times this size with a swimming pool, tennis courts, anything we want."

"*This* is what I want, Sondra. I'm happy here."

"Oh, Jake, think about it. Los Angeles. The hub of the entertainment industry. You'll meet all kinds of exciting people. We'll attend premieres and parties with all the big names. If you want to keep busy, you can find something to do there. Work on whatever house we buy, or maybe we could get you into acting. You used to love that. Together we can take the entertainment industry by storm. The women will love you. We'll be the next Joanne Woodward and Paul Newman."

"You know, Sondra, you haven't changed a bit. You're still self-centered and totally unaware of what other people want."

"You're letting your pride get in the way. I understand that, but I could tell by the way you kissed me that you still care. We have a chance to make things right. Don't shut the door before you think it over."

Jake's jaws tightened. "Apparently you haven't been listening, Sondra, so I suggest you listen *very* closely now. I don't need to think it over. I'm not interested in a relationship with you. I'm not interested in moving to California. I don't want to become an actor. I love the dairy and this way of life."

"Oh, Jake, you can't be serious."

"I'm very serious. Now, I have a guest waiting for me, so I would appreciate it if you'd leave."

Abby didn't want to get caught eavesdropping. She scurried to the office and closed the door. Shortly after, she heard the front door slam. A minute later Jake stepped inside the office.

"Sorry for the interruption, Abby. I'd take some coffee now, if you don't mind. While you're making it, I'll finish making notes on the business plan."

He forced a smile, and Abby's heart ached for him. She wanted to throttle Sondra. But more than that, she wanted to comfort Jake.

"One mug of coffee coming up." Abby doubted Jake needed the caffeine, but if he wanted coffee, that's what he'd get.

While Abby waited for the coffee to brew, she gazed out the window above the kitchen sink. Storm clouds had gathered all day, threatening rain that could cancel the softball game scheduled that evening. She heard a distant rumble and hoped the storm would blow over. She wanted to watch Jake play ball. More than anything, she wanted to help him forget his encounter with Sondra.

Lightning flashed and thunder crashed almost simultaneously. Abby jumped, then laughed at herself.

"Takes you by surprise when it's that close."

Abby turned toward the sound of Jake's voice. He was leaning against the breakfast bar.

"It's so loud here." She smiled. "I love it."

"It bounces off the mountains."

Another flash turned Abby's attention to the open window. A long low rumble crept across the sky, ending in a faint murmur. The air had turned chilly. Abby shivered and rubbed the goose bumps on her arms.

"There's a light jacket in the hall closet if you're cold,"

Jake offered.

"Thanks. I'm okay." Abby reached for two mugs hanging on the side of the cupboard. "I love your kitchen, Jake. It's so roomy, with plenty of counter space. Anybody who loves to cook would give their eyeteeth for a kitchen like this. Everything's so handy with lots of room to work. You did a great job designing it."

"You like to cook, Abby?"

"I love to cook."

"Then this kitchen is made for someone just like you."

Abby looked at Jake. He smiled, shoved away from the counter, and moved toward her. Just as he reached her, lightning flashed across the sky, a loud crack a split second later, startling Abby. Jake grabbed both her hands and held on.

"Don't want you dropping my best china." He grinned, took the mugs, and set them on the counter in front of the coffeemaker. He filled both mugs and added sugar to one. "You take yours plain, right?"

She nodded.

"Let's go sit on the front porch swing and watch the storm for a while."

Abby swallowed hard, willing her hands to stop shaking, and took the mug from Jake. Between the last lightning strike and Jake's touch, she wasn't sure she could move without crumpling into a heap.

"Will we be safe?"

"Should be. I love watching thunderstorms. They're fascinating." Jake put his hand at the small of Abby's back and guided her toward the door. "We'll grab you that jacket on the way."

~

Jake and Abby sat on the wooden porch swing, gently swaying, sipping coffee, and watching the rain. Quarter-sized raindrops fell, splattering into large spots on the porch steps and gravel drive, then gradually settling into a gentle rain. Flashes of lightning and low rumblings interrupted the steady rhythm of rain on the porch roof.

Spur huddled under the swing, whimpering each time thunder rolled across the sky. Jake leaned against the back of the swing, enjoying the storm and Abby's company. He closed his eyes and thought about the encounter with Sondra.

She had definitely taken him by surprise when she appeared in his office. Sondra was definitely a beautiful woman. Jake allowed himself the luxury of kissing her, a small part of him hoping to make Abby jealous. However, she didn't appear to care. And why should she? She was in love with Kevin, not him, no matter how much he wanted it to be otherwise.

But Sondra's kiss left him cold. He wondered what he had ever seen in her. He evidently hadn't seen past her blonde hair, fine features, and perfect body. He thought he had, but if he had dug deep enough, he would have seen the shallowness in her. On the other hand, she was a good actress. She'd fooled him into thinking they had a future.

He couldn't believe her audacity, thinking he could, or would, set everything aside and blindly follow her to

California now that she had made it. She didn't get him and never would.

He glanced at Abby. Neither one had spoken since settling on the porch swing, the silence between them comfortable. Jake could get used to times like this with someone like her.

Watching Abby in his kitchen had soothed the anger Sondra sparked in him. Abby looked like she belonged there. That would happen only in his dreams. Dreams that were slowly turning into nightmares. *Why do I always fall for the wrong woman, Lord? What's my problem?*

"Would you like more coffee, Jake?"

"Sure." He downed the last few drops and handed Abby the mug.

The storm gradually moved eastward, the lightning and thunder coming at longer intervals. Spur inched his way out from under the swing and settled at the edge of the porch steps. Abby returned a few moments later and handed Jake his mug.

"Thanks, Abby."

Abby settled next to him on the swing. "Want to talk about it?" she asked.

"What? The business plan?"

"No." Abby took a sip of coffee.

"The weather?"

"Sondra."

"Nothing to talk about."

"I think there is." Abby turned slightly in the swing, and rested her leg across the seat. She hooked her other leg over her foot. "Are you still in love with her?"

Jake looked at Abby for a moment. *How can I be in love with her when I'm in love with you?* "No," he answered and looked away.

"She hurt you."

"I should have been smarter from the very beginning. I guess we're all entitled to be a fool once."

"She's the fool, Jake. Not you."

"Maybe." He leaned forward, rested his arms on his legs, and cradled his mug between his hands. "I started building this house the week after I proposed to her. I should have suspected something when she didn't act overly enthusiastic about it." He took a drink of coffee and leaned back, resting his ankle on his knee. "She looked at the plans once, then said 'whatever makes you happy, Jake, is fine with me.'"

"That's it? She didn't come out to look at the house while you were building it?"

"Oh, she came out a few times, even talked about how she was going to decorate it. Then she'd drag me off to do something she was more interested in. Now that I think about it, she didn't like being around the dairy or the smells associated with it. From the first she showed guarded interest and always had something to do elsewhere."

He rose and stepped to the edge of the porch. "The house was half done when she took off for California. The inside—finish work and decorating—was all done to suit me. At that point it became my house, not ours."

"No wonder she didn't know the way to the office."

Abby fidgeted with her half-empty mug. "You've done a wonderful job of creating not just a house, but a home, Jake. It's warm and inviting. You'll find someone who'll appreciate it and see the love you put into it."

Jake turned toward Abby. "I hope so. I haven't given up the idea of having a family someday. God knows this house is big enough."

"It will happen, Jake."

He smiled at Abby's simple statement. If she only knew how much he wanted her to be a part of his life, share this house with him, and have his children. Jake downed the last of his coffee. S*tupid fool!*

"Looks like the storm has moved through. We've got blue sky in the west. Give me a minute to change for the game, then we'll drive to the folks'. There's enough time before we have to leave for the park to broach the subject of expanding the dairy operation. I've already talked to Dad about it a little, but nothing concrete. Now that we have an actual business plan, they'll have something tangible to think about."

Abby reached for Jake's mug. "I'll rinse the mugs and put the papers in an envelope while you're changing."

Jake opened the screen door for Abby. She stepped past him into the house then turned toward him. "She doesn't deserve you, Jake."

He gave a slight nod of his head. "Spoken like a true future sister-in-law. I appreciate the sentiment."

"Do you still have feelings for her?"

"You already asked me that."

235

"No, I asked if you still loved her. This is different."

He snorted. "She's convinced I still love her and will pant after her like a love-starved puppy. The only emotion she stirs in me is pity. I feel sorry for her. That's it." Jake thought he saw a hint of relief on Abby's face. Or was that wishful thinking?

"That's good, Jake. And healthy. Real healthy." She smiled and headed for the kitchen.

Chapter 20

"*H*it out of the park, Jake!" Abby held her breath as Jake swung at the first pitch and missed. "Come on, Jake, you can do it!" The second pitch whizzed by, and Jake leaned back to keep his head from making contact with the softball. On the third pitch, Jake's bat connected with the ball, sending it into center field and over the fielder's head. Two runners crossed home plate, and Jake held at third with a stand-up triple.

Abby let loose a shrill whistle through her teeth and yelled, "Way to go, Jake!" He looked in her direction and grinned. So did several other people sitting in the stands. Abby blushed.

"That's a good way to start the bottom of the first," Pat said.

"Sure is," Leonard remarked.

"Do you play?" Pat asked Abby.

"Heavens no, but I love to watch sports of any kind. It's thrilling."

Pat smiled. "You must get a kick out of watching Kevin."

Abby's heart stopped. What sport did Kevin play that she should know about? He'd mentioned softball a few times, but his fishing seemed to take precedence.

"I understand Kevin's softball team is one of the top ones in Denver," Pat continued. "I'm glad he still plays. I've always enjoyed watching my boys participate in sports. I'm sure you'll be the same way when you and Kevin have kids."

Abby swallowed hard. "Oh, yes, I'll definitely encourage my kids to participate in sports. It builds good character. I never had the chance to participate. We moved so often that I didn't even try."

Pat gave Abby a funny look, then smiled. "I'll bet you would have been good at sports if you'd had the chance."

"Maybe."

The inning ended, leaving Jake stranded at third base. He donned his catcher's garb and took his place behind home plate. Watching Jake play fascinated Abby. His movements were fluid and powerful, stirring longings deep in Abby that she found hard to ignore, but ignoring those longings was her only option. She had made a fateful decision that complicated her life beyond what she could gracefully salvage. She hated the lie, but until Kevin came back, she could do nothing about it. He had to be the one to tell his family the truth.

She set aside her troubled thoughts and concentrated on the game. By the top of the third inning, Mac's Marauders were ahead four to one, Jake responsible for two of the four runs.

Abby's relaxed mood shattered as Leonard nudged Pat and nodded toward the bottom of the bleachers. "Sondra's here," he said.

"This sounds awful," Pat remarked, "but I hope she keeps her distance. I really don't want to talk to her."

Abby glanced in Sondra's direction. "Looks like she's headed this way."

Before Pat could utter anything, Jake ripped away his catcher's mask to chase a foul ball, and they all stood and cheered at Jake's catch. During the excitement, Sondra worked her way to the row below them and positioned herself in front of Pat. As everyone settled back onto the bleachers, Sondra turned and greeted the three of them.

"Pat, it's good to see you and Leonard. And nice to see you again, too," she said to Abby.

"Hello, Sondra. How are you?" Pat's voice was crisp with strain.

"Wonderful. Did Jake tell you I saw him?"

"He said something about you stopping by."

Sondra smiled. "That Jake. I don't know what I'm going to do with him. He's probably waiting to tell you the good news until we can do it together."

"And what news is that?"

"Oh, I'd rather not spoil the surprise, Pat."

"Actually, I don't think Jake will mind, Sondra," Pat said. "Why don't you tell me, and I'll act surprised when Jake tells us."

Abby rolled her eyes and chewed the inside of her lip.

"Okay," Sondra said. "I can't wait for Jake, anyway. You'll be happy to know that Jake and I are an item again. Isn't that right, Annie?"

"Abby, and that's not what I understood." The sarcastic comment slipped out before Abby could bite it back.

"Well, you understood wrong. Jake will set things straight."

"I'm sure he will," Abby replied.

Sondra frowned at Abby and then directed her next remark to Pat. "You must be excited to have both your boys engaged at the same time."

Pat returned Sondra's smile. "You can't imagine what I'm feeling right now. Why don't we discuss this later? I'd really like to watch the game, if you don't mind."

"Not at all. I've always loved watching Jake play."

Sondra's coy look made Abby want to throw up. Instead, she concentrated on the ball game, cheering for the Marauders and ignoring Sondra for the remainder of the game, except to answer Sondra's inquiry as to Kevin's whereabouts.

When the game ended, Mac's Marauders had prevailed, nine to five. Abby, Pat, and Leonard met Jake at the bottom of the bleachers. Sondra barged in on the foursome, planting a kiss on Jake before he could defend himself. Feeling sorry for Jake, Abby squelched the desire to put Sondra in her place.

Jake untangled himself from Sondra and gave her a warning look she didn't heed. She slipped her arm through his and hung on tight.

"Great game, son," Leonard said as he slapped Jake on the back.

"Sure was," Pat added. "The team seemed to rise to the occasion."

"Dedicating the game and the season to Rick was plenty of incentive. We couldn't lose."

"I guess not." Pat looked at Abby. "Are you going home with us?"

Jake looked at Abby. "You're still going for pizza with me, aren't you?" he asked.

Abby didn't remember an invitation from Jake, but his look implored her to answer yes.

"Of course. I'm looking forward to it."

Sondra shot Abby a dirty look, which Jake missed. "Are you sure you won't be bored, Annie? There's nothing worse than feeling like a third wheel."

Abby glanced at Jake. Anger sparked in his eyes. She stood her ground. "Oh, I don't mind, if Jake doesn't."

"The invitation stands."

"Well, then, we'll see you at home, Abby," Pat said. "We'll leave the porch light on in case we're already in bed. I know how long these after-game parties last."

Pat and Leonard walked away hand in hand. When they were out of earshot, Jake turned to face Sondra.

"I don't recall inviting *you* for pizza, Sondra. Now if

you'll excuse *Abby* and me—"

"Jake, what's gotten into you? Surely the three of us can have pizza together. After all, we're going to be family."

"The team always gets together for pizza after a game. It's understood that we can invite one person. I've already invited Abby."

"I'm sure Annie won't mind my going in her place."

Abby opened her mouth, but Jake spoke before she could.

"I'm not sure what it's going to take to get through to you, Sondra, but obviously our little talk this afternoon didn't do it. You're not welcome to go for pizza; you're not welcome in *my* home anymore. If I see you on the street, I'll say 'hi,' but that's as far as it goes. I won't stop to talk. It's over."

"Jake—"

"Abby, are you ready?"

"Ready."

"She's your brother's fiancée, Jake. Be careful."

Jake glared at Sondra. "This is Abby's chance to get acquainted with people who've known Kevin all his life."

"Oh, get real, Jake." Sondra rolled her eyes.

"Watch what you insinuate, Sondra," Jake warned.

Before Sondra could say another word, Jake gripped Abby's arm and ushered her away. She gritted her teeth to keep from yelping at the pain he unknowingly inflicted on her arm. When they reached his pickup, he opened the passenger door and helped Abby in.

She rubbed her arm where Jake had grasped it. He

rounded the pickup and climbed behind the steering wheel. His hands gripped the wheel and his knuckles went white. He said nothing for a couple of minutes. Abby waited quietly as he shoved his anger aside and relaxed.

"Thanks, Abby." Jake smiled at her. "Sorry to put you in that position, but I knew she'd try to finagle an invitation, and I didn't want her company."

Abby smiled. "She sat in front of us during the game and tried to convince your mother that you two were still an item."

"Did she succeed?"

"Your mother wasn't the least bit convinced."

"What I ever saw in her I'll never...." Jake started the engine and backed out of the parking space. "Do you still want to get pizza?"

"I'd love to, if you don't mind having me along."

"Not at all. What I told Sondra was true. You'll get a kick out of meeting the team and hearing stories about Kevin."

"Sounds like fun." Abby absently rubbed her arm again as Jake guided the pickup toward the park exit.

"What's wrong with your arm?"

"Nothing." Abby stopped rubbing it.

Jake slammed on the brakes. "It's red. What happened?"

"Nothing. It's fine. Let's go."

Jake looked away for a moment then back at Abby. "Did I do that?"

She ignored the question and looked straight ahead. "Let's go before the rest eat all the pizza."

Jake put his hand under Abby's chin and turned her face toward him. "Did I hurt your arm?"

"You didn't mean to."

Jake dropped his hand, and Abby could see him mentally berating himself.

"Jake, it's okay."

He shook his head. "It's not okay."

Tears pooled in Abby's eyes. "You were upset with Sondra. You didn't realize you were squeezing my arm so hard. I'll be fine, so don't worry about it."

Silence invaded the pickup cab. Jake watched her for a moment. "You're crying."

"Not because of my arm. I don't like the way Sondra has treated you."

With a gentleness that sent shivers of desire through Abby, Jake took hold of her arm, studied it, rubbed it with his thumb, and then let go.

"I'm really sorry, Abby. My anger at Sondra is no excuse for bruising your arm. No excuse at all."

"I'll heal. Now, I don't know about you, but I'm hungry."

Jake looked at Abby a moment longer, then put the pickup in gear and drove out of the park. Halfway down the street, he said in a quiet and gentle voice, "I don't need your tears, Abby, but I do need your forgiveness for hurting you."

"Someone has to care that Sondra hurt you. If not me, then who else besides your mother?"

Jake glanced at her and shook his head.

She smiled. "You're forgiven. Let's go have some fun."

Jake nodded once and smiled. "Fun and pizza coming

right up."

~

"Hey, Jake, you were sure getting an eyeful of that pretty little third baseman when she was up to bat. What were you tellin' her?"

"What makes you think I was tellin' her anything, Kale?"

"By the smile on her face and the grin on yours. What'd you do? Make a date?"

Abby felt a twinge of jealousy at the thought of Jake flirting with someone.

"Nope." Jake grinned. "Didn't you notice the wedding band on her left hand?"

"You gonna let something like that stop you?"

"You bet. Especially when she's married to the big guy playing first base."

"Heck, Jake, you could take him, easy." Kale shot back.

"Maybe." Jake leaned back in his chair and took a sip of Coke.

"So what *did* you say to her, Jake," JD asked, "that made her miss the next pitch?"

"It wasn't what he said," Kale interjected. "It was my fast ball."

"You wish, Kale," Jake countered. "I told her she was holding the bat like a feather duster."

Everyone at the long, crowded table laughed, including Abby. She found the camaraderie and teasing between Jake and his friends unexpected and affirming. It must be like this after every game, Abby thought. Jake had told her that JD and Stacey MacCord treated whenever the team won. So far, according to Jake, the MacCords had paid for the pizza since the season began.

"Hey, coach, when are we playing against your celebrity pals?" Steve, the second baseman, asked.

"We haven't finalized the date, yet," JD answered, "but it looks like it'll be the last week in July. You might want to mark your calendars. So far we've had acceptances from Michael Bolton's and Vince Gill's teams. I'm waiting on the other two."

"So how good are these guys?" Jake asked.

"Pretty good, but you can beat them if you don't get distracted."

"You mean by pretty girls?" Kale asked.

"Is that the only thing on your mind?" Jake challenged.

"Are you kidding? Of course it is. I've got no attachments. Bring 'em on."

Jake laughed. "Keep your gun handy, deputy. You may need to shoot 'em to get their attention." Jake ducked the ice cube Kale hurled across the table. "I think he needs more time in the bullpen, coach."

Loud laughter sounded from the front of the café. Sondra entered on the arm of a tall, blonde, and handsome man. She hung on his every word, laughed when he said something. She worshipped him with her eyes.

Jake glanced in her direction, then quickly turned his attention back to the chatter that had resumed at their table. Out of the corner of her eye, Abby watched Sondra glance at

Jake, only to find him ignoring her. She walked toward Jake, her date in tow, and stopped behind Jake's chair.

"JD, how nice to see you. Congratulations on your team winning tonight."

"Thank you, Sondra. How are you?"

"Great. I assume you've heard about my new television series." She lifted her chin and smiled.

"I heard. Good luck."

"Thank you. Do you mind if Jason and I join you?"

"Actually," JD said, "we do. Sorry, but this is a team party and you need to be a member of the team or a guest. But do enjoy your evening. We'll try not to disturb you."

Sondra flipped her hair back from her face. "Don't worry, I doubt we'll even know you're here." She tugged on her date's arm. "Come on, Jason, let's get a table." They settled at a table on the far side of the room.

When she was gone, Abby glanced at Jake. Giving a nearly imperceptible shake of his head, he remarked under his breath, "Some people never learn."

"She caught me after the game and tried to wrangle an invitation," Kale said, "but I told her I was going alone tonight because I was on call."

"What? You turned down a date with a beautiful woman?" Steve teased. "I thought you were available. What happened to 'bring 'em on?'"

"Heck, she's way out of my league," Kale added under his breath, "thank goodness."

For a moment, Abby felt a little sorry for Sondra, until she noticed that Sondra was all over her date, kissing and fondling him without regard to the public spectacle she made of herself. If she intended to make Jake jealous, she was failing miserably. Jake wasn't paying attention.

Stacey MacCord leaned toward Abby and whispered, "Best thing that ever happened to Jake was when JD gave Sondra her big break. JD felt bad for Jake when he realized his part in their breakup. Fortunately, it turned out to be a good thing for both of them."

Abby smiled. "I think you're right. Jake doesn't seem to have any feelings at all for her. Her loss."

"Yes," Stacey agreed.

Around midnight, JD stood. "A toast to a fallen comrade." He raised his glass of Coke. "To Rick."

Everyone stood and raised their glasses.

"To Rick," they chorused. A moment of silence followed as they drank their toast, and then the party broke up.

Chapter 21

*O*n the drive home, Abby tucked away the memory of the ball game and the party afterward. She resigned herself to the inevitable—Jake would be hers only through her memories. And tonight was one of the most precious.

"Everything okay?" Jake asked.

Abby turned from looking out the pickup side window and smiled. "Everything is fine. Thanks for inviting me tonight. I had a great time."

"We didn't share much about Kevin, I'm afraid."

"You shared enough." She'd found out that Kevin was a star pitcher on the baseball team in high school. She deduced that he pitched for the softball team Pat alluded to earlier.

"Kevin still pitching for the High Rollers?"

"As often as he can," Abby remarked, hoping she wasn't too far afield. The comment seemed safe, considering everything.

"How's your arm?"

"It's fine, Jake. It doesn't hurt. No permanent damage."

"Good. I don't know what got into me."

"Sondra, I think."

"I shouldn't let her get to me like that. She isn't worth it."

"It's a natural reaction. Don't give it another thought."

He grinned at Abby. "Where'd you learn to whistle like that?"

She felt a rush of heat across her face and was grateful for the dark. "An old boyfriend."

"Boyfriend, huh?"

"Yep. We were juniors in high school, and I thought it was cool that he could make such a shrill noise through his teeth. It took me several weeks to perfect it, but once I did, well, it's a little like popping your gum. Once you learn how, it just slips out without any effort. I didn't mean to call attention to myself. I was just rooting the team on."

"You did a good job. We won, didn't we?"

Abby smiled. "You sure did. So, where did the name Mac's Marauders come from?"

"Mrs. MacCord. We'd been considering "MacCord's Marauders since JD is the coach and an ex-Marine, so she suggested we shorten it to Mac's Marauders. We all agreed."

"What's this celebrity thing JD was talking about?"

"Evidently, there are a bunch of softball teams that have

celebrity players, or at the very least, celebrity coaches. They get together from time to time and play each other for charity. JD's thrown us into the mix and set up a celebrity tournament here."

"I'd love to watch that." Abby knew she wouldn't get the chance.

"Maybe you can talk Kevin into coming over for it. He likes rubbing elbows with celebs."

"Maybe." Abby turned away and stared out the side window again. If Jake only knew, and he would as soon as Kevin got back. *I'm not going to perpetuate this lie any longer than I have to. And then Jake will want nothing to do with me. I'll be no better than Sondra in Jake's eyes.*

~

Abby set the warm garlic bread on the table and sat down. When Leonard finished the blessing, Abby took the bread and passed it to Jake, then passed a large bowl of chicken Caesar salad.

"This is wonderful dressing, Abby," Pat said after a couple of bites. "What brand is the dressing?"

"It's homemade. A favorite recipe of mine."

"It's excellent."

Jake finished his helping of salad and leaned back in his chair. "That was good, Abby. What's next?"

Abby stared at him. "What?"

"The main course. What is it?"

Abby frowned. "The salad is the main course. I did fix a cherry pie for dessert, but this is dinner."

"No meat and potatoes?"

A puzzled expression crossed Abby's face. "There was meat in the salad. Not beef, but definitely meat. I like a lighter meal when it's hot, don't you?"

Jake shrugged his shoulders. "I need more than salad to keep me going. I still have a lot of work to do before bedtime."

Tears pricked Abby's eyes. "I-I'm sorry. That's what I fixed." She pushed her chair back and fled the kitchen.

"Jacob Leonard Karlson. Shame on you. What's gotten into you?"

Jake winced at his mother's admonition. "Nothing. But I can't last the rest of the evening on what she fed us."

"She worked hard to fix this meal, and insisted she do it by herself. Abby wanted to pay us back for all our hospitality."

"I told her it was good." He squirmed as he felt the heat of embarrassment flood his face.

"And then you cut her off at the knees. Go apologize."

"I'm still hungry." Jake looked to Leonard. "Aren't you, Dad?"

"Do as your mother says. You owe Abby an apology."

"Maybe Kevin is okay with grazing for supper, but I need more."

"Then go home and fix yourself a sandwich," Pat said, "*after* you apologize."

As he left the kitchen to find Abby, Jake heard his mother say, "I don't know what's gotten into him, but if he wasn't so big, I'd turn him over my knee..." Leonard's laughter was the last thing Jake heard as he climbed the stairs.

Jake stood at Abby's door, his fist poised to knock. The door ajar, he knocked lightly. "Abby?"

Silence greeted him. He pushed the door open. Abby sat on the edge of the bed, wiping the tears from her eyes. Jake grabbed a tissue from the dresser and handed it to her. She took it and blew her nose.

"Look, I didn't mean to upset you. I'm just used to having a heavier meal. It keeps me going until the milking's done."

Abby tore at the tissue, refusing to look at Jake. "Clearly I'm not used to cooking for farmers. I didn't realize..."

Jake closed his eyes for a moment. "No, you didn't, and I had no right to set you straight. The salad was delicious."

Abby looked at him and shrugged.

"Really, Abby. You're a good cook."

"You haven't tasted my cherry pie yet. Then you can decide if I can cook or not."

"After what I pulled, you're going to let me taste it?"

"If you promise not to gush over it just to make me feel good."

Jake grinned. "I promise. Come on, let's test it."

Jake ate two pieces of cherry pie a la mode. "Gotta fill up all the cracks the salad missed." He winked at Abby, and she rewarded him with a smile. "Seriously, this is great pie."

"Wait till you try my pot roast," she said. "You'll forget all about the pie."

"Can't wait." He rose and carried his empty plate to the

kitchen sink. "And neither will the cows. You coming down to the barn later?" he asked Abby.

"I think I'll turn in early tonight and do some reading."

"Okay. See you tomorrow. Good night." Jake gave his mother a quick kiss on the cheek. "Night, Dad."

"Believe I'll help you with the milking tonight." Leonard followed Jake out the door.

Jake and his dad walked to the barn, neither saying a word. After they had finished the last bunch of cows and were cleaning the milking barn for the night, Leonard asked, "What's eatin' at you, son?"

Jake frowned. "Nothing. Why?"

"You might be able to get away with that with most folks, but you can't fool your mother or me. What's going on? Sondra still got you upset?" When Jake didn't answer, Leonard added, "You still have feelings for her?"

"Sondra? Not hardly. She's history and has been for a long time."

"Then what's eating at you?"

"The heat. It's wearing on me. Don't worry, I'll be fine."

They worked in silence until they finished the cleanup. As they were leaving the barn, Leonard put a hand on Jake's shoulder.

"If you can't talk to me about it, then talk to somebody. But don't let whatever is bothering you fester too long. Night, Jake."

"Night, Dad."

Jake watched his father as he walked to the house. He's getting older, Jake thought. He doesn't step as firmly or work as quickly as he used to. And he tires out faster. Jake also noticed that Leonard favored his injured arm more in the past few months.

But he can still read me like a book. And there's no way in you-know-what that I can tell him I've fallen in love with my brother's girl. He would turn me over his knee, injured arm or not. Jake smiled and shook his head at the image he conjured in his mind. And in spite of the comic picture, he knew he deserved a good whipping.

"Dad, hold up. Think maybe I'll grab another piece of that pie before I hit the sack."

~

Abby slipped into her robe and followed the sound of voices coming from the kitchen. She thought she'd heard Kevin's voice and wondered if he'd finally shown up. She peeked into the kitchen. Jake and Leonard sat at the kitchen table, sharing the last of her cherry pie. She smiled. At least she knew Jake liked the pie.

She crept upstairs, not wanting to disturb them. Tomorrow she would go shopping again, this time for pot roast.

Instead of crawling into bed, Abby sat by the window and stared at the night sky. "Lord," she prayed, "help me make things right with Jake, Pat, and Leonard. I don't like the lie between us. Bring Kevin home soon. We need to tell them the truth. Help me, *please*."

Before she could crawl into bed, she heard Leonard on the stairs. She glanced out the window as Jake stepped

255

outside and turned toward the path to his house. Headlights flashed and a vehicle turned down the lane. Spur barked. Jake paused and turned in the direction of the visitor. A black Lincoln Navigator stopped next to the house, and Kevin stepped out. The answer to Abby's prayer.

"Kev!"

"Jake. Hey, Spur."

She turned from the window, threw on some clothes, brushed her hair, and rushed downstairs. It was time to set things straight, no matter the consequences.

When she reached the bottom of the stairs, Jake and Kevin were in the kitchen.

"I'd offer you a piece of Abby's cherry pie, but Dad and I just cleaned it up."

"That's okay. All I need is a glass of water." Kevin moved toward the sink as Abby stepped into the kitchen.

"Abby." He smiled. "I figured you were probably asleep."

"Not yet." She tried to smile, but anger bubbled up inside her. "It's about time you showed up."

Kevin looked in Jake's direction. "Whoa. Guess I deserved that one."

"Guess you did," Jake said. He glanced at Abby.

Kevin closed the distance between him and Abby and gathered her into his arms. "You can be mad at me later. Right now, I need a kiss. I missed you."

Abby couldn't avoid the inevitable, at least not until they settled things. She lifted her chin and let Kevin kiss her. The kitchen door opened and closed as Jake left. She ended the kiss and shoved away from Kevin.

"We have to talk. *Now,*" she said. "Away from here. Take me for a drive."

"I just got here. Can't it wait?"

"No." Abby headed for the door.

~

Car doors slammed and Jake glanced back toward the house. The Navigator's engine came to life, and tires crunched against the gravel of the drive. Jake shook his head. From the look on Abby's face, he figured Kevin was in for an earful. Not that he could blame Abby. She had a right to be mad at Kevin. He'd deserted her for two weeks.

Spur trotted up to Jake from the field, and Jake reached down and stroked his head. They walked in silence, and when they reached the house, Jake sat on the top porch step. Spur curled up beside him. A dark cloud of depression settled over Jake. He absently stroked Spur's head and scratched behind his ears.

"So, Spur, you up to listening to my sad tale?"

Spur groaned and rested his head on his paws.

"Whether you like it or not, you're the only one I have to talk to. Cam's gone back to Durango, BJ's playing ball in San Francisco, and Rick..."

Jake rubbed his hand across his face. "I've really screwed up, haven't I? I'm in love with Abby, and there's no future in that. I hurt her feelings tonight for no reason. I criticized her cooking instead of complimenting her on a great meal. Maybe she could have included a baked potato with a pound of sour cream and bacon bits, but that didn't give me cause to say what I did."

Spur whimpered as if to say, "You did what?" and rolled over on his side.

"You're right. It was stupid and immature. And then I lied to Dad about why I acted that way. And to top it off, Kevin shows up and acts like everyone should be glad to see him."

Jake leaned against the porch support post. "You should have seen the look in Abby's eyes when she saw Kev in the kitchen. If looks could kill... In fact, she didn't look all that happy to have him kiss her."

I wasn't happy about it, either. He stared at the night sky. The stars blinked at him. Millions of tiny lights scattered across a black canopy.

"Lord, something's not quite right between Abby and Kevin. Not just tonight, but their whole relationship seems off. She doesn't talk about him much. Only when she's asked. She never talks about their plans. Does that seem right?" He shook his head. "Doesn't to me, either."

Jake closed his eyes. He couldn't shake the feeling that there was more to Kevin's engagement to Abby than met the eye. Then again, maybe it was just wishful thinking.

Spur sat up, growled, and bounded off the porch toward the field.

Jake snorted. "So much for a sympathetic ear." He rose and stretched his arms overhead. As he opened the front door, he prayed. "Lord, show me the truth." He looked up. "And help me accept it."

Chapter 22

*K*evin pulled into the city park and killed the engine. Abby stared at her hands as she clenched and unclenched them, the heat of her anger rising from her neck to her face.

Kevin flipped a dismissive hand. "Look, Abby, I know you're a little miffed that I deserted you. My family can be boring and overbearing. I wouldn't have left if it wasn't important, but my business reputation—"

"Can it, Kevin. You weren't taking care of business and you know it. As for your family, they're wonderful. I've enjoyed every minute of the past two weeks. Well, everything except the mine accident. That was horrible."

"What accident?"

"Apparently, you haven't checked your messages, or

you blocked mine. I'm guessing the news didn't travel all the way to Mexico."

"Mexico? What are you talking about?" Kevin turned in his seat. "I was taking care of a client and didn't have time for the news."

Abby shook her head. "You've been lying so long, Kevin, it's become second nature."

"Abby, I'm not lying—"

"Give me a break. I'm not stupid. Naïve, maybe, but not stupid. By the way, how is Gail?"

"Gail?"

"I know you were with her in Mexico at her parents' condo. Did you have a good time?" She could see enough of Kevin's face to know her suspicions were right. Her emotions in chaos, she bit her lip to stop the tears of anger she wanted to shed.

Silence wrapped itself around the two of them. Kevin stared out the windshield.

"How did you figure it out?" he finally asked.

"It wasn't hard. Remember, I work for you."

"My secretary tell you where I was?"

"I'm not giving up my sources, but it wasn't your secretary."

"Good. I won't have to fire her."

"You're a real piece of work, Kevin. You pay other people to cover up your lies, and never feel a bit of remorse."

"I wouldn't get too self-righteous if I were you, Abby. What was it I paid you?"

"You're right, Kevin. You paid me to lie for you. I was

a fool. Knowing your track record, I figured it wouldn't hurt anyone, and I'd be out from under my father's debts. The problem was, I didn't expect your family to be so nice." The tears that Abby fought against spilled onto her cheek. "I thought they'd be just like you—deceitful, uncaring, shallow, dishonest." She wiped at the tears with her fingers and turned toward Kevin. "Do you *know* how wonderful your family is? Have you thought about how much you hurt them when you stay away? They love you, Kevin. And you treat them like they're infected with the plague."

"They're boring and unsophisticated."

"Your parents are the most genuine, loving, and fun people I've ever met. Added to that, I find it hard to believe you and Jake are brothers. He's honest and responsible, and has more integrity in his little finger than you'll gain in a lifetime." Abby found a tissue in her pocket and wiped her nose.

"Don't mince words, Abby."

Abby settled her elbow on the armrest and leaned her head into her hand. She needed to collect herself. She couldn't let Kevin have the upper hand.

Kevin's next words were sharp. "Apparently, you think I'm the scum of the earth."

Abby took a deep breath and let it out. "I think you've lost your way, Kevin. You're dishonest and selfish, but I know you weren't raised that way. What happened?"

"Nothing happened." Kevin's jaw tightened. "And you have no right to lecture me about my life. What do *you* know, anyway?"

"I know I don't like who you are. You're a cheat and a liar, just like my father. I know you cheated Jake out of his dream because of your selfishness. I know you deceive your clients if you can get away with it just to make an extra dollar. I know I no longer want to work for you." Abby sighed. "And I know we have to tell your family the truth. And if that means I have to pay you back, I will. Every last cent. It will take me a while, but you'll get every penny back."

"With interest?"

"What?!"

"Never mind. I don't want the money back. I want you to honor your part of the bargain."

"I can't do that anymore. I don't feel right about deceiving your family."

Kevin's face turned hard. "Listen closely," he said through clenched teeth. "You *will* follow through on our deal. You *will* continue to be my fiancée for the next three days, and then you're off the hook."

"I can't do that, Kevin. I can't keep lying to your family."

"You will, because if you don't, you'll never work in accounting or business management again. I promise you that. I'll make sure word gets around that you embezzled from the company, and that we made an agreement that you'd pay it back if I wouldn't press charges. The rumor mill can be *very* effective if done correctly. No one will ever hire you."

Abby stared at Kevin. "I can't believe you'd do that."

"Don't try me, Abby."

"Why is this charade so important to you?"

"None of your business."

Abby's temper flared. "That's where you're wrong. You've just threatened my future. If I'm to continue to be a part of this, I need to know why. I told you why I agreed to this in the first place. You owe me an explanation as to why this lie is so important to you."

Kevin glared at her. "All right. You said I cheated Jake out of his dream. Well, poor Jake. All my life it's been Jake this and Jake that. No matter how hard I tried, Jake was always better. I worked my tail off in school and in sports just to keep up with his accomplishments. I was always compared to perfect Jake. But Jake wasn't nominated for outstanding alumnus at his ten-year reunion. He doesn't own a multi-million-dollar business. And perfect Jake doesn't have a beautiful woman by his side. I've finally got a chance to show everyone I'm better than Jake."

Kevin glared at Abby, anger defining the hard lines of his face. Abby's tears stopped. She studied Kevin, surprised at what he'd said.

"I pity you, Kevin, because no matter how many awards you get, or how much money you make, or how many beautiful women you have hanging on your arm, you'll never be happy. The only person you have to measure up to is yourself, although it wouldn't hurt to follow Jake's example. He's happy with his accomplishments and doesn't feel the need to flaunt them."

Kevin set his jaw. "So, that's how it is, huh? I leave you alone with my brother for a couple of weeks, and he steals you away from me."

"He couldn't steal what you never had. And Jake hasn't done anything. He's been a gentleman. He's treated me like a future sister-in-law."

A patrol car, lights flashing, pulled in behind the Navigator, and an officer stepped out.

"Great," Kevin hissed and rolled down the window.

"You folks having trouble?" the officer asked.

Abby couldn't see his face, but the voice sounded familiar.

"Kale. How're you doing?" Kevin asked.

"Kevin, you old son-of-a-gun. 'Bout time you showed back up." Kale leaned down and peered across at Abby. "Hi, Abby."

She smiled. "Hi, Kale."

"I hate to run you off, Cuz, but we have a rule about parking here after 10:00 p.m., unless there's an event going on."

"Sorry, Kale. I just got back in town and needed a little private time with my girl." He reached across the seat, took Abby's hand, and squeezed it. "We went for a ride and ended up here. We'll move along in a minute."

"No problem. Just letting you know. You two take care now." Kale returned to his patrol car. He flashed his light bar a couple of times and tapped the siren as he drove away.

"Save me from small-town cops," Kevin muttered.

"Sheriff's deputy," Abby corrected.

"Whatever."

"He called you 'Cuz'. Why?"

Kevin frowned at her. "Our mothers are sisters. That doesn't mean I have to like him."

Abby slowly shook her head. "Is there anything you care about, Kevin?"

Kevin leaned toward Abby and narrowed his eyes. "Listen very carefully. If you want to have any kind of future, you'll continue as my fiancée for three more days. Then you can go your own way with my blessing. If you decide not to, you'll not only suffer professionally, you'll have the added burden of seeing my family hurt and disappointed. They won't think much of you for lying. I don't think you want that. Have we still got a deal, or do I turn you in to the Denver DA for embezzling $70,000 dollars of my money?"

Abby's heart stopped. "You wouldn't dare!"

"Don't tempt me."

"You're sick, Kevin. I hope your family never learns just how sick you are. Not that it would matter. They'd be disappointed, but they'd stand by you, because they love you. You don't deserve them, and they don't deserve your lies. Maybe you'll see that someday. God willing."

"You didn't answer my question."

Abby turned away from his glare. She'd already lost where Kevin's family was concerned. As for the future, she needed to support herself. Kevin's threat left her little choice. She didn't doubt Kevin's ability to make it look like she embezzled the money. Only three more days, then she could lick her wounds and start over…somewhere.

"All right, we still have a deal, but after that, I don't care if I *never* see you again."

"Fine. At least we agree on something." Kevin started the engine of the Navigator. As he put it in gear, he asked, "What mine accident?"

~

Sleep eluded Abby once they returned to the house. On the drive home, she had told Kevin about the mine accident and Rick's death. He seemed genuinely sorry about Rick. Had he not, Abby would have given up hope that Kevin had a chance to change his life. She prayed God would open his heart and show him the error of his ways.

When the morning sun broke through her bedroom window, Abby awoke exhausted and despondent. She couldn't ask God to see her through the next three days. She didn't have the right, since her actions went against everything she thought God expected of her.

After dressing and applying her makeup, Abby summoned up her courage, put a smile on her face, and headed downstairs. When she entered the kitchen, Kevin, Jake, Leonard, and Pat were already eating breakfast.

"Morning, Sleeping Beauty." Kevin smiled. "Thought you were going to sleep the day away."

"Sorry I'm late for breakfast," Abby said. "I'm afraid Kevin and I were up awfully late catching up."

Kevin pulled a chair out next to him for Abby. When she sat down he kissed her on the cheek. Abby resisted wiping it off.

"What would you like for breakfast, Abby?" Pat asked.

"Just coffee."

"You can't get through the day on just coffee. Let me fix you a couple of pancakes."

"I'm feeling a bit under the weather this morning. Coffee's enough."

"I'm sorry to hear that, Abby," Jake remarked. She glanced at him. He looked down and forked a helping of pancakes into his mouth.

"Can I get you anything?" Pat asked. "Aspirin?"

"No thanks. I just need to take it easy for a little while. I'll perk up before long, I'm sure."

Kevin put his arm around Abby's shoulders. "I guess I should know better than to keep you up so late."

The smile Abby directed at Kevin didn't reach her eyes. "I guess so."

"By the way, Jake. I'm really sorry about Rick. I didn't know until Abby said something last night."

"Thanks." Jake took a drink of coffee. "It was all over the national news. Figured you would've seen it."

Kevin cleared his throat. "I didn't see any news. Too busy trying to appease my client." Abby choked on the drink of coffee she'd taken. "You okay, honey?" Kevin patted her on the back. "Last night was the first I knew of it."

Abby coughed a couple more times and sucked in a deep breath. "Fine. Coffee just went down wrong." Along with your lie, she wanted to add.

"Abby tells me she had a good time while I was gone."

"She seemed to enjoy herself," Jake said.

"Jake taught me how to milk cows, and he took me

fishing. I helped Pat in the garden and helped Jake with his books. And I still had time to miss you," she added.

Kevin gave Abby a funny look, then turned to look at Jake.

Jake drained his coffee cup and rose. "I've got work to do. No rest for the wicked." He snatched his cap from a hook by the door. "Oh, by the way Dad, I fired George Denton this morning."

Leonard frowned. "Kinda sudden, don't you think?" He downed the last of his coffee.

"Nope. He lied to me about why he didn't come to work for two days in a row."

"He needs this job, Jake," Pat said. "He's got little ones at home and another on the way."

"He should've thought about that before he went on a two-day drinking binge. And he shouldn't have lied to me. This isn't the first time he's missed a couple of days in a row, and not the first time he's lied about it. I can't abide a liar or a drunk. I gave him a second chance a month ago. He blew it. I told him we'd give him two weeks' severance pay, which is more than he deserves. And if I could get away with it, I'd put his wife's name on the check instead of his."

Abby's stomach churned, and she lowered her head. Jake couldn't abide liars, which is exactly what she was. A liar.

"I can't argue with you, son," Leonard said, "but it's a shame, nonetheless."

"He gets his drinking and lying under control, I might change my mind. Until then, he's gone." Jake grasped the doorknob and opened the door. "You coming down to the barn, Kev?"

"Maybe. Depends on what Abby wants to do."

"Bring her along. She knows her way around."

~

Abby and Kevin went to town together, had lunch, and took a drive. Kevin told Abby he wanted to be sure she was prepared for the activities of the next few days and wanted to discuss things away from his family. Abby hadn't had a chance to ask Kevin about Gail the night before, and her curiosity got the better of her.

"You never did tell me why you went to Mexico to see Gail," Abby said as Kevin turned the Navigator down the drive to the house. "Are you two an item again?"

"Nope," Kevin answered.

Abby waited for a minute. When Kevin didn't offer any further explanation, she said, "Details, please."

"Okay, I guess you have a right to know. She called me here and said she wanted to talk things over. Said she missed me."

"So you had to find out if she was sincere."

"I couldn't very well tell my family I was trying to patch things up with my real fiancée, while my pretend one was staying in their house." He stopped the Navigator in front of the house and killed the engine.

"It would have saved *all* of us a lot of trouble." Abby wasn't feeling very forgiving or compassionate at the moment.

Kevin frowned at her. "It would have complicated things. I decided to see what she had to say for herself. I thought I'd only be gone for a couple of days. But when I got to Denver, Gail convinced me she was really sorry about the breakup and begged me to go to Mexico with her. I figured it would be a whole lot more fun than being here, so I agreed. I also wanted to see if I loved her enough to take her back."

"And?"

"I discovered I don't love Gail like I thought I did. She's shallow and self-centered."

"More than you?" Abby blurted.

Kevin glared. "According to your standards, yes. She treated the Mexican servants like they were scum and put on airs to everyone she met. She threw lavish parties and then complained that people only came because she was footing the bill. I was there for window dressing. Anyone could have stood in for me."

Touché, Kevin, Abby thought and prayed there was still hope for him to change. If he could see it in others, maybe he'd recognize it in himself someday.

"I don't need to be associated with someone like her. So I dumped her before she could dump me again."

Oops, I hoped too soon. "Sounds like you're both well rid of each other." Before Kevin could reply, Abby stepped out of the Navigator. "I need a shower," she mumbled and headed for the house.

Chapter 23

With little enthusiasm for facing an evening with Kevin and his classmates, Abby dressed in a colorful floral sundress with a full skirt and low back meant to impress Kevin's friends. Low-heeled sandals and a pale yellow shawl completed her ensemble. Pulling her wild red curls back with gold filigree clips gave her hair some semblance of order.

She wandered outside and settled on the canopied swing beneath a majestic maple. Abby set the swing in motion and soaked in the beauty of Mount Lamborn. Though it was early evening, the air was heavy with the heat of early July.

A meadowlark trilled, but Abby's heart was in too much turmoil to enjoy the birdsong. She glanced toward the barn and her heart warmed at the sight of Jake walking toward the house. When he saw Abby, he stopped.

"Hi. Looks like you're all ready for a big night."

She shrugged. "Kevin's class is meeting for dinner and dancing."

"That should be fun."

"Hope so."

"You look pretty, Abby."

She smiled at his compliment. "Thanks."

Jake sat on the grass in front of the swing. "You don't seem too excited about this evening."

"I won't know anyone but Kevin. I'm not too good around strangers."

"That's not true, Abby. You fit in right away with our family, and you were great with Sarah and the kids."

"You and your folks made me feel welcome, and Sarah was easy to talk to. As for the kids, piece of cake." She grinned.

"You'll do the same with Kevin's friends."

Abby picked at invisible lint on her dress. There were so many questions she wanted to ask Jake. So many things she wanted to store in her heart, but there was no more time. She needed his advice. In two days, she'd never see him again, and she needed to know how to deal with the loss.

"How did you handle it when Sondra left?" she asked.

Jake frowned and stared at the ground. Abby held her breath, afraid she'd overstepped by asking something so personal, something that would conjure bitter memories.

Jake stuck a stalk of grass in his mouth and chewed on it. "I didn't deal with it very well at first. I was devastated. Mad at her and mad at the world. Then I realized I was only hurting myself and making everyone around me miserable. I finally gave my anger over to God. It was easier after that." He settled his gaze on her.

"You just asked God, and He took away the hurt and anger?"

"Well, it took a lot of praying on my part, and a lot of listening on God's part." He chuckled. "I think God probably got tired of hearing me complain so much, but He stuck with me."

"What if someone doesn't deserve God's help?"

"It's not about deserving. It's about God's grace."

"No matter what you've done?"

"No matter. Just ask. God is loving and forgiving. 'Cast your cares on the Lord and he will sustain you; he will never let the righteous fall.' Psalm 55:22."

She marveled at his ability to quote scripture at a moment's notice, but the words did little to encourage her. "That's the catch, then," she said. "You have to be righteous."

Jake frowned. "You talking about Kevin or you?"

Abby looked away from Jake, afraid he'd see the tears welling up in her eyes. Staring at her clenched hands, she remarked, "It doesn't matter."

"Does this have something to do with the kiss I—"

"No."

"You sure?"

"Yes."

"Did Kevin do something? You seemed a little mad at him last night."

Abby bit the inside of her lip and dared to look at Jake. "Everything's fine between Kevin and me. We settled things last night. Don't worry."

Jake shook his head. "Are you sure?"

Kevin approached Jake and Abby. "Hey, what are you two talking about so seriously?"

"Not much," Jake said.

"Looks pretty serious to me."

Abby rose from the swing and picked up her shawl and small shoulder purse. "I'm just worried about fitting in."

Jake stood. "And I was assuring her she'd have no problem."

"Jake's right, sweetheart." Kevin took Abby's hand.

"You look gorgeous. Shall we go?"

Odd, Abby thought, how Kevin's compliment didn't thrill her like Jake calling her pretty had. "I guess I'm as ready as I'll ever be."

"Hey, Jake, why don't you join us later? We're meeting at the Columbine Inn. There'll be dancing after dinner and anyone's welcome. All they have is a jukebox, but it should be fun. Guess the class didn't want to spring for a deejay or a live band."

"I've got a volunteer fire department meeting tonight about the fireworks."

"Great. As long as you're in town you just as well stop by. I'm sure the others would like to see you."

"I'll think about it. You two have fun."

Kevin pulled Abby toward the Navigator. "We will."

Abby turned her head toward Jake and mouthed, "Thank

you."

He gave her a thumbs up.

~

Kevin watched Abby as much as he could and still drive safely. There was something going on between her and Jake. They had acted like a couple of kids caught with their hands in the cookie jar when he approached them earlier. It rankled him. Going to Mexico might have been a mistake. His absence gave Jake a chance at Abby.

Kevin set his jaw. He shouldn't care if Jake had feelings for Abby. Or vice versa. But something about Abby intrigued him. She was beautiful in a different way than Gail. Not classy, more natural. And unlike Gail, she seemed to care about people. She had a genuineness about her that didn't exist in Gail. Or most people he knew, for that matter. According to Abby, she'd come to care about his family. Maybe too much.

"Something going on between you and Jake I should know about?" he asked.

Abby turned from staring out the side window and looked at Kevin. "No." She returned her gaze to the landscape speeding past.

"You two sure have a funny way of looking at each other for nothing to be going on."

"We've developed a friendship." She glared at him. "Isn't that what you wanted?"

"I wanted you to distract my family so that I didn't have to endure their constant badgering. I didn't expect you to fall for my brother."

Abby ignored his remark, so he tried another tack. "What do you mean you helped Jake with his books?"

Abby continued to stare out the side window. "He was having trouble balancing his books. I offered my accounting expertise. I found his mistake and noticed the beginning of a business plan. While he was busy taking care of the dairy, I put the finishing touches on it."

"What business plan?"

"You'll have to ask him. It's not my place to say."

Kevin bit back an expletive. He wanted to enjoy the evening, and getting Abby riled up wouldn't help. Still, he couldn't shake the feeling that there was more to Abby's willingness to help Jake than met the eye. Kevin saw something in her eyes every time she looked at Jake. And something in Jake's eyes whenever he glanced at Abby.

"So, Jake took you fishing? Where?"

Abby turned slightly in the seat. "What is this? Twenty questions?"

"Why don't you want to answer me?"

"I spent a very enjoyable two weeks with your family. They made me feel welcome and kept me from getting bored. I simply returned the favor by helping them. Now, if you don't mind, let's just drop it. I've agreed to play my part, Kevin, and I will. I'll be your doting fiancée for the evening. I'll make you into a god if you want me to. After all, you've paid for my services."

"You act as though I'm treating you like a whore."

"That's *exactly* how I feel, Kevin. But don't fret over it.

It was my choice."

He gritted his teeth, fighting the urge to press the issue. He wasn't about to let Abby ruin his evening. He had a chance to show his classmates what success really looked like, and Abby was the final touch to the picture.

He parked the Navigator in the Columbine Inn's parking lot. "Put a smile on your face, sweetheart, because the woman walking toward the restaurant is my old girlfriend. Time to start earning your pay."

~

Instead of turning toward home, Jake drove west out of town toward the Columbine Inn. Against his better judgment, he decided to take Kevin up on his offer. He tried to convince himself he just wanted to see Kevin's classmates, people he hadn't seen in a while, but he knew better. He was worried about Abby, and he couldn't purge how beautiful she looked sitting in the swing. Like a field of wildflowers.

He had the impression she dreaded the evening. Her reticence seemed more than nervousness over meeting Kevin's friends. Something was wrong, yet Jake couldn't quite put his finger on what was bothering Abby. She assured him that things were fine between them, but he wasn't convinced. How had she put it? "Kevin and I settled things." What did that mean?

Jake turned into the inn's parking lot and parked his GMC pickup next to Kevin's Navigator. He remained in the pickup for a few minutes, trying to convince himself that he should go home.

Get out or go home.

He pulled the keys from the ignition and locked the doors. Inside the inn, he stepped to the bar and ordered a Coke, almost shouting over the din of music and talking. Jake glanced around the room and spotted Kevin, Abby, and several familiar faces, including Kevin's old girlfriend, Melissa. The group sat at a large table in a more secluded section of the restaurant. Kevin acted like he was king of the castle holding court.

Kevin hollered at Jake and motioned for him to join the group. Jake sauntered over, calling a greeting to several people as he walked by their tables. He stopped near Kevin's chair. Abby sat at Kevin's left and Melissa sat on his right.

"Jake," Kevin said, "you remember the gang."

Jake smiled and nodded at each one. "Nice to see all of you again."

He realized the tall blond man sitting at the other end of the table had been Sondra's date at the pizza parlor. He hadn't seen Jason since high school, and he had changed considerably over the last ten years. Jason appeared to be alone this evening. Smart guy, Jake thought.

"Pull up a chair and join us," Kevin invited.

"Thanks, but I don't want to intrude."

"Better join us, Jake," Brent said. "Kevin's so full of BS that someone has to tell us the truth." Everyone laughed and several encouraged Jake to join them.

"Thanks, anyway. Doesn't look like there's room."

Kevin rose and grabbed a chair from another table. Brent scooted over and Kevin pushed the chair next to Abby.

"See, plenty of room."

Jake intended to firmly refuse and walk away, until he looked at Abby. Her eyes implored him to sit down. At least he thought that's what she wanted. Maybe it was wishful thinking on his part, but before he could talk himself out of it, he settled onto the empty chair.

In the next few minutes, Jake learned how the others had spent the last ten years of their lives. All of them had varied careers, and Brent and Michelle, who'd married right out of high school, had two kids. The rest were still single, although Kimberly was engaged.

Abby's quietness bothered Jake, and he noted she didn't look like she felt well. She smiled at the appropriate times, but the smile never reached her eyes.

"Kevin here is doing all right for himself," said Dirk. "Of course, we all knew he would. Bet you're proud of him, Jake."

Jake nodded. "He's made our family look good."

"Oh, come on, Jake. You're looking pretty good yourself," remarked Melissa. "What are you doing these days? Is it Dr. Jake now? Weren't you going for your veterinary degree?"

"That didn't work out," Jake answered. "I'm helping Dad run the dairy."

"He's built a very successful operation," Abby said. "As a business manager, I've been impressed with what he's done. Karlson Dairy is one of the top dairies in the nation. Won the National Dairy Quality Award for the West Region this past year. No doubt he'll win the national award in the near future."

Jake glanced at Abby. She smiled at him and her face lit up. Everyone but Kevin congratulated Jake. Kevin glared at Abby.

"Yes, Jake's quite the milker." Kevin raised his mug of beer and sneered. "Here's to Jake, successful dairy farmer."

A moment of awkward silence passed around the table, until Jake lifted his Coke and smiled. "Thanks, Kevin, I'll drink to that." Abby lifted her glass and the others followed suit.

Dirk rose and sauntered over to the jukebox. He inserted some coins and punched a few buttons. Music from the Judd's filled the room. Dirk returned to the table and asked Kimberly to dance. Brent and Michelle joined them on the dance floor.

Kevin looked at Abby, then turned to Melissa and asked her to dance. When they reached the dance floor, he pulled Melissa close, and they moved as one to the music. Abby fiddled with her glass. Jake fumed.

Jake leaned toward Abby so she could hear him above the music. "Would you like to dance?"

Abby smiled. "Thank you, Jake, but no. I'm not feeling very well. I have a pounding headache."

"I'm sorry to hear that. Can I get you something?"

"I'll be fine. I took some aspirin earlier."

"Your glass is empty. Can I get a refill for you?"

She shook her head. "I think I've had enough Coke for the evening. I'll have trouble sleeping if I have any more caffeine."

The song ended and Alabama crooned, *If I Had You.* Kevin remained on the dance floor with Melissa, holding her close, the way he should have been holding Abby.

Kevin was never satisfied. No wonder Abby had a headache. Kevin was flaunting his old girlfriend in Abby's face. "Are you sure you don't want to dance, Abby?"

"I'm sure."

"Has he been acting this way all night?"

Abby nodded.

"There's no excuse—"

"Let it alone, Jake. Since this headache came on, I haven't felt up to dancing, and Kevin just wants to have fun."

Before Jake could say anything more, Jason asked him a question about his dairy award, and he spent the next few minutes telling Jason about the requirements for the award.

The song ended, and everyone returned to the table. Kevin and Melissa laughed as they sat down. Jake decided he'd had enough. He scraped his chair back and stood.

"Thanks for letting me crash your party, but this dairy farmer has an early day tomorrow. Nice seeing all of you again." He turned to go, but the sound of Abby's voice stopped him.

"Jake, wait. Would you mind taking me home?"

"Abby, you can't leave," Kevin said. "The evening's just getting started."

"I'm sorry, Kevin, but I have a splitting headache. I need to go to bed. You stay and have fun with your friends. I'll be fine. Jake can take me home."

Kevin looked at Jake. "Do you mind, big brother?"

"Not at all."

"Great." Kevin stood and kissed Abby on the cheek. "Get to feeling better, sweetheart. Tomorrow night's a big night."

Abby picked up her shawl and purse. "It was nice meeting all of you," she said.

Jake followed Abby out of the Inn and opened the pickup door for her. She climbed inside and hooked the seatbelt. Jake climbed behind the wheel. He noticed Abby lean her head back and close her eyes. He gripped the steering wheel to keep from gathering her in his arms. He wanted to throttle Kevin.

Jake started the engine and said a prayer of thanks that Abby had turned down his invitation to dance. He no longer trusted himself. Had he danced with her, he was certain his feelings for Abby would have flashed like a neon sign.

Chapter 24

After leaving the Columbine Inn, neither Abby nor Jake said a word. She appreciated the silence as they drove. If Jake said anything, she'd fall apart.

Thankful for the cover of darkness, Abby let her tears trickle down her cheeks. All she knew how to do anymore was lie. Or cry. Her head didn't ache; her heart ached.

Refusing to dance with Jake was the only smart thing she'd done in the past two weeks. If she had accepted Jake's invitation, it would have added to Kevin's suspicions. Her feelings for Jake would have shown clearly. Kevin already suspected something between them, and she didn't want to give him more reason to resent Jake. *Two more days. Only two more days.*

Jake parked the pickup in the drive and killed the

engine. Abby reached for the door handle. She didn't want Jake to see her tears.

"I apologize, Abby, for Kevin's behavior tonight."

"What?"

She turned toward Jake. He looked at her and frowned. Reaching across the seat, he wiped away her tears with the back of his hand.

"Please don't, Jake. It's all ri—." Her voice caught in her throat, and she fought back a sob.

"Son of a—"

Jake released his seatbelt, lifted the console between them, and slipped his arm around Abby's shoulders. His other arm circled her waist. Too tired to resist, Abby buried her face in his shoulder and sobbed. He rested his cheek against her head.

After a few minutes, Abby felt his arm move, and he pressed a tissue into her hand. She wiped her eyes, but the tears continued to flow. His arms were warm and comforting, and if she believed in answered prayers, she'd pray to stay in his arms forever. *But God only answers the prayers of the righteous, and I have no right to ask.*

He took the tissue from her and handed her a fresh one. She wiped her nose, blotted her tears, and sucked in a deep, shuddering breath. She should ease away from Jake's embrace.

"Kevin's behavior tonight is unconscionable. He'll answer to me for hurting you like this."

"N-no." Abby pushed away from Jake enough to look at him. "Please don't say anything to him. It's all right, Jake.

I'm just not feeling well. Kevin meant no harm."

She could see Jake's jaw tighten. He looked away.

"Jake..."

"I know you're in love with him, Abby, but that's no reason to excuse his abominable behavior."

Abby diverted her gaze to Jake's chest, not wanting to witness his anger. How much more heated it would be if he knew the truth. For the moment, she was content to let his anger focus on Kevin.

"Kevin was excited to see his friends. He was just enjoying their company. It's only for a day or two."

Jake's hands cradled Abby's face, forcing her to look at him. "Kevin didn't give a crap about his friends. He just wanted to show them how successful and wonderful he is. At your expense, I might add."

And yours, too, Abby thought. True to form, Jake showed more concern about Abby than himself. That thought made her eyes burn with new tears. She fought them back. He could never know her tears were for Jake and the way Kevin belittled him. He'd know she was crying because she loved him, and she would never know the joy of having his love returned.

She touched his face with the palm of her hand. "Let it go, Jake. Kevin and I will work it out."

"Abby, I can't—"

"*Please*, Jake." She closed her eyes. "Please."

He let out a ragged breath. "I'll try."

She looked at him and mustered a smile. "Thank you. And thank you for everything you've done for me these last two weeks. You and your folks have been wonderful. Kevin's very lucky to have such terrific parents, and you for a brother."

Abby leaned forward and kissed Jake on the cheek. "You're very special, Jake. Thank you for everything."

Abby thought she saw Jake's eyes soften. Summoning the last of her willpower, she scooted across the seat, opened the door, and stepped out of the pickup.

"Goodnight, Jake. Thanks for the ride home." She closed the door and walked to the house.

~

Abby opened the door to the house and slipped inside. Jake waited until he saw the light in her bedroom shine across the lawn before he relaxed and leaned back against the seat. Scrubbing his hands over his face, he relived the kiss she bestowed on his cheek. The feel of her lips against his cheek begged for more, and he used every bit of self-control not to respond. Kevin didn't deserve her, yet she loved Kevin and defended him when he didn't deserve defending.

The urge to hit something built in Jake. He didn't care what Abby said. Kevin was going to get a piece of his mind.

He cranked the engine over and backed out of the drive. After parking the pickup at his house, Jake walked back to his parents' place. He settled on the canopied swing, not caring how long he had to wait for Kevin. It was time Kevin had a lesson in decency.

~

Abby kicked off her shoes, threw herself on her bed, and sobbed silently into her pillow. Pat and Leonard had retired, a relief to Abby. She couldn't have faced their questions. Kissing Jake on the cheek instead of the lips took all her strength, but she wanted him to know she appreciated everything he'd done.

Unable to dredge up the energy to change for bed, she fell asleep fully clothed and wrapped in the bedspread. Spur's barks woke her. She sat up and focused on the clock. Two fifteen. Bright lights shown through her open window before disappearing. She peered out and saw Kevin climb out of the Navigator.

As long as she was dressed, she decided she'd have a talk with him when he came in. While she fumbled for her shoes, she heard Jake call Kevin's name. Fearful of what Jake had in mind, Abby slipped to the open window, her heart in her throat.

"Jake," Kevin said. "What're you doing up? I thought you had to get up early and shovel manure." As Kevin talked, Jake moved closer. "So what's up? You have something on your m—"

Jake's fist met Kevin's jaw. Kevin stumbled backward and fell. He lay on the ground for a moment, shook his head, then levered himself onto one elbow and stared at Jake.

He wiped at his mouth with the back of his hand. "What the hell'd you do that for?"

"For treating Abby the way you did tonight."

"That's none of your damn business." Kevin pushed himself to a sitting position. "If you ruined my teeth I'll—"

"You're a real piece of work, Kevin. I don't even know you anymore. But I know one thing. You don't deserve Abby."

"And you do?"

Jake scoffed. "She seems to love you, Kevin. Why, I don't know. But I suggest you start treating her with respect."

"How I treat Abby is my business, so butt out."

"Sorry, Kev. You need to be reminded about the right way to treat a woman."

"Like you're an expert."

Abby watched in horror as the scene unfolded before her. The brightness of the moon and the yard light illuminated Kevin and Jake. Jake clenched his fists at Kevin's remark. She should try to stop what was happening. She leaned toward the open window and tried to call out to them to stop, but the words died in her throat.

"Wake up, Kevin, before you lose the best thing that ever happened to you." Jake turned away from Kevin and stalked toward the path that led to his house.

"Come back here and fight like a man!" Kevin scrambled to his feet.

Jake stopped and turned toward Kevin. "I would, if there was a man around to fight with."

Kevin stared after Jake, but didn't follow. He reached in his back pocket, pulled out a handkerchief, and wiped his mouth. He walked toward the house, muttering something under his breath.

Abby sank to the floor and crossed her arms over her stomach. She couldn't stop the ache, and she couldn't stop the tears. Now was not a good time to talk to Kevin. He would have no patience to listen to her. But then, no time would be a good time.

After what she'd witnessed, she couldn't face Jake. Her lies had caused a rift between brothers, and that was unforgivable. The only way to mend that rift was to tell the truth. And the truth had to come from Kevin first.

Abby pulled herself up and let out a deep breath. Kevin would only tell the truth if she forced him. But how would she do that? If she told his family everything, he'd find a way to turn things to his advantage. There had to be another way. She was a coward, for she couldn't bear the condemnation in their eyes when they heard the truth. They would forgive Kevin. He was family. They would never forgive her.

Jake had championed her tonight. She'd have to be content with that. She knew he'd regret his actions when he learned the truth.

She saw only one course. Pulling open the dresser drawers, Abby took out her clothes and laid them on the bed. As she packed, she composed the notes in her head.

~

Jake shoved his hand into the bowl of ice and grimaced. Kevin had a jaw of steel. The skin had broken on two of his knuckles. His hand ached, but nothing like his heart.

The last time he'd hit Kevin, he was nine and Kevin was six. His mom had taken him to task for picking on his little brother. As usual, Jake took the blame for something that Kevin instigated. After that incident, Jake learned Kevin wasn't worth getting in trouble over.

But tonight...tonight Kevin got what he had coming, even though he hadn't taken the lesson to heart. Kevin was more concerned with his looks than he was about his treatment of Abby.

"What a jerk!" Jake hissed. He didn't understand how Abby could love Kevin when he treated her so bad. *It's like she's punishing herself for something. Why can't she see he's not worth it?*

Jake shook his head as he removed his burning hand from the bowl and dumped the ice into the sink. In the upstairs bathroom, he rubbed antiseptic cream on his knuckles, applied a bandage, and downed two aspirin.

The ache in his hand—and his heart—refused to abate as he undressed and climbed into bed. He raised his hand above his head to ease the throbbing and closed his eyes. Nothing, however, could ease the ache in his heart as Abby's face appeared in his mind, tears streaming down her cheeks. Jake groaned. "Lord," he whispered, "take away my longing, and heal Abby's broken heart. Show Kevin the error of his ways, and help me to forget. Please, God, I need to forget."

~

At the top of McClure Pass, Abby pulled the Navigator over and turned off the engine. She leaned her head back and closed her eyes. Jake would be rising about now to start the morning milking. She could almost hear him talking to the cows as he readied them for the milkers. He loved his work. Unlike Kevin, who was obsessed with his job only for the success and recognition it brought.

How could two brothers be so different? They were raised the same, no doubt about that, but something had turned Kevin away from the values Pat and Leonard had taught him.

"Lord, please help Kevin find his way back. He'll lose his family and everything that's important, if he doesn't."

Abby couldn't pray for herself. Her lies didn't give her the right. But she could pray for Kevin and Jake.

"And please help Jake find a woman who deserves his love. He has so much to give. Maybe after Sarah has gone through the grieving process... Jake would make a wonderful father for those kids. He deserves to be happy, Lord."

She smiled and closed her eyes. Numbness and exhaustion set in. She needed sleep.

Abby had waited in her room until she was sure Kevin was asleep. Opening his door as quietly as she could, she had tiptoed into his room and set the note she'd written on his nightstand. Finding the keys to the Navigator took a few moments. She finally found them in his pants' pocket.

The second note was placed on the kitchen table for Pat, Leonard, and Jake. Abby thought seriously about writing a separate note to Jake, but decided that would only give Kevin more reason to suspect her feelings for his brother. She'd caused enough of a rift between the two. One note for the three of them was less obvious and better for everyone.

Abby hoped her departure would force Kevin to tell the truth. She opened her eyes and shivered at the thought of enduring Kevin's wrath when he returned to Denver. *I can handle it. I have to handle it. This is the only way.* Dealing with Kevin's anger was far preferable to facing Jake's contempt.

As soon as she arrived in Denver, she would go through all the office records to gather evidence proving she had *not* embezzled from Kevin. She wasn't going down without a fight.

Abby closed her dry, aching eyes and fought the panic welling inside her over the consequences of leaving Kevin high and dry. The fight would be fierce. She inhaled a deep breath. A few minutes' rest before tackling the heavy traffic on I-70 wouldn't hurt. Jake's grinning face was the last image in her mind before she dozed.

Chapter 25

*K*evin stuffed the note in his pocket, the bulge in the envelope told him Abby left the engagement ring. Both demanded attention like a festering sore. *Damage control first.* He tucked in his shirt and rushed downstairs. The missing Navigator keys were the least of his worries. He had to know what she'd told his family. Maybe they didn't know she was gone. He could only hope. *Damage control first.*

When Kevin entered the kitchen, Jake and Leonard sat at the table. Jake frowned when he saw Kevin. Leonard glanced at Kevin, drained his coffee cup, and set it on the table.

Pat looked up from the stove. "*Kevin*, what happened?"

"What?"

"Your lip is split and swollen."

Kevin reached up and winced. "I hit myself on the door of the Navigator. Guess maybe I had a little too much to drink last night."

Pat slid the skillet from the burner. "I'll get a wash cloth and make a cold compress."

"No. It's fine. I'll take care of it. So, what's for breakfast?"

Jake slammed his cup onto the table. "What's going on, Kevin? Why'd Abby leave?"

Guess they know she's gone. He had to find out what else they knew. "She had to go back to Denver."

Pat handed Kevin a cup of coffee. "She left us a note. Said she was sorry for lying to us. What did she mean, Kevin?" Pat frowned. "I just can't imagine Abby lying."

Kevin took the coffee and sat down at the table. "Where's the note?"

"Answer the question, Kev," Jake growled.

Kevin needed to know what Abby wrote in her note. His attempt at stalling was failing miserably, and Jake's lousy attitude didn't help either. Evidently, his mood had not improved overnight. Kevin hedged. "I don't know how much I should tell you, without knowing what Abby told you."

Pat sat next to Kevin, a piece of paper in her hand. "She thanked us for everything we'd done and for making her feel so welcome. And for allowing her to be a part of our family for a while. 'I'm so very sorry I lied to you,'" Pat read. "'I only hope that someday you will forgive what I have done. I never meant to hurt you. Kevin will explain everything. Love, Abby.' Why does she think we won't forgive her?

What's going on?"

Kevin glanced around the table and searched for something to tell them. At least Abby had been vague. An idea hit him. He bit back a smile. Instead, he took a deep breath and explained, managing a grave expression on his face.

"When I got home last night, Abby was waiting up for me. Jake brought her home early because she had a headache. I didn't think too much about it. But when I got home, Abby said her condition had flared up, and she needed to go back to Denver."

"Condition?" Jake asked. "What condition?"

"Abby has a rare blood condition. It's not life threatening, but every once in a while it flares up. When it does, she has to go to the hospital and have her medication readjusted. Stress can bring it on. It usually starts with a headache, and then worsens. She's had a headache since yesterday morning. Last night her condition flared up."

Jake glared at Kevin. "And you let her drive to Denver by herself? You should have gone with her."

Kevin returned Jake's glare. "I tried to convince her I'd drive her back, but she refused. She knows how important tonight is to me. I told her I could get her to Denver and be back in time for the banquet, but she wouldn't hear of it. I know when I can't win an argument with her. I waited upstairs this morning until I heard from her. She called my cell phone a few minutes ago to let me know she'd made it all right."

"This condition have a name?" Jake asked.

Kevin held his forefingers about a foot apart. "It's about this long and hard to pronounce."

Jake scraped his chair away from the table, grabbed his cap, and jerked the door open. He slammed it behind him as he left.

"Why didn't she tell us about her condition?" Pat asked. "Why did she think she had to lie about it?"

Kevin smiled. "That's Abby. She was afraid you wouldn't want me to marry her if you knew."

Pat folded the note and stuffed it in her pocket. "That's nonsense."

"You got that right," Leonard said. Kevin squirmed at the look his father leveled at him.

Pat rose. "I'm going to get that cold compress." She hurried from the kitchen.

"Son," Leonard said, "I don't cotton much to lying. Something you want to say to straighten this out?"

Kevin shoved away from the table. "This is *exactly* why I don't come home very often. I don't need this third degree." He followed Jake out the door, hoping Jake was already in the barn. He didn't want to deal with Jake or his father at the moment. He had to get away. Much to his chagrin, Jake was waiting outside.

"You want to tell me the real reason Abby left?"

"I told you. She's has a condition—"

"*Bull.* There's nothing wrong with her except for the way you've treated her. When are you going to learn, Kev?"

"You stay out of this, Jake. I saw the way you looked at her. Your problem, big brother, is that you're jealous. You can't keep a girl, so you're jealous of mine. And you're jealous of my success."

Jake narrowed his eyes, then shook his head. "Jealous? No, Kev. I've never been jealous of you. I've always been proud of you. *Really* proud of you and what you've accomplished. Until now. I don't know who you are anymore."

"I'm a *hell* of a lot better than you, Jake."

"I don't know why you hate me so much, Kev. I hope you get that burr out from under you. But it doesn't matter how you feel about me. You have no right to lie to Mom and Dad. They've always done right by you. They love you and don't deserve the way you've treated them the last few years." Jake lifted his cap, rubbed his hand through his hair, and reset his cap. "I suggest you take a long hard look at how you've treated them. Wake up, Kev, before it's too late." Jake turned and strode toward the barn.

"Go to hell!" Kevin yelled after him.

Jake kept walking, which infuriated Kevin more. Kevin headed for his Dad's pickup, kicking anything and everything in his way. He opened the driver's door, thankful Leonard hadn't changed his habit of leaving the keys in the ignition. He climbed in and started the motor, spewing gravel as he sped away.

~

Jake slammed the barn door and took the steps to his office two at a time. The message light on the phone blinked. He hit the message button and wrote the name and number on a piece of scrap paper. He hadn't expected such a quick response to his ad for a dairy hand. The second message was from George Denton's wife, asking Jake to call her about her husband's job.

Jake rested his forehead on his hand and closed his eyes. He didn't want to deal with George or his wife. He felt sorry for Barbara Denton, but he couldn't solve her problems for her. He had enough of his own.

"Lord, I sure could use some help right now. Kevin's lying through his teeth about Abby, but how can I convince him to come clean? And what's with Abby? What in the world has she been lying about?"

"Those are good questions, son."

Jake whirled around. Leonard stood in the doorway to the office.

"May I borrow your pickup? Seems Kevin's using mine, and I need to set some water on the hay over by Taylor's."

"Tell you what, Dad. I need to do some thinking. I'll take care of the irrigating. That is, if you don't mind helping Carlos finish the milking."

"Don't mind at all."

Jake rose. "Thanks, Dad." As he approached the door, Leonard blocked his exit.

"You and Kevin have a fight last night?"

Jake looked down at his feet. "'Fraid so. I hit him."

"That explains your bandaged knuckles and Kevin's fat lip. Any particular reason you hit him?"

Jake glanced at his Dad and wished he could crawl in a hole. "I'd had enough of the way he was treating Abby. He had her in tears last night. Kind of figure that's the reason she left. Kev spent the evening shoving Melissa in her face."

"How long've you been in love with her?"

"Melissa?"

"You know who I meant." Leonard's scowl made Jake regret his flippant remark.

Jake swallowed hard. He'd never been able to hide anything from his dad, so he couldn't deny his feelings for Abby. He steeled himself and looked directly into Leonard's stern face.

"I didn't set out to fall in love with her. It just happened. But I haven't acted on it. She doesn't know and never will."

"Doesn't matter how you feel about her, Jake, she's not yours to protect. She's Kevin's girl. She and Kevin have to work out their differences."

"I can't stand by and let Kevin hurt her."

"Not your place to interfere. Let them work it out." He clamped a hand on Jake's shoulder. "You can't be Kevin's conscience. I can't abide his lying any more than you can, but he's old enough to figure things out. He has to change himself."

Jake sucked in a deep breath. "I know you're right about Kevin, but somebody has to remind him he's going down the wrong road."

"Maybe. Looks like you at least got his attention." Leonard smiled, removed his hand from Jake's shoulder, and stepped aside. "I've let you take on an awful lot of burden since my accident, but you don't need this one. I'm Kevin's father. Let me handle it."

Jake grasped the door handle. "Sorry."

"It's not easy, Jake, but you're going to have to set aside your feelings for Abby. No other choice."

"I know, Dad." Jake walked out the door. "I *know.*"

~

Kevin parked the pickup on Main Street and debated about going into Granny's Café. He needed some breakfast, but he didn't want everyone asking about his split and bruised lip. His jaw ached, something he hadn't noticed until a few minutes ago. Abby's betrayal had diverted attention from the pain for a while.

Kevin hit the steering wheel with his open hand. *She's going to pay for this, stranding me here. She doesn't know the meaning of suffering. Yet.*

Maybe he hadn't treated Abby right the night before, but he couldn't help it. He couldn't get over how good Melissa looked. Besides, he and Abby weren't really engaged. Granted, everyone thought they were, but still....

He glanced up in time to see Melissa stroll by on the sidewalk. Lowering the window, he hollered at her. She stepped off the sidewalk and stopped next to the pickup.

"Hey, Kevin. How're you doing this morning?"

"Good. Sure did enjoy last night."

Melissa frowned. "What happened to your lip? Abby give you that?" She grinned.

"Why would you think that?"

"She looked a bit unhappy last night. Tell her I'm sorry. I didn't mean to make her think I was after you."

"Weren't you?"

She frowned. "No, Kevin, I wasn't. It was over between us a long time ago."

"Thought maybe you were looking to pick up where we left off."

"Hardly." She shook her head. "When you dumped me, Kevin, I was devastated. I can say that now, because I got over you. I finally realized that you were way too self-centered for me. I need someone who's sensitive to my needs from time to time." She touched Kevin's lip with her finger. "Looks like Abby feels the same way."

"Abby understands me."

"If you say so, Kevin."

She laid her hand on Kevin's cheek. "What *did* happen to your face?"

He grabbed her hand and removed it. "I bumped my lip on the Navigator door when I got home."

"I guess that's a good enough story. Where's Abby?"

"None of your business."

"You're right, Kevin." She stepped away from the pickup and turned to go. "See you tonight."

"Melissa, wait. Will you let me buy you some coffee?"

She turned toward Kevin and smiled. "Don't think so, Kevin. You should be with Abby. She's the one you're engaged to. Tell Abby I'm really sorry about monopolizing your time last night. It was very insensitive of me. I hope she'll understand."

"She'll understand."

Melissa stepped onto the sidewalk, turned, and looked

at him. "You know, Kevin, I came back for the class reunion hoping to find you'd changed. Hoping to find you weren't a jerk anymore. Guess some people never learn."

She walked away before Kevin could defend himself. He stared at her receding back until she disappeared into a store.

"What's wrong with everybody?" he hissed. *They're jealous, that's all. They can't stand the fact that I'm so successful, so it's pick-on-Kevin week.*

Melissa's parting shot left him furious and in no mood to be around people. He'd lost his appetite. He remembered Abby's note in his pocket and decided he needed a private place to read it and figure out what to do.

~

Sunlight sparkled on the water as it worked its way along the irrigation furrows. Jake stuck the shovel into the fertile ground and leaned on the handle. He couldn't get Abby or his conversation with his dad out of his mind. If he knew Abby's phone number he'd call her to make sure she was all right. He didn't trust Kevin's explanation. It didn't make sense. It made less sense that Kevin hadn't gone with Abby.

"It's just as well I don't know her number, Lord. Dad's right. I have no business interfering."

No matter how many times he told himself that Abby's leaving wasn't his business, he couldn't let it go. Her leaving left a hole in his heart the size of Alaska. Abby didn't belong with Kevin.

You shall not covet your neighbor's wife.

The words pounded in his head. Or your brother's fiancée, Jake thought. "I hear you, Lord, and I know my love for Abby is wrong. But it's not wrong to want her to be happy. Kevin has made her miserable. I know that's why she left. There's nothing wrong with her but an aching heart. I could see it in her eyes."

When Kevin had stormed from the kitchen, Jake had wanted to throttle him. He still wanted to, but his dad was right. Kevin's love life wasn't his business. He'd have to step back and let Kevin and Abby work it out. Or let his dad handle it.

Jake pulled the shovel from the ground and walked along the head of the rows to make sure the water was working its way down. Along the way he cleaned out dirt clods, sticks, and leaves that impeded the water's flow along the furrows between the stalks of silage corn. Satisfied he had a good set, he climbed in his pickup. He'd return to check on the set later.

As he drove back to the dairy, he tried to figure a way out of the awards banquet that night. But short of breaking an arm or a leg, he knew he'd have to attend for his parents' sake. Until a couple of weeks ago, he'd been proud Kevin would receive the Outstanding Alumnus award. At the moment, he didn't think Kevin qualified.

His brother didn't demonstrate the qualities of integrity and honesty, the two things besides career success that the award honored. What bothered Jake more was Kevin's hatred of him. He couldn't imagine what he'd done to make

Kevin despise him so much. He'd bent over backwards to help Kevin achieve his goals, and all he got in return was Kevin's resentment.

"Lord, please help Kevin before he self-destructs."

Chapter 26

*K*evin drove a short distance from town until he found a pullout that overlooked North Fork. He backed the pickup toward the valley and dangled his legs over the lowered the tailgate. Sucking in a breath of fresh air, he opened a box of donuts and took a sip of convenience store coffee. Not bad, he thought.

He and Melissa had parked here more than once when they were dating. He smiled at the memories. Melissa had become a beautiful, confident, and successful woman. Too bad he dropped her all those years ago.

After devouring a second donut, Kevin reached into his pocket and pulled out Abby's note. Fishing the diamond ring from the envelope, he stuffed it in his pocket and unfolded the pages.

>*Kevin*

>>*Leaving like this was the only way I knew to set things straight. Your parents and Jake have been wonderful to me and accepted me as one of the family, simply because I was engaged to you. They haven't deserved my lies, but they deserve yours even less.*

>>*I couldn't tell them the truth because I couldn't bear to see the hurt on their faces or their contempt when they learned we've been lying to them. They love you, Kevin, and will understand and forgive you. They won't forgive me. I realize that by leaving I've put my career in jeopardy, but when I saw Jake hit you last night...*

"Shit!" Was she watching from her bedroom window? Kevin touched his sore lip and continued reading.

>>*...I knew the truth had to be told, and it had to come from you. I cannot continue this charade, when the lie causes brothers to turn against each other.*

She could have talked to him when he came in the house. He shook his head, knowing deep down he probably would have brushed her off.

>>*I can only hope that you'll change your mind about ruining my career. You will get back every bit of the money. I will set up a payment schedule, as I have no way to return the full amount in one payment. I hope that will satisfy you.*

He'd never planned to ruin her career. He'd used the threat to keep her in line. A pang of guilt struck him.

As for the banquet, you don't need me. You'll do fine on your own. Maybe Melissa will fill in for me. You two seemed to be getting along well tonight.

Kevin, I implore you to look within and ask yourself if this is really you. You and Jake were raised by the same parents, yet you have abandoned what they taught you. I let myself get suckered into your world of deceit. It wasn't worth the price.

"What price?" he asked, but he already knew the answer. Jake.

Somewhere deep inside you is a man of integrity and honesty. You have so much going for you; don't throw it away because you want to look good in everyone's eyes. It won't take long for people to see right through you, and you'll lose everything you've worked for.

Years ago, you backed out on your promise to Jake to work at the dairy after you graduated from college, and until he finished veterinary school. Oddly enough, Jake doesn't begrudge you for having forgotten the promise. He's proud of what you've accomplished, and he's happy working the dairy. For that alone, you owe him and your parents the truth. They have sacrificed much for you.

A knot formed in Kevin's stomach. That's what Abby had referred to the other night. He'd forgotten all about his deal with Jake. Was Abby right when she said Jake didn't hold a grudge? Jake had never reminded him about their deal. So why was Jake angry with him? In the next second, he answered himself. *Because Jake is in love with Abby, not because I broke my promise.* Rather than contemplate that revelation, he returned to Abby's note.

I hope you'll find it in your heart to forgive me for putting you in this position. I believe I'm doing you a favor and hope you'll see it that way. Because of my promise to my Mother, I was obsessed with paying off my father's debts, so I went along with the charade. My father was a con man and bilked people out of their money. You don't have to be like him. You're better than that.

I went along with you because I figured your family was no better. I was wrong. I'm not trying to minimize my part in all this, but I believe it's your responsibility to tell your family the truth. I have already apologized to them. Maybe someday they'll think kindly of me and forgive what I've done.

Just so you know, I intend to seek employment elsewhere because of your business practices, and I don't think we can work together anymore. You've lost your integrity. My resignation will be official a week from Friday. Don't worry, I will pay you back.

Abby

Kevin wadded up the pages and raised his hand to throw them away, but something stopped him. He set his coffee down and stared at the crumpled papers in his fist. He had expected hateful words. Abby's words were reprimanding, but not hateful. She accepted her own responsibility, while clearly pointing out his shortcomings, according to her.

With both hands, he smoothed out the papers and read Abby's words again. When he finished, he stared at the valley below him. Guilt shadowed him like a coyote stalking a wounded deer. Dozens of childhood memories flooded his thoughts.

He thought about North Fork and growing up on a dairy. He hated cows and their smell. He couldn't wait to go to college and wipe the dust of North Fork off his feet.

For most of his life, he resented growing up in a small town. Everybody knew everything about everyone. You couldn't get away with anything, and people's curiosity felt like a chokehold. Yet he often felt alone and alienated in Denver. Too often he wondered if the people he called his friends were genuinely interested in him, or if the interest was because they wanted something of him.

Gail's interest in him had proved superficial. That truth he'd realized while in Mexico. She wanted him only because of the material things he could provide.

He'd also noticed the change in his classmates when Jake arrived at the Columbine Inn. That they liked Jake, simply because he was Jake, was evident. He didn't put on airs. Even when Kevin made a snide remark about Jake being a milker and a dairy farmer, Jake accepted the remark as a compliment. Abby's praise of the dairy irritated him, but in an effort to belittle Jake, he'd belittled himself.

Kevin never saw himself as a con man. She said he lacked integrity. Was she right? Had all the wrong things become important—money, prestige, possessions?

He had squirmed when his dad insinuated he was lying. He couldn't remember ever blatantly lying to his parents before. How had his lies become so important?

He always looked up to his dad, who was well respected in North Fork. When his dad had his accident, Kevin was too wrapped up in himself to see the effect the accident had on his family. Dads were invincible, and his dad was no different. After the accident, Kevin couldn't come to terms with his father's vulnerability. But why had he abandoned everything his parents taught him as Abby suggested? *Because I didn't want to end up a crippled old farmer like Dad.*

Kevin scoffed at the thought. His dad had gone through some difficult years, including a bout of depression after the accident, but Leonard eventually pulled himself from the depths and accepted his limitations, learning to work around them. Jake and his mother handled everything until Leonard healed. Kevin had kept his distance, safe in his own ignorance and indifference.

Jake, the solid son. The one with broad shoulders. The brother he spent his life trying to live up to. Maybe that was the problem. He should have been trying to live up to his own expectations and abilities, not someone else's. Kevin dismissed the idea that he was a bad person. He'd worked hard to get where he was.

Melissa's comments had surprised him. She wasn't pining away for him like he thought...hoped. Melissa had been his first love. Maybe his only real love up to this point.

Yet he dropped her without a second thought for fear she'd get in the way of his ambition. His dreams. Melissa had been the driving force in Kevin wanting Abby to pose as his fiancée. He hadn't wanted to admit to Melissa that his fiancée dumped him. But Melissa wouldn't have cared. She didn't care. What was it she had said? She hoped he'd changed, but he hadn't.

Kevin lay back on the pickup bed and closed his eyes. *Where did I go wrong? I didn't think I'd become so uncaring and dishonest, but according to everyone but me, I have.* He opened his eyes and squinted at the cloudless cerulean sky. *Now what do I do?*

Seek and you will find; knock and the door will be opened to you.

Kevin sat up, the words reverberating through his head. Words he had learned in Sunday school. Words he thought led to success and money. "What would you have me do?" He gazed into the depths above him. A moment later, he prayed, something he hadn't done in a long time. "Lord, I know I've ignored you for a long time now, but I need your help. I'm miserable, and I'm not sure why. Help me sort this out."

~

"Where in the world is Kevin?" Pat peered out the kitchen window. "The banquet starts in less than an hour. He's going to make us late."

Leonard put his arm around Pat's waist and guided her to a chair. "Sit down and relax, honey. Tonight's very important to Kevin. He'll be here."

Five minutes later, Kevin walked in the door.

"We were worried about you," Pat said.

"Sorry, I've been busy."

"Son, we need to talk," Leonard said.

"Not now, Dad. I need to get a shower and get ready for the banquet. Maybe afterward."

"Definitely afterward," Leonard said to Kevin's back.

Kevin stopped. "Where's Jake? He's going tonight, isn't he?"

"He's home changing. He said he'd be there," Pat answered.

"Good."

~

Abby returned the Navigator to the rental agency and took a cab home. She dropped her suitcases inside the door of her apartment and stumbled to her bedroom. Collapsing on her bed, she cried herself to sleep.

When she awoke several hours later, she showered, ate a bowl of cereal, and sorted through her mail. A hand-addressed envelope caught her eye. She slit it open and removed a thank you note from a man her father had owed a large sum of money. As she read the note, her heart constricted and tears filled her eyes.

> *My wife's illness had eaten away our savings, and although she's on the road to wellness, we didn't know where we'd get the money to pay for her final treatments. Your check has answered that prayer.*

God bless you!

Abby set the note on the table, lowered her head onto her arms, and sobbed. When she stopped crying, she offered a prayer of her own.

"Thank you, Lord, that some good has come from my dishonesty."

She tucked the note away in her desk and stared at the blinking message light on her answering machine. No doubt Kevin had left at least one of those messages. She punched the message retrieval button. Two of the messages were from Kevin imploring her to call him as soon as she arrived home.

"Fat chance," she whispered and erased all the messages.

When the phone rang a few minutes later, she reached for the receiver, then decided to let the answering machine pick it up. She didn't feel like talking to anyone.

"Abby, this is Kevin. Where are you? Call me, please. It's important. Call my cell."

He didn't sound mad, only worried, but then he was good at deceit. She resisted the urge to pick up the receiver. Couldn't trust herself to talk to him. The last thing she needed was to have Kevin ream her out for leaving. He was going to be hard enough to deal with Monday morning. By then she hoped to have her own arsenal to counteract his threats.

On the drive home, Abby had resolved to find a small town somewhere to settle in. Maybe Colorado, New Mexico, or Wyoming. Remembering her resolve, she logged onto her computer and searched for a place like North Fork. The people of North Fork had made her feel welcome. Maybe, just maybe, after she got over Jake, she'd find someone like him to settle down with. That is if she ever got over him at all.

The doorbell rang. She glanced at her watch and realized she'd been surfing the net for over an hour.

"Abby, are you there? It's Meg."

The voice of Abby's assistant surprised her. She hadn't let Meg or anyone know she was home.

"Abby." Meg knocked again.

"Just a minute." Abby logged off the computer. As soon as she opened the door, Meg pushed past her.

"Kevin called me at work and ordered me to come over here and make sure you were home. What's going on?"

"Hi, Meg." Abby smiled in spite of herself. "Won't you come in?"

Meg ignored Abby, pulled her cell phone from her purse, and punched in a number.

"Who are you calling?"

Meg held up her hand. "Kevin? Meg. Abby's here. She seems to be fine. Do you want to talk to her?"

Abby shook her head and motioned to Meg she didn't want to talk to Kevin.

"She doesn't want to talk to you." She tilted the cell phone away from her face. "He says it's important."

Abby closed her eyes, shook her head, and mouthed "no." She turned her back to Meg's glare.

"Sorry, Kevin, she's determined she's not going to talk to you." Meg paused, listened, and then closed her cell phone.

"He said to tell you he'd see you when he got back. He sounded a little put out."

Abby turned to face Meg. "I'm sure he is. He'll get over it."

"You want to tell me what's going on? Why'd you come back early and without Kevin?"

"It's a long story."

"I've got the rest of the day and all night. Kevin said I don't have to go back to work. What in holy heck is going on?"

Abby sighed and motioned toward the couch. "Okay, sit down." She needed to talk things out with a friend, and now was as good a time as any. "Like I said, it's a long story. You want some iced tea while you're listening?"

"Sure."

Abby filled two glasses, handed one to Meg, and sat on the opposite end of the couch.

"Posing as Kevin's fiancée backfired. I've lost any chance of being with the love of my life because of it." She bit her lip and wiped a tear from her eye.

Kevin fiddled with the spoon at his place setting, and unconsciously tapped his right foot. He hoped he could pull this off without losing his nerve. More than anything, he wished Abby had been willing to talk to him. Considering everything, he didn't blame her, but still.... He squelched his rising anger and reminded himself he had more important things to worry about at the moment.

He and his parents had arrived at the banquet hall with five minutes to spare. Jake walked in two minutes later. Kevin, already seated at the head table, caught Jake's eye, smiled, and motioned Jake to join him. Jake glared and took his place with Leonard and Pat at a table near the head table. Numerous people had greeted Jake. The old jealousy nagged Kevin. He gritted his teeth and shoved it aside.

The meal of roast beef, mashed potatoes, and green beans may as well have been rice cakes for all Kevin tasted. The piece of cherry pie sat untouched. He wanted to get the ceremony over with. Funny, he'd looked forward to this award for months. Now he couldn't wait for the evening to end.

When Kevin thought he couldn't stand the wait any longer, the master of ceremonies stood and introduced him, praising his accomplishments and complimenting his parents for the way they had raised him. To the sound of applause, Kevin rose, accepted the Outstanding Alumni plaque and took his place at the podium. His hands shook as he placed the plaque beside the podium and pulled his notes out of his suit jacket. He unfolded the papers and smoothed them. Swallowing hard, he gazed out at the crowd, cleared his throat, and began.

"Thank you, Pete, for such a glowing introduction. For a minute there, I thought you were talking about someone else." He managed a smile and the audience laughed.

"You can't imagine how much this award means to me. I've dreamed of receiving this award since I was old enough to understand what it meant. I promised myself that one day

I'd stand up here, and here I am." Beads of sweat seeped from his forehead. "Unfortunately I can't, in good conscience, accept this award."

A murmur swept through the crowd. Kevin picked up a glass of water and swallowed the cooling liquid.

"I know you're wondering what I'm up to, so let me explain. I'm a liar and a cheat and unworthy of this honor."

K. L. McKee

Chapter 27

Spent tissues covered the couch between Abby and Meg. Abby blew her nose, gathered up the tissues, and tossed them in the kitchen trash. She turned toward Meg.

"Want more tea?"

"If I have one more glass, I'll rival Niagara Falls."

Laughter spilled from Abby.

"About time you laughed," Meg said. "You're much too morose for my liking."

"Oh, Meg, only you can make me laugh when my heart hurts so much I want to rip it out."

"A year from now you'll look back on this and wonder why it upset you so much."

"Fat chance of that." Abby plopped onto the couch and laid her head back. "If you met Jake, you'd understand. He's everything my father wasn't. I finally found the perfect guy, and my own selfishness made it impossible to ever have him in my life."

"How can you be so sure, Abby? When he finds out the truth, maybe he'll understand and look you up."

"Why would he do that? He cared about me because I was Kevin's fiancée. He has no reason to contact me now that I'm no longer engaged to his brother. And now that he knows I'm a liar, he'll want even less to do with me. He believes in honesty, period. No matter how you look at it, I totally screwed up."

"I've never seen you so down. Come on, girl, you've got to stop feeling sorry for yourself. Life goes on."

Abby smiled. "Yes, it does, and I've figured out what I want to do with mine."

She told Meg about wanting to move to a small town, and that someday, if she was lucky, she hoped to find someone like Jake.

"What small town?"

"I don't know."

"Why don't you try my hometown? It's small, you'll still be in Colorado, and I'll know where you are. That will make it easier for Jake to find you."

Abby glared at Meg. "*Stop* it. Jake doesn't care about me. Won't ever care about me. As soon as my job with Kevin is over, I'm going to put all my things in storage and travel to towns I want to check out. When I find the right one, I'll hire a moving van and settle in. Of course, that will have to be sooner than later, since my funds are limited."

"Are you sure you can't keep working for Kevin? I'm going to miss you something fierce."

"Oh, Meg, I'll miss you, too." Abby took a deep breath. "Which reminds me. Since tomorrow is a holiday, no one will be at the office. I'm going to retrieve that signed check and anything else that will help my cause. Thank goodness I insisted on Kevin continuing the policy of requiring two original signatures on every check. There's no way I'm going to let Kevin turn me in for embezzlement."

"He'd never do that, Abby."

"You didn't see the look in his eyes when he said it."

"Surely he was bluffing. But you're right. The check *will* help prove he knew about the money. You want some help?"

"Sure, if you want."

"I will if you promise to go with me to the parade in the morning and the Rockies' game and fireworks at Coors Field tomorrow night. Kevin gave me the company tickets before he left."

"I don't feel like celebrating."

"It'll do you good, Abby. Take your mind off your troubles for a while. Please?"

"Okay, I'll go. I can sit around and feel sorry for myself only so long. Once we find the cancelled check with Kevin's signature, I may be more inclined to celebrate."

Abby glanced at the kitchen clock and raised her glass in a mock toast. "Here's to you, Kevin. Enjoy your award. Not that you deserve it."

~

Murmurs, a few coughs, and clearing of throats rumbled through the banquet crowd at Kevin's declaration. His mouth had gone dry as he uttered the self-deprecating words. The glass of ice water shook as he took a drink and waited for his audience to quiet.

"Now that I've admitted I'm a cheat and a liar," he said and waited a moment for the crowd's complete attention, "I would like to explain." This was new territory for him, and he wasn't sure he could continue. *I could always turn my admission into a joke. No one would be the wiser.* He glanced at his family, cleared his throat, and forged ahead.

"When I was first informed I'd receive this prestigious award, I was beside myself. Finally, my dream had come true. I'd be able to show my hometown what success really was." In the audience, people exchanged glances. Some frowned. "I didn't expect the award to turn into an unwanted and humbling lesson.

"All my life I saw my brother Jake as the enemy. I made a concerted effort to better him in everything—grades, sports, fishing, you name it. I even cheated a couple of times in order to achieve my goal." Kevin made a point to look at Jake. "I think my jealousy might have started when he rode that calf, and I didn't." He smiled. Jake frowned. A few people chuckled. Kevin looked away from Jake. "Whatever it was, by the time I graduated from high school, my only goal in life was to be more successful than Jake. So, when this award came along, I thought it gave me the perfect opportunity to show him up."

Kevin glanced again at Jake, whose frown had

deepened. He squared his shoulders and continued. "I planned to come home for a couple of weeks, flaunt my success, show off my fiancée, and rub it all in Jake's face...and everyone else's. Subtly, of course." Kevin took another drink of water. The silence in the room grew thick.

"Unfortunately, things started going wrong. A week before my planned trip home, my fiancée dumped me. I couldn't possibly show up without a fiancée, I thought. My high school girlfriend would be there, and I needed a beautiful woman to make her jealous. Without a fiancée, I'd have to admit to everyone I'd failed at something. Being a man of considerable resources and persuasive abilities, I came up with a plan.

"You'll notice that Abby is not here with me tonight. That's because she's not actually my fiancée, and she refused to continue the lie."

As he made the last statement, Kevin glanced again at Jake and noticed he sat up straighter, surprise registering plainly on his face.

"Because Abby works for me, I was able to convince her to pose as my fiancée so I wouldn't lose face. She agreed, I found out later, because she thought no one would get hurt in the process. You see, she doesn't think very highly of the way I conduct my life and assumed my family would be no different. As soon as she realized that my family lives honesty and integrity daily, she begged me to tell them the truth. I refused and threatened her job if she didn't continue to go along with my little charade.

"And then..." sweat trickled down Kevin's face, and he

wiped it away with his hand, "...and then I did the unthinkable. I left town, using an unhappy client as the excuse, and insisted Abby stay and keep my family happy. Abby informed me then she no longer wanted to work for me and begged me to tell the truth."

Kevin turned his head and coughed. He sucked in a deep breath, hoping to calm his nerves and his stomach. "I threatened Abby's career," he said, his voice low. "I'm ashamed to admit I meant it at the time. This was two days after we'd arrived in North Fork."

Another murmur swept through the crowd and people shifted in their seats. Kevin watched Jake lean forward, rest his arms on his legs, and stare at the floor. His mother reached for Leonard's hand, her face stricken. His father shook his head slowly.

Kevin wasn't sure he could go on, or sure he'd made the right decision to confess everything in public. But he was committed, the choice made. He gripped the podium and forced himself to continue.

"When I returned to North Fork a couple of days ago, Abby again begged me to tell my family the truth. I refused and added extra insurance to my threat. I won't burden you with the details."

More murmurs, louder, threatening to undermine Kevin's resolve. He took a long drink of water. Oddly enough, rather than feeling like a fool, he actually felt relieved. Ashamed, yet relieved. He didn't like hurting his family, but if he only admitted his shortcomings to them, he would be doing them, himself, and Abby a disservice. His decision to make the speech was, in part, out of respect for Abby.

"Early this morning, Abby had all she could take of my manipulation and left town. And yet again, I lied to my family about why she left. Mom, Dad, Jake," he waited for them to look at him. Jake refused, so Kevin continued. "I'm very sorry. You haven't deserved the way I've treated you."

Kevin lifted the refilled glass of water to bathe his dry throat, surprised that his hand no longer shook. *Honesty is the best policy, however difficult. Whoever lives by the truth....*He forged on. As he set the glass down, he smiled.

"Why am I publicly admitting all of this? Because I have no claim on the award presented to me tonight. And I want everyone to know I have no claim on Abby. We're not an item and never were." Jake jerked his head up and Kevin looked him squarely in the eye. "Abby only pretended to be my fiancée. Everything else all of you saw in her—a kind, generous, honest, and caring person—is real. She is the one person who has kept my business dealings on the straight and narrow because she refused to be a part of anything dishonest, unwilling to bend the rules. I can truthfully say that the accounting end of my business is honest and above board. Unlike its president.

"I could have admitted the lie only to my family, but something happened to me today that made me realize the only way to redeem myself was to admit in public the kind of man I've been. Today I learned something about myself. I didn't much like the lesson, but I've resolved to take it to heart. That lesson came in four parts."

Kevin shuffled his notes, looking for the right spot. The words blurred, and for a moment, he wondered if he could continue. Blinking to clear his eyes, he shifted the papers again. Finally, with the right notes before him, he looked up and forced himself to speak in a normal voice.

"First, when I told my family yet another lie, this time about why Abby left so suddenly, my father remarked, 'I don't much cotton to lying.' My response was to storm out the door so I didn't have to listen to my father's reprimand. I'm sorry Dad, Mom..." Kevin's voice broke "...for not being the son you raised me to be." Kevin blinked back the stinging in his eyes.

"The second lesson came as I stormed out the door. Jake was waiting for me and reminded me I'd been taught to tell the truth. This from the brother I cheated out of a dream." Kevin willed himself to look at Jake. "I'll never be able to replace that dream for you Jake, but you can be sure I'll never do it to another soul."

Jake raised his head and frowned at Kevin. Kevin lowered his eyes, unable to bear Jake's disappointment. Shuffling and murmuring rose from the audience. Pinching the bridge of his nose, he prayed. *Help me, Lord. I didn't think this part would be so hard.*

He cleared his throat and continued. "The third lesson came from an old girlfriend. One I unceremoniously dumped years ago. I really screwed up on that account. She outclasses me by far. She told me she'd come back to the reunion hoping to find I'd changed." He looked at Melissa. "You nailed it. I hadn't changed." She smiled in sympathy, giving him courage to finish his speech.

"And the fourth lesson came from Abby, the very person I promised to ruin. In a note written to me, she implored me to look within and ask if the person I'd become was really me. She reminded me that I had abandoned everything my parents had taught me, and told me that somewhere deep inside me is a man of integrity and honesty. I hope she's right."

Kevin wiped his sweating hands on his trousers and held up the plaque. "My name is on this plaque. I contacted Pete this afternoon to ask if the name could be changed, but he refused. He said he couldn't break the rules. You see, I wanted to put Jake's name on it instead of mine, for he's been far more successful than I have, and he lives the integrity and honesty that is synonymous with this award."

Out of the corner of his eye, Kevin saw Jake straighten in his seat and shake his head. "So, on behalf of my parents, and my brother Jake, who really deserves this award, I will accept the award, not because of who I am and what I have accomplished, but because of who I will endeavor to be from now on."

Silence accompanied Kevin as he returned to his seat. A lone person clapped, and then a few more joined, until the room filled with thunderous applause. Pete, the Master of Ceremonies, concluded the evening by thanking Kevin for his honesty and wishing him well.

As soon as he could, Kevin worked his way toward Jake and his parents, but people kept stopping him, wishing him well, and congratulating him on a brave speech. Kevin didn't feel brave. He felt that he'd let down the people he cared about most. When he finally reached his family's table, Jake was gone.

Chapter 28

*J*ake shoved his way through the crowd, ignoring people as they called his name. He was in no mood to talk with anyone. Especially Kevin. All he could think about was the fact that Abby had lied every day for over two weeks.

He vaguely remembered the drive home. His head reeled with images and thoughts of Abby. Abby wasn't engaged to Kevin. Never was. Abby didn't love Kevin. Abby lied, and Jake suffered. He had struggled with his own guilt because of her lies. He had lost sleep because of her lies.

Spur greeted him as he parked in front of his house. He slammed the pickup door and gave Spur an absent-minded pat on the head. He plopped onto the porch swing, loosened his tie, and stuffed it in his jacket pocket. Scrubbing his hands over his face, he bit back an oath, closed his eyes, and leaned his head back.

Abby lied to me. And to the folks. She's no better than Sondra. He leaned forward, rested his elbows on his legs, and cradled his head in his hands. *Why do I always get suckered by dishonest women?*

He wanted to tear something up, hit something, do something to relieve the disappointment, anger, and ache in his heart. Why did Abby's lies hurt so much more than Sondra's? *Because I thought Abby was different. What a fool!* He was through with women. They weren't worth the trouble, and he didn't need the grief.

Fatigue settled like an unwelcome blanket in the heat of summer. He wanted to pray, needed to pray, but no words came. His mind refused to cooperate. The telephone rang several times. He ignored it. Minutes ticked by as the night edged toward morning.

Spur growled, barked, and then took off down the trail toward the barn. Jake looked up to see a light illuminating the trail.

He lowered his head into his hands. *Please, God, whoever it is, make them go away. I don't want to talk to anyone. Not Dad. Not Mom. Not Kevin. Please let me be alone.*

"Hey, Jake."

Jake looked up. Kevin stood at the bottom of the porch steps.

"Mind if I sit with you?"

"Go away."

"Guess I phrased that wrong." Kevin climbed the steps and sat down beside Jake.

"Apparently, you didn't hear me," Jake growled.

"I heard you. Chose not to listen. I need to talk to you."

"I don't want to talk to you. Go home."

"Sorry, we need to talk."

Jake leaned back. "Don't you think you've said enough for tonight?"

"Nope. There's more you need to hear."

"I've heard enough." Jake rose and stepped toward the door.

"Sit down, Jake. Whether you like it or not, you're going to hear me out."

"You going to make me?"

Kevin rubbed his sore lip. "If I have to."

Jake shook his head and, in spite of his anger, fought back a smile. Returning to the swing, he sat down. "Make it quick."

"I'm sorry for what I've done to you. I'm especially sorry for cheating you out of veterinary school. You should have reminded me of my promise. Why didn't you?"

Jake shrugged. "You were excited about the job opportunity you had. I didn't feel right about denying you an opportunity that would eventually let you take over the company. Besides, by that time, I was pretty settled into the dairy."

"Abby said you didn't hold a grudge, but I had to hear it from you."

Jake flinched at Kevin's mention of Abby. He felt more

betrayed by Abby than he had when Kevin reneged on their deal.

"Look, Kev, I'd have made a terrible vet. Little old ladies and their lap dogs would have driven me crazy. I'm happy doing what I'm doing, so don't sweat it."

"I still need your forgiveness, Jake."

"You're forgiven, Kev. Don't think another thing about it."

"Thanks."

Chirping crickets filled the silence between them. Stars carpeted the night sky, but Jake felt no comfort from the familiar. He hurt. He wanted to rage at someone, but oddly enough, not Kevin. Kevin faced up to his deceit. Abby ran from it. He couldn't forgive that.

"You're in love with Abby, aren't you?"

Kevin's question startled Jake. Had his feelings for Abby been that obvious?

"Now why would you think that? She was engaged to you. Or so I thought."

"Come on, Jake. I'm not upset about it. I should be, but I'm not. I can understand why you'd fall for Abby. She's a terrific woman. Wish I'd discovered it sooner."

Jake glanced at Kevin. "She lied, Kevin. For over two weeks she lied to me. To us. Then instead of facing the consequences, she turned tail and ran. She's no better than Sondra."

"Thought so."

"*What?*"

"Abby's not Sondra. Not by a long shot. Abby's the kind

of woman a man could settle down with and raise a family. The kind of woman a man could trust. A kind and loving woman and loyal to a fault."

Jake scoffed. "She lied, plain and simple, and I'm sick and tired of deceptive women."

"You need to forgive her, too, Jake. She hated lying to you and the folks. She begged me to tell the truth before I left for Mexico. I had the audacity to threaten not only her job, but I told her I'd claim she embezzled money from me, which would insure she'd never work in accounting again. She didn't have a choice but to stick to her promise."

"She had more than enough opportunities to come clean."

"I'm betting she only lied about being engaged to me. I'll bet everything else she told you was the truth. And I'm betting she brushed off questions about our wedding plans, children, you name it."

Jake thought back to the times he'd asked Abby about those very things, and her answers had been vague, or she deftly changed the subject, which had made him suspicious in the first place.

"Remember the day Abby and I arrived? You asked her how she got mixed up with me. Remember her answer?"

Jake shook his head.

"'He paid me' is what she answered. I remember, because I nearly swallowed my tongue, since it was the truth."

Jake stared at Kevin. "You paid her?"

"Yep. When I first asked her to pose as my fiancée, she

refused. I wouldn't take no for an answer, so I asked how much it would cost me. She told me $50,000 after taxes. She was quite surprised when I agreed."

"You paid her $50,000 dollars?"

"After taxes. I was that desperate."

Jake set his jaw and glared into the night. "She's not only a liar, she'd do anything for money."

Kevin sucked in a deep breath and shook his head. "In Abby's defense, that's not what I was trying to explain. But as long as I've stepped in that pile of manure, you need to hear all of it. Seems Abby's father—"

"Let it alone, Kevin." Jake rose. "I've heard enough for one night."

Kevin grabbed Jake's arm and pulled him back onto the swing. "Shut up, Jake. You're going to sit here and listen until I'm through." Kevin let out a breath when Jake complied.

Kevin cleared his throat. "Seems Abby's father bilked a lot of people out of money. Abby's mother paid toward the debts, but never got them paid off before she died. Anyway, Abby promised her mother she'd finish paying off the debts. That's where the money went. She didn't do it for herself. She did it for her mother."

"Bet her mother'd be *real* proud if she were alive," Jake scoffed.

Kevin ignored the remark. "In return, she promised me three weeks of pretending to be my fiancée. When she realized what a nice family I had, she wanted to tell you the truth, but she thought it was my responsibility. After all, you're *my* family. I told her she'd have to pay back every cent of what I gave her if she didn't stick with the plan. Even threatened her job. Well you heard me talk about that."

Kevin stepped to the porch rail, leaned back, and gripped it with both hands. "And if all that wasn't enough, I deserted her. Left her holding the bag. For over two weeks, no less. Nice guy, huh?"

Jake rested his arms on his knees and stared at the porch floor.

"Abby saw you hit me last night, Jake. That's why she left. She figured the only way I'd tell the truth was if she forced me into it. She couldn't let the lie come between you and me."

Jake looked up at Kevin. "I hit you because of the way you were treating Abby."

"I know. And because you're in love with her and couldn't stand to see her hurt."

Jake started to protest, but Kevin stopped him. "Abby couldn't bear to face your contempt when you found out about the lie." Kevin paused and when Jake didn't react to his last statement, he said, "I think she's in love with you, Jake."

Jake sat up and glared at Kevin. "She has a funny way of showing it."

"She figures you and the folks won't want to have anything to do with her now that you know the truth."

"She's got that right."

"Come on, Jake, don't be so hard on her. She doesn't deserve it."

"She lied, Kevin. That's all there is to it. She can't be trusted."

"Do you trust me?"

"Of course I do."

"Why? I lied to you. Far more than Abby ever did."

"That's different."

"What makes it different?"

"You're my brother. I love you."

"And your point would be?"

Jake frowned at Kevin.

"Think about it, Jake. Abby's worth forgiving. You two belong together, so don't blow this one." Kevin reached in his pocket and pulled out several wrinkled pieces of paper and tossed them at Jake. "This is the note Abby left me. Read it before you pass judgment. And don't be so damn stubborn." Kevin stalked down the steps, flipped on his flashlight, and strode down the trail toward home.

The papers that Kevin tossed at him landed on the porch floor. Jake sat for several minutes and stared. He wasn't interested in Abby's excuses. There were no excuses for lying. Spur trotted up, sniffed at the papers, and uttered a guttural whine.

"You too? *Traitor.*"

Spur looked at Jake, turned and trotted down the steps, disappearing into the night. Jake shook his head, scooped up the papers, and stuffed them in his jacket pocket, intending to shred them. He sat for a while trying make sense of everything Kevin had said.

I can't believe she let Kevin pay her to lie. How could

she? She looked me in the eye and told me she was engaged to Kevin. How could she not tell the truth?

With a deep sigh, he finally gave up. "She lied, Lord. That's all there is to it. I can't forgive that." Abby's lies dogged him as he climbed the stairs to his bedroom, and until he fell into a restless sleep.

Jake's mood hadn't abated by the time he rose for the morning milking. Every task contained a little anger, although he tried hard to put the previous night and thoughts of Abby aside and concentrate on the cows and the milking.

"You mad at the cows for something this morning?" Carlos asked.

Jake ignored Carlos and continued working.

"Why don't you let me finish up?" Carlos suggested. "You've disinfected that cow's teats twice now."

Jake glanced at Carlos and then at the cow. "Sorry, I guess my mind's on other things today."

"Must be pretty serious for you to forget what you're doing. Does it have something to do with Kevin's speech last night?"

"News travels fast."

"You forget, Elena helped serve the meal last night."

Jake remembered seeing Carlos's wife at the banquet. "You're right, I did forget. She still feeling okay?"

"Yeah, the baby's pretty active and keeps her awake at night sometimes, but she doesn't seem to mind."

"Are you going to the parade today?" Jake asked.

"Sure. Wouldn't miss a Fourth of July parade."

"How about the street dance tonight?"

"Got to do the milking."

"I can handle tonight. You and Elena have some fun."

"You sure it's safe to leave you alone with the girls?" Carlos's eyes twinkled. "You don't seem to have your mind on them this morning."

Jake smiled in spite of himself. "It's safe. Just go have some fun."

"Okay. Thanks, Boss."

After the morning milking, Jake showered, dressed in jeans and a blue western shirt and headed to town. He caught the end of the parade, sorry he'd missed Kevin as the Grand Marshal. In the park, he wandered through the crush of people, stopping occasionally to visit with old friends, thankful no one mentioned Kevin's speech. For a while, he put away thoughts of Abby.

Several classmates he hadn't seen in many years had returned for the annual North Fork Independence Day celebration. He enjoyed chatting with them, in spite of his sullen mood. About mid-afternoon, he spotted Sarah and the children. Danny saw Jake approaching and ran toward him.

"Uncle Jake!"

Jake scooped Danny up and dangled him at his side like a sack of potatoes. Sarah, Tyler, and Courtney joined them.

'Unca Jake, pick me up," Courtney begged. Jake obliged, letting Courtney dangle from his other arm.

"Put me down!" Danny demanded. "I'm too big for this!"

"You think so, huh?" Jake chuckled and set Danny down, then shifted Courtney to his hip. "Hi, Sarah. How're you doing?" He gave her a one-armed hug.

"Coping," she said, returning his hug. "It's awfully lonely now that my family's gone home. I keep expecting Rick....Would you like to come by for supper some evening? The kids would love it."

Jake nodded. "I'd like that. Just let me know when."

Sarah smiled. "I will."

Danny tugged at Sarah's arm. "Mom. I want to go to the carnival. They have this really cool ride and—"

"Not now, Danny. I need to get Tyler home for a nap."

"Aw, Mom, it's not fair."

"Danny..."

"I'll be happy to take Danny and Courtney to the carnival. You can take Tyler home."

"Jake, you don't have to."

"I'd like to. Do us all good. I'll drop the kids off later."

"Please, Mom?" Danny pleaded

"Pwease, Mommy?" Courtney joined Danny's plea.

"If Uncle Jake is sure."

"I'm very sure," Jake assured her.

Sarah tried to give Jake money to pay for the carnival, but he refused. With Courtney riding his hip, and Danny dashing ahead of him, Jake headed toward the carnival for a few hours of fun and distraction, thankful Sarah hadn't mentioned Abby.

Chapter 29

*T*he barn door slammed. Jake flinched. "I thought I told you to take the night off," he said without looking up.

"Didn't say a word to me," Leonard answered.

Jake gritted his teeth. He hadn't seen his dad since the banquet, and he was in no mood to talk to him. With Kevin gone for the day and probably most of the night, Jake looked forward to being alone. Leonard showing up spoiled that hope.

The afternoon with Courtney and Danny had provided a perfect distraction. He had won Courtney a teddy bear and Danny a new baseball glove. Between the Ferris wheel, the roller coaster, and the booths, he cleaned out his wallet. But the distraction was only momentary. During the ride to Sarah's, Courtney asked about Abby, and the memories of the afternoon spent with Abby and the kids in the park came flooding back. Memories he didn't want. He'd declined Sarah's invitation of grilled hamburgers for supper. He needed the peace of the milking barn, with only the cows for company and a country western station playing on the radio. Leonard's arrival had shattered that solitude.

"I take it you gave Carlos the night off."

"Yep."

"Need some help with the milking?"

"Nope."

"Jake, I know last night was difficult, but—"

"Look, Dad," Jake said, a bit gruffer than he intended, "just let it alone, okay?"

"No, it's not okay. I have something I want to say, and I expect you to listen."

Jake finished hooking up the last cow to the milker and turned to face his dad. He crossed his arms and leaned against the concrete wall. "Say what you have to say, but make it quick. I'm busy."

Leonard shook his head. "After we got home from the banquet, your mom, Kevin, and I talked for a while before Kevin went to see you. He's convinced that Abby's in love with you. Can't say I disagree with him."

Jake glared at his father and waited.

"You as much as admitted outright to me that you were in love with her."

"Things change," Jake snapped.

"Not if you truly love someone. Infatuation, yes, but not love."

"Then I'll get over it."

"Maybe you shouldn't. Maybe you should forgive. Things haven't always been perfect between your mother and me. But when things went wrong, we found a way to set things right because we loved each other enough to forgive. One of the things about loving someone is knowing you can forgive them, and they can forgive you."

"That may be, but you have to trust them first."

"Abby can be trusted. She has a good heart."

Jake gazed at the floor, away from Leonard's determined stare. "I really don't know Abby that well, and neither do you. We've only known her a couple of weeks, during which time she lied to us. Maybe what I felt *was* infatuation. Maybe it's best to let it go."

"Maybe not."

Jake jerked his head up at the sound of his mother's voice. She stepped next to Leonard and put her hand in his.

"Love isn't always easy, Jake," she said, "but it's always worth the effort. When I first realized you and Abby were attracted to each other, I worried about one of my boys getting hurt. I wanted to dislike Abby because of it, but I couldn't. I really liked her. What was more unsettling was that I thought she was much better suited to you than Kevin. She still is."

"She lied to all of us, Ma. She could have come clean. Instead, she sneaked away in the middle of the night and let Kevin take all the heat."

"She forced Kevin to take a good look at himself. For that, I'll be forever grateful to her." Pat walked over to where

Jake stood and touched his arm. "Abby used bad judgment. She made a mistake. Surely you've made a mistake or two," she paused and waited for Jake to look at her, "and been forgiven. I don't believe the kind and loving person that Abby showed us was a lie. Maybe you should think about that."

"Maybe I've been burned once too often."

"Don't let the hurt one girl caused make you so rigid you can't forgive the one that's right for you," Pat said.

Leonard joined Pat and wrapped his good arm around her. "God forgives us our mistakes because He loves us. In return, He expects us to treat others the same." He waited a moment, and when Jake didn't respond, he said, "That's all we have to say, son. Just promise us you'll think about it. The decision is yours." Leonard brushed a kiss across Pat's cheek. "Well, since you don't want any help tonight, I think I'll take my favorite girl dancing." With his arm still around Pat, Leonard escorted her out of the barn.

Jake stood rooted to his spot long after his parents left. One by one the milking inflations dropped off the cows, and still Jake didn't move. He couldn't purge the image of Abby helping him with the milking. He smiled at the memory of the surprise on her face when he'd shown her the teat lice and the laughter that followed. And his surprise when she had gotten even. He had connected with her more than any girl he ever dated. And in such a short time.

One of the cows kicked at the air and bellowed her discontent. Jake shook his head and turned his attention to the cows, trying his best to block out any thoughts of Abby.

~

Abby closed the study Bible she'd purchased that morning and leaned her head against the back of the couch. As soon as she had arrived home from the bookstore, she sat down and opened the Bible to Psalms. She wanted faith like Jake's, and he quoted the Psalms often. In his Psalms, David praised God and asked forgiveness. In Psalm 86 she read, "You are kind and forgiving, O Lord, abounding in love to all who call to you." And in Psalm 103, "He forgives all my sins and heals all my diseases, he redeems my life from the pit and crowns me with love and compassion.... The Lord is compassionate and gracious, slow to anger, abounding in love."

Her eyes grew heavy as she finished Psalm 139. Abby knew why Jake loved the Psalms so much. She read the last few lines again.

"Search me, O God, and know my heart; test me and know my anxious thoughts. See if there is any offensive way in me, and lead me in the way everlasting."

Abby realized she needed to ask God's forgiveness for what she'd done. She mistakenly believed she had no right to ask God to forgive her, but after reading the Psalms, she knew that all she had to do was ask.

Shutting her eyes, she prayed, "Lord, I know I have offended you because of my lies, but I need your forgiveness. I am truly sorry for the lie I perpetuated in order to pay my father's debts. Forgive me, please, and if You can, help Jake, Pat, and Leonard forgive me for lying to them.

They are kind and wonderful people, and I'm thankful for the short time I spent with them. I'm a better person because of them."

Peace washed over Abby, and she opened her eyes. For the first time since she'd left North Fork, her heart felt lighter. Forgetting Jake wouldn't be easy, but with time, she'd heal. Jake had told her that he talked a lot with God after Sondra left. She resolved to have daily conversations with God for the rest of her life. With His help, she would make it through the weeks and months ahead.

She dreaded her first confrontation with Kevin, but it couldn't be helped. The cancelled check with his signature had been located with only a few minutes of searching, so he couldn't claim she'd embezzled the money. Her books were beyond reproach. Too many checks and balances. But there was still the matter of paying back the money, since she hadn't fulfilled her part of the bargain.

With the check located, Abby had spent the rest of the Independence Day with Meg. They picnicked at Cherry Creek Reservoir, attended the Rockies' game, and then watched the fireworks together at Coors Field. Meg was a comfort and a distraction from her thoughts of Jake, although watching BJ Murcheson play had reminded her of his friendship with Jake.

She regretted having to leave Meg behind, but moving away from Denver, and from Kevin, was her only chance to put the last three weeks behind her. Kevin had originally planned to extend his holiday a day beyond the fourth, so there was little chance he would bother Abby before tomorrow or the next day and, with any luck, he would wait until she saw him Monday at work.

Abby sighed and picked up her Bible again, determined to finish reading the Psalms, but the doorbell interrupted her. She peered through the peephole. Kevin stood on the other side of the door. She inwardly groaned and stepped back.

So much for waiting until Monday.

Abby decided to pretend she wasn't home, sure he would go away. The doorbell chimed again. Abby moved away from the door and held her breath. Kevin knocked, waited, then knocked again, louder.

"Abby, I know you're in there. Open the door. I'm not going away until you do." A pause. "I can hear the stereo playing."

Abby let out a sigh. *Rats.*

Kevin pounded the door again. "We need to talk, Abby. Open up!" He pounded on the door once more. "Come on, Abby. I'm going to keep pounding on this door until the neighbors complain. Let me in!" He punched the doorbell again.

Abby gritted her teeth. *May as well get it over with.* She released the dead bolt, left the safety chain in place, and opened the door.

Kevin grinned. "Hi, Abby." He slipped his foot in the opening of the door. "Might as well let me in. Save you a lot of trouble."

"I don't want to talk to you right now, Kevin, so go away. I'll see you first thing Monday morning at the office."

"I've already been to my office." He held up an envelope

with Abby's handwriting on the front. "Your official resignation, I believe."

She nodded. She had left it for him when she'd arrived at the office to look for the check.

"Let me in."

"We'll discuss it on Monday."

"We'll discuss it now, or I'll knock on every one of your neighbors' doors and tell them how mean you are for not letting your fiancé in to patch things up."

"You're *not* my fiancé."

He grinned. "They don't know that."

Knowing he would follow through on his threat, and too tired to fight him any longer, Abby shoved his foot out of the way, released the safety chain, and let him in.

"Have you got anything to drink? I'm really thirsty."

"Iced tea."

"That'd be great. By the way, where's the Navigator? I need to turn it in before it costs me a fortune."

Abby filled two glasses with ice cubes and tea and handed one to Kevin. "Say what you have to say, and then leave me alone."

Kevin raised his glass. "Thanks for the tea." He sauntered over to the couch and sat down.

Sarcasm laced her voice. "Make yourself comfortable while you're at it."

"Thank you, I think I will." He crossed one leg over the other and leaned back. "About the Navigator...." He raised his eyebrows.

"I turned it in. They put the charges on the credit card

you used to rent it. Sorry, but since I owe you a great deal of money, I couldn't afford to put the charges on my card."

"No problem. Found your check, too. That's another thing we need to talk about."

"It's the first installment on what I owe you. I'm sorry it can't be more, but my finances are a little challenged right now." Abby sat stiffly on the opposite end of the couch, waiting for the bomb to drop. *He's going to tell me he's notified the police.*

"First things first." The smile faded from his face. "I need to apologize to you." He leaned forward and stared at the floor. "I'm truly sorry for the way I treated you, and I'm *really* sorry for threatening you. I should be horsewhipped." He glanced at Abby, an imploring look in his eyes. "Fortunately, that went out with the invention of automobiles." A wry smile flitted across his face, then faded.

Abby couldn't believe what she just heard. Kevin apologizing and meaning it. At least he looked like he meant it.

Kevin set his glass on the coffee table, stood, and began pacing. "I guess I should fill you in on what happened the last few days. I was furious when I found out what you'd done, but to save face with my family, I told another lie about why you left. They didn't buy it, which made me even angrier."

Leaving nothing out, Kevin told Abby what happened, including his speech at the banquet. Abby quietly listened to Kevin's story, watching him closely, looking for any deception. She saw none. As the story unfolded, he paced, barely looking at Abby. Regret laced his voice. He paused once and stared out her window for a moment before continuing. His voice faltered when he told her about Jake's reaction to his lies and Melissa's comments about his character. When he finished, he slumped onto the couch.

"You did the right thing by leaving, Abby," he assured her. "You brought me to my senses. Painful as it was, I got the lesson."

Abby shook her head and tried to think of the right response. "Y-you're welcome, I guess."

Kevin picked up his glass and swallowed half the remaining tea. He retrieved Abby's resignation from the coffee table where he set it earlier. "I'd prefer to tear up your resignation, Abby. I need you. My business needs you. I'm not sure I can trust anyone else to keep me in line."

"You don't need me, Kevin, if what you've told me is true. If you're willing to change the way you do business, you'll see to it that the person who takes my place continues what I've done. You've seen my recommendation for a replacement."

"Meg. I'm sure she's competent, but she's not a CPA and doesn't have a business degree. And she may not be as adamant about putting her foot down as you are."

"She'll do fine. She understands my philosophy. She's nearly finished with her business degree and will take the CPA exam this fall."

"I'd rather you stayed."

"I can't."

"Why?"

Abby fidgeted with her glass, then set it on the coffee table. "Too many reminders of what happened. I'm not proud of deceiving your family. Seeing you would constantly remind me of what I've done."

"And remind you of Jake?"

Abby frowned at Kevin. "W-why would you say that?"

"Because I think you fell in love with my brother, and seeing me would remind you of that."

"You have a wonderful family, Kevin. I became fond of all of them. I regret not having told them the truth."

"You didn't have a choice. And you did fall in love with Jake, didn't you?"

Abby looked away from Kevin's accusing gaze. "I don't have to answer that." She waited for Kevin to comment, and when he didn't, she looked at him. "Even if I did, it's a moot point. He doesn't care about me. He accepted me because I was engaged to you. Besides, he can't abide liars, and that's what I am." Abby walked to the kitchen and set her glass in the sink. She didn't want Kevin to see the tears in her eyes.

"He'll get over it. He's a bit angry right now at both of us. You're right, he doesn't like lying, but give him a little time. He'll come around. He's in love with you."

Abby's heart constricted at Kevin's words. She turned toward him. "Did he tell you that?"

"Not in so many words, but I know my brother pretty well. Mom and Dad agree with me."

Abby leaned against the kitchen counter. "I don't think you know Jake as well as you think you do. Even if he had feelings for me, he won't now. He has very high standards, and I haven't lived up to them. He won't ever be able to trust me, and trust is essential to any relationship. He'll move on, and so will I."

"You're sure?"

"I have to, Kevin."

Kevin shrugged, opened the envelope containing Abby's resignation, and pulled out the check for the first installment on what she owed him. He shoved the envelope into his shirt pocket and deliberately tore the check into little pieces.

Abby stared in disbelief. "What are you doing?"

Kevin walked to the kitchen and deposited the pieces in Abby's trash. He stepped in front of her and placed his hands on her shoulders.

"You lived up to your part of our bargain, even though I abandoned you to spend time with Gail. You jeopardized your standing with my family, because you had an agreement with me, and because I threatened your career. The way I see it, there were only two days of the original bargain you failed to complete. I'm more than willing to forgive the whole amount, but if you insist on paying it, you'll need to restructure your payment schedule. You only owe me around $5000. I'll leave it up to you. That amount or nothing."

Abby blinked at Kevin and tried to speak, but no words formed.

He cradled Abby's face in his hands. "I'm sorry for all the grief I've caused you." He kissed her forehead, then dropped his hands and walked toward the front door.

Before leaving, he stopped. "By the way, Mom and Dad don't hold the lie against you. They said to tell you you're welcome in their home any time." He winked at her and opened the door. "And don't give up on Jake. He'll see things as they should be. He just needs a little time. Take the rest of the week off. I'll see you in the office on Monday. According to your resignation, you still owe me a week of work." The door closed quietly behind him.

K. L. McKee

Chapter 30

"Jake, shed your catcher's gear."

Jake frowned at JD. "I'm not up until next inning."

"I'm taking you out. You'll be coaching first base the rest of the game."

"JD, I—"

"No arguments, Jake. Your mind isn't on the game tonight. You'll do a whole lot less damage coaching first base."

Jake removed his shin guards. Whether he liked it or not, JD was right. Jake's mind was more on Abby than on the game. His first time at bat, a shrill whistle from the crowd had distracted him. He had glanced up, expecting to see Abby, then realized his mistake. The next pitch sailed by. Strike three.

Handing over his gear, Jake apologized. "Sorry, JD."

"No harm done. Something I can help with? I'm a good listener."

Jake shook his head. "Naw. Something I have to work out on my own." Rick had been a good listener, too. Jake missed him.

"Well, let me know if I can help." JD called toward the dugout. "Tim! Get over here. You're catching the rest of the game."

After the game, Jake sought out his parents. "I'm going to take off early tomorrow morning and go fishing. Won't be back until late Sunday."

"Where're you going?" Leonard asked.

"Think I'll hike into Finney Cuts. Hopefully, no one else will be there, and I can have some time to myself."

Pat touched his arm. "What time will you be back?"

"Before dark. I'm taking Spur with me."

"Jake!" JD called. "You joining us for pizza?"

Jake shook his head.

"You tell JD you won't be here tomorrow night?" Leonard asked.

"Yes, Dad. I already made arrangements for Tim to catch tomorrow night."

"Okay. You be careful, son."

"I will."

~

Jake took his time hiking the mile and a half into Finney Cuts on Saturday morning. Finney Cuts was a small snow-fed mountain lake near the top of Grand Mesa, a bit east of

Leon Peak, the highest point on the mesa. Since the trail was uphill most of the way, he set a steady pace, enjoying the beauty and quiet of the Colorado high country as he hiked. Spur bounded ahead, returning every now and then to make sure Jake still followed.

Once he arrived at the lake, however, memories of Abby flooded his mind. Granted, he'd taken her to a different lake, but all he could think of was how much fun she had learning to fish, and how much she appreciated God's handiwork. Finney Cuts would have affected her the same way Lost Lake had, its setting as breathtaking.

The last part of the trail into Finney Cuts ran through slide rock, and the west border of the lake was hilly and rocky. A mountain meadow bordered the east and north sides. Fuchsia paintbrush, purple elephant head, and yellow cinquefoil added color to the rich greens of the grasses. Besides a luscious meadow, pockets of marshland surrounded the lake. Wild currant and rose bushes filled the meadows and marshes, and a stand of pines grew a short distance back from the crystal clear water.

The first fish Jake hooked reminded him of Abby's excitement over catching a fish, and her concern and reluctance at the thought of killing it. He knew her reaction wasn't faked. She genuinely enjoyed her first fishing trip, unlike Sondra, who wanted nothing to do with fishing.

At nightfall, Jake settled down to sleep under the stars, and Spur snuggled against him. The words of Psalm 121 came to mind. *I lift up my eyes to the hills—where does my help come from? My help comes from the Lord, the Maker of heaven and earth.*

For the first time since Abby left, Jake prayed about his feelings for her. The ache in his heart needed healing. He wanted to forget. Had he hurt this much when Sondra left? He didn't think so. But he also didn't see any future with Abby.

"Lord, how can I trust Abby when she lied about something so important? Sondra lied—kept things from me—and Abby did the same thing. I was right not to trust Sondra any longer. I'm right not to trust Abby. She's no different."

But he already knew that Abby was entirely different from Sondra. Not at all self-centered. She demonstrated that during the mine accident and the days following. And unlike Sondra, Abby seemed to enjoy helping him with the milking.

But Abby had lied. "A lie is a lie, no matter how you look at it."

Didn't you lie?

Jake blinked, wondering where that had come from. He always prided himself on his honesty.

"I don't lie, Lord."

But you did.

Jake bolted upright. Spur scrambled up and barked. Jake reached out and petted him, reassuring him everything was okay, and then snuggled back into his sleeping bag. Spur settled down beside him.

He stared at the canopy of bright, twinkling lights and closed his eyes as the realization swept over him. He had lied to Abby the night he kissed her. He told her he was testing her, making sure she really did love Kevin. She had caught him off guard. He could argue all he wanted, but the truth was the truth. He lied, plain and simple.

"But that was different," he muttered. "I was sure something wasn't right. Abby had a chance to tell me the truth then, but she didn't. Instead, she slapped me for questioning her relationship with Kevin."

A lie is a lie.

Jake groaned. He was no better than Abby. The only difference was she didn't know he had lied. Still, she had plenty of opportunities to tell the truth. Especially the night Jake had taken her home from the Columbine Inn. She should have come clean then. Besides, hadn't he apologized for kissing her?

Abby apologized, too, for slapping you.

"What am I supposed to do, Father? Abby took the coward's way out by not facing us and apologizing in person. I feel betrayed."

Peter betrayed me when he denied me, and I forgave him.

The reprimand was worse than any he had received as a child from his parents. Jake shook his head, closed his eyes, and hoped for sleep, or answers, or at the very least, peace. But in his mind, he argued all night with his conscience and with God. He fell asleep just before dawn.

On Sunday, Jake fished, hiked, and played with Spur, all the while, trying his best to sort out his feelings about Abby. He pulled into his driveway as the last rays of sunlight painted a spectacular sunset across the western sky.

After informing his parents he'd arrived home, Jake unpacked his gear and showered. The trip had given him time to think, but confusion, anger, and hurt still muddled his mind. As he crawled into bed, Jake prayed for guidance, but no answers came. Only one word repeated in his mind. *Forgive.*

Exhaustion took over, and he slept without dreaming. The alarm jolted him awake. He groaned and stumbled out of bed. As the sky faded from black to gray, Jake trudged to the barn, Spur trotting ahead of him. He worked on automatic, years of doing the same thing over and over pushing him on. Too tired to think, he shoved aside thoughts of Abby. Halfway through the morning milking, Leonard came in to help. He didn't mention Kevin, Abby, or anything that had transpired the previous week.

"Your mother is taking a bunch of clothes to the cleaners this afternoon. If you have anything to add, she'll need it by lunch."

Jake nodded and continued working. Leonard didn't push.

When lunch rolled around, Jake walked to his house, took his suit out of his closet and cleaned out the pockets. He found Abby's note that Kevin had left for him to read. He stared at the wrinkled pages for a moment.

I thought I shredded these. Crumpling the papers in his fist, he aimed for the wastebasket.

"Two points," he muttered.

As he headed for the door, he paused and stared at the wastebasket. Sauntering over, he retrieved the papers and stuffed them in his back pocket. Maybe he would read her note. Or not.

As Jake and Spur approached his parents' house, Spur raced ahead. At the back door, Spur barked, and then scratched at the screen as though trying to open it. When it wouldn't budge, he whined and pawed at it.

"Spur what's gotten into you?"

Jake planted a foot on the top step and rubbed Spur's head. Spur looked at Jake, sniffed at the door, and whined. Jake shook his head.

"You never want to go inside, boy, unless there's a thunderstorm." Jake glanced at the cloudless blue sky. "Don't think there's much chance of that today."

Jake reached up and opened the screen door. Spur darted onto the porch and nosed around the far corner. He looked toward Jake and barked, then turned his attention to the corner again, his tail wagging.

"What in the world?" Jake walked over to where Spur stood. He set his suit on a nearby bench.

"Jake, what's Spur upset about?" Pat stepped onto the porch. "He was acting the same way this morning. I didn't let him in. I just sent him off to the barn. What's he looking at?"

"Don't know, but something over here is bothering him."

As he surveyed the corner, Jake's eyes rested on a pair of boots. He knelt, patted Spur, and retrieved them. Spur sniffed at the leather, whined, and then looked up as Jake stood.

"Abby's boots. She left them." Jake held them up for Pat to see.

"Well, I'll be. I hadn't noticed them," Pat said. "She always took them off before she came in the house. She must have set them in the corner the last time she wore them."

"I'll pack them up and send them to Kevin. He can get them back to Abby."

Spur barked several times, then settled on his haunches and stared at Jake.

"What?"

Spur cocked his head and whined again. Jake's shoulders slumped. "You miss her, don't you boy?"

Spur uttered a guttural sigh.

"We all miss her," Pat said. "You could deliver the boots in person."

Jake stared at his mother and slowly shook his head. "Is that what you want me to do?"

"It's only a suggestion. What you do is entirely up to you. It's your decision. Not mine. Not your dad's. Not Spur's."

Spur barked and his tail cut a swath through the dust on the porch floor. Jake scratched Spur's ears and patted his neck.

"I'm being ganged up on," he muttered.

~

Friday. Abby's last day working for Kevin. She didn't think leaving would be so hard. Kevin and the rest of her coworkers had thrown her a going-away party that morning, then she had lunch with Meg and two of the other girls from the office.

She leaned back in her chair and stared at her desktop. Except for the telephone, the computer, and her purse, it was bare. She had cleaned all of her personal items out of the desk, boxed them, and carted everything home the day before. Part of her regretted her decision to leave. She would miss Meg and the fast-paced routine of Kevin's business.

Abby treasured Meg's friendship. Abby's family had been too transient for her to make any lasting friendships. The thought of leaving Meg behind brought tears to Abby's eyes, yet she knew leaving was the right thing to do. Seeing Kevin every day reminded her of Jake and her lie. A lie that would haunt her the rest of her life.

Meg had spent the week helping Abby pack and store her possessions. Until Abby found a place to settle, she crammed nearly everything she owned into a storage unit. Meg decided to take over Abby's apartment lease and would move in as soon as Abby left, so some of Abby's furniture remained in the apartment for Meg to use.

Most of her clothes and other personal items were packed away in storage. Monday morning she planned to load her suitcases into her car and spend a few weeks visiting the towns she'd picked out in Montana, Wyoming, and Colorado. There was even one in New Mexico that looked interesting. One of the towns was bound to be like North Fork. When she found the right one....

The knock on her door startled her. She sat up straight. "Come in."

Shock, momentary joy, and then bewilderment settled over her as Jake stepped into her office. He pushed the door closed behind him, walked to the desk, and dropped her boots on the empty desktop.

"You left these when you sneaked out in the middle of the night."

She stared. "I-I didn't sneak. I left quietly."

His gaze bore through her. "Same thing."

The heat of anger crept up her neck. "All right. I sneaked out. I'm sorry. I couldn't face the three people I disappointed with my lie. I'm a coward, so shoot me."

Jake's expression didn't change. Abby bit her lip and wondered what he was doing in Denver…and her office.

"You didn't have to bring them over," She glanced at the boots, and then back at Jake. "You could have donated them to a charity. I don't have much use for them here. Besides, you paid for them."

His eyes narrowed. "They were a gift."

Her legs trembled, and she pressed her hands down on her knees to stop the quivering. "You could have sent them with Kevin."

"Didn't find them until after he left."

"UPS would have worked."

He cocked his head. "I had another reason for coming."

Afraid to hope he'd come for her, she asked, "And that would be?"

"I came to get back what you stole from me."

Abby jumped up, outrage coursing through her. "*What*?"

"You heard me. I came to get what you stole from me."

Her nostrils flared, and she gritted her teeth. How *dare* he accuse her of stealing. She clenched her hands at her side as her temper took over. "I may have lied to you, Jake Karlson, but I'm not a thief! I didn't steal *anything* from you."

In a quiet and controlled voice, he said, "But you did, Abby."

They stood staring at each other for a moment, Abby's outrage at Jake's accusation building inside her. "Just what is it I'm *supposed* to have stolen from you?"

Jake planted his hands on either side of the boots and leaned toward her. "My heart, Abby, and I want it back."

Abby stared dumbfounded at him for a moment, then sank onto her chair, her gaze not leaving his. She digested his words, then searched for something to say. *How am I supposed to answer that?*

"Well?"

She blinked. "Y-you can't have it," she whispered. "It's mine."

Jake walked around the desk, turned her chair so she faced him, and placed his hands on the arms of her chair. "I can't live without a heart, Abby. I need mine back."

In her lap, she clenched and unclenched her hands. He was so close she could feel his breath on her face, smell his aftershave, see the grayish blue and green of his eyes. Tears threatened, and then faded as she thought of an answer. "But you already have mine," she said. "You don't need two hearts."

For the first time since walking into her office, Jake

smiled. "That explains why I'm still walking around." Pulling her from the chair, he gathered her into his arms. "Seems we have a dilemma," he said. "You have my heart, and I have yours."

"That's a dilemma?"

"Only if you refuse to come home with me. My heart belongs in North Fork."

"So does mine."

He bent his head and brushed her lips with his, then claimed them with a deep, demanding kiss. Her toes curled; her stomach warmed and fluttered; joy filled her heart.

"Marry me," he whispered against her lips.

Her heart constricted. "A-are you sure? I lied to you."

"Yes, you did. Promise me you won't *ever* do it again."

She stared into his eyes. "I promise."

"Good. Now, about marrying me...."

Overwhelmed by joy and unable to find her voice, she nodded yes.

He leaned back and studied her for a moment. "Be sure, Abby. I'm a dairy farmer. I often smell of manure, silage, and sour milk. I don't make much money. I seldom take vacations. You'll be stuck in North Fork for a long time."

Abby slipped her arms around Jake's neck, kissed him, and found her voice. "You clean up real nice, money doesn't matter, and I've done enough travelling. It's time I put down roots. North Fork's a perfect place for that. Besides, I'll be fine as long as you take me fishing every now and then."

He grinned and nodded. "I want kids, lots of them."

"A dozen?"

He frowned. "Well, maybe not that many."

She giggled. He kissed her again.

"Jake," she said when they surfaced for air, "I need to explain why—"

"Not now." He tried to kiss her again.

"But you have to understand—"

"Be quiet and let me enjoy this. You can explain later. Besides, I read the note you left Kevin." His lips sought hers again.

Her telephone rang. Jake groaned.

"I should get that," she whispered against his lips. She fumbled for the phone, never taking her eyes from Jake's face, and punched the speaker button. "Yes?"

"Abby." Kevin's voice intruded. "I need to see you before you leave today."

Before Abby could say anything, Jake answered for her. "She's busy, Kev. Make it another time."

"Jake! You made it."

"Yeah."

"Good. I won't have to stall Abby. Well?"

"Want to be my best man?"

"Absolutely! Congratulations."

"Thanks. Now bug off."

"Be happy to."

"By the way, Kev, Abby's leaving early."

"No problem." A click and silence followed.

Jake cradled Abby's face in his hands. "Is there someplace we can go where we won't be interrupted?"

"My place."

Jake smiled. "Let's go."

He took her hand and Abby grabbed her purse as Jake pulled her around the desk. When he opened the office door, she stopped him.

"Wait!"

She pulled Jake with her as she stepped back to the desk and grabbed her boots. "Can't forget these. I may need them."

Jake grinned. "By the way, Spur misses you," he said as the door closed behind them.

Epilogue

"*H*it out of the park, Jake!" The baby kicked, and Abby absently rubbed her protruding belly.

Jake swung at the next pitch. Whap! Bat and softball connected. The ball sailed over the outfielder's head. Abby let loose a shrill whistle. Jake jogged around the bases, smiled, and winked at Abby as he stepped on home plate. She blew him a kiss.

The baby kicked again. A twinge hit Abby's lower back and snaked around her belly. Her eyes watered. She arched her back and rubbed where the pain had started. The twinges had started mid-morning, but they'd been slight compared to the last one. She hadn't said anything to Jake. Today was the championship game in the second annual celebrity softball charity tournament. Mac's Marauders had a title to defend, and Jake was a key player.

"Are you feeling okay, Abby?" Pat asked.

"I'm fine. I think I'll get up and walk for a few minutes. I'm a bit uncomfortable sitting."

Abby carefully made her way down the bleachers and walked to a grassy area a little behind and to the side of third base. As she paced, she kneaded her back and thanked God for the blessings of the last year.

Her life had moved with the speed of a rocket after Jake confronted her in her office. He had presented her with a pear-shaped solitaire diamond as soon as they arrived at her place.

"I'm sorry," he apologized when her eyes filled with tears. "I know it's not as fancy as the ring Kevin gave you to wear, but it just looked like you, and it's got a whole lot of love attached to it."

"It's perfect," she assured him. "I hated that gaudy ring Kevin gave me. This one suits me much better, especially because it's from you."

They married four weeks later, Abby wearing Pat's wedding dress, altered by shortening the sleeves and lowering the neckline to accommodate the heat of August instead of the cool of November. Besides serving as best man, Kevin had insisted on walking Abby down the aisle, suggesting it was a perfect way to stifle any gossip about Jake stealing Abby from him.

Kevin had offered Abby a monthly stipend to stay as head of accounting. Meg would oversee the day-to-day business, allowing Abby to supervise from North Fork, with an occasional trip to Denver. With Jake's blessing, she had agreed.

Abby fingered the diamond and the wedding band on her left hand. She stopped pacing and took a deep breath. The twinges were coming harder and closer. She was in labor.

"Just wait a little longer, baby. The game's almost over, and I want your daddy to see you come into the world." She rubbed her belly as she spoke. "And this is a very important game."

She gasped. Wet warmth trickled down her legs. Another pain, harder and longer gripped her. She sank to her knees and groaned. Before she could stand up, Pat was by her side.

"Abby, are you in labor?"

Abby nodded and with Pat's help got to her feet.

"Leonard's gone to get Jake," Pat said. "The next time a pain starts, pant. You don't want this baby coming before we can find the doctor and get you to the clinic."

Abby acknowledged Pat's instruction and immediately began panting. As the pain subsided, she closed her eyes. When she opened them, Jake was at her side, his catcher's gear discarded, a worried frown on his face.

He scooped her into his arms. "Let's get you to the ambulance. Doc got called away fifteen minutes ago. We're trying to locate him."

~

Jake's heart pounded. He climbed into the ambulance that was always present whenever they had a game and laid

Abby gently on the gurney. His EMT training kicked in as he took her pulse and her blood pressure.

"Honey, how long have you been in labor?" he asked as he took her vitals.

"I think since mid-morning."

Another pain hit her. Jake talked her through it. When he saw her relax, he wiped the sweat from her brow.

"Why didn't you tell me?"

"I wanted you to be able to concentrate on the game." She shrugged. "It wasn't that bad."

"Don't you know that you and the baby are more important than some stupid softball game?"

"I-I'm sor—ohhhhhhhhhh!"

Kale stepped inside the ambulance. "Need some help, Jake?"

"Yeah, find Doc! And close the door. I need to get Abby undressed and check to see how far along she is."

Jake cleaned his hands with the supplies kept in the ambulance as he gave orders. He quickly undressed Abby from the waist down, covered her with a sheet, and then folded it back to check on the baby's progress.

Abby groaned. "I need to push, Jake. *Please.*"

"No! *Breathe.*"

After a minute, Jake lowered the sheet and looked at Abby. "Our baby isn't going to wait. Doc's not here. I'm going to see who's available to help you deliver." He forced a reassuring smile on his face. "I'll be right back."

He opened the ambulance doors. "Kale! Who's here that can deliver a baby?"

Kale smiled. "You, Jake. You're the only one of us that's actually done it."

"Well that one wasn't my baby."

"Couldn't be much different than delivering a calf. You've done plenty of that."

Jake frowned at Kale's grinning face. "I didn't father any of the calves, either. Now get me some help."

Pat moved toward the ambulance. "I'll help. Kale, see if they've contacted Doc."

Jake stepped back in the ambulance, Pat right behind him. Sweat ran down his face, and he wiped it away with his forearm.

"Jake," Abby croaked, "I don't think we can wait. The baby's coming *right now!*" She groaned, louder this time.

Jake took her hand. "Looks like it's up to me. Do you trust me? Can you do everything I tell you?"

She nodded.

Fifteen minutes later, Jake held his daughter in his hands, proud Grandma Pat smiling at them from Abby's side. Tears streamed down Jake's face. Pat helped him clean the newborn's nostrils, and then Jake laid her on Abby's stomach while he cut the umbilical cord. Pat cleaned and wrapped the baby in blankets and set her in Abby's arms.

The ambulance sped away from city park, Kale driving with Pat in the passenger seat. Jake knelt beside Abby and wiped away the tears on her face.

"She's beautiful," Abby said. "Look at all that curly red hair." She glided her hand over the baby's head.

"She's beautiful, just like her Momma." Jake smoothed

Abby's hair away from her face. Their new daughter made tiny sucking motions and let out a whimper.

"Shhhh, sweetie," Abby crooned. She looked at Jake and tears filled her eyes again.

"What's wrong, honey? Do you need something? Are you in pain?"

"No." She frowned. "I'm sorry you didn't get your son. I know you must be disappointed."

Jake frowned and shook his head. "I'm not your father, Abby. I'm not obsessed with having a son. All I wanted was a healthy baby and a healthy mother. That's what's important." He kissed her. "I couldn't be happier. If we have a half-dozen girls and no boys, I'll still be happy."

Abby smiled. "You really mean that, don't you?"

"Absolutely." Jake grinned at her. "Of course, when our girls are old enough to date, I'm going to lock them up. I know how boys are at that age." He wiggled his eyebrows at her.

Abby laughed. "Let's not rush things. This little one is going to grow up fast enough."

"We're here," Kale called from the driver's seat. Jake could see the clinic out the windshield of the ambulance. "Doc's been located," Kale continued. "He'll be here in five minutes."

Jake looked at Abby. "So, are you going to hog her, or do I get to hold her for a minute?"

Abby kissed her tiny daughter on the forehead, then handed her to Jake. He cradled his daughter in his arms and said a silent prayer of thanks. Then he smiled at his firstborn and whispered, "Welcome to the world, Nancy Patricia Karlson. I hope it's to your liking."

About the author:

K. L. (Karen Lea) McKee has had a passion for writing since she was a young girl. After raising two rambunctious boys and earning her B.A. in English from Regis University, she renewed her desire to write faith-based stories.

Karen worked in the Reference Center of her local library for twenty-nine years, retiring to pursue writing full time. She is a member of Rocky Mountain Fiction Writers and several local writing groups.

She and her husband reside in Western Colorado, known for its fruit orchards, wineries, majestic mountains, spectacular canyons, and strikingly beautiful desert terrain. She enjoys knitting, music, tennis, pickle ball, the beautiful Western Colorado outdoors, and spending time with her family.

Karen was raised in the small town of Paonia, Colorado known for its fruit orchards, cattle ranches, small farms, and coal mining. She appreciates the hard work and sacrifice needed for each of these occupations. She also understands what it's like growing up in a small town.

Other books by K. L. McKee:

Miracle, a novella

In Name Only

Worth Waiting For

CPSIA information can be obtained
at www.ICGtesting.com
Printed in the USA
LVHW041523141119
637372LV00001B/99